ICE COLD Kiss

New York Times & *USA Today* Bestselling Author

CYNTHIA EDEN

This book is a work of fiction. Any similarities to real people, places, or events are not intentional and are purely the result of coincidence. The characters, places, and events in this story are fictional.

Published by Hocus Pocus Publishing, Inc.

Copyright ©2024 by Cindy Roussos

All rights reserved. This publication may not be reproduced, distributed, or transmitted in any form without the express written consent of the author except for the use of small quotes or excerpts used in book reviews.

Copy-editing by: J. R. T. Editing

If you have any problems, comments, or questions about this publication, please contact info@hocuspocuspublishing.com.

PROLOGUE

"I need discretion. I need tact. I need someone who will remain in total control at all times."

Midas Monroe lounged in the leather chair and let a slow smile curve his lips. "Discretion is my middle name." Oh, no, it really, really wasn't. He rolled one shoulder in a casual shrug. "Or maybe it's tact. I *am* a master when it comes to tact." As far as keeping control… "I've never had a single complaint about my lack of control. I keep all of my jobs completely professional, and I *always* protect my charge." That was his business after all—protection. Guarding the ones who found themselves in danger.

Maybe they were being stalked.

Maybe they had an ex who wouldn't let go.

Maybe they'd dipped into dangerous business that they now regretted.

People came to him for all sorts of reasons. The *why* didn't particularly matter to Midas. He always watched their asses. And got a nice, fat payday when the job was done.

His gaze slid around the study and dipped toward the large picture window on the right. The window that overlooked the tall, thick trees and the snow-capped mountain in the distance. A million-dollar view. Truly. Of course, the house itself probably went for about four million, give or take some change. The place smelled of money, and the man before him? Ryker Bellamy. He was old money. Passed down generation to generation. Not that Ryker hadn't done his part to add to the family pot. The guy had been in the real estate business ever since he stepped foot out of his Ivy League college.

Freaking money to burn.

A life that was far, far different from Midas's.

Of course, most people had lives very, very different from his. Because not everyone had a serial killer for a father. *I'm just the lucky one.*

Unlucky one.

Cursed.

"I...know about your past," Ryker murmured as he tugged at his tie.

Midas contemplated pretending to be shocked. Thought about letting his jaw drop dramatically. Sometimes, he truly enjoyed fucking with people. But, nah. This time, he just rolled his eyes. "And obviously, it doesn't matter, or I wouldn't be here."

"You...you work quite a bit with the Feds."

He worked with one Fed in particular quite a bit. Technically, a former Fed now. His buddy, Oliver Foxx.

"Special Agent Foxx is the individual who recommended you to me."

Now Midas straightened. He'd figured that maybe his last client had told Ryker about his services. After all, the bulked-up action star had a place in Colorado Springs, Colorado, too. *That man wouldn't know real action if it bit him on the ass.* Course, that was why he'd needed Midas, and Midas had been happy to take the payday, protect the guy from a female fan who'd gone off the deep end, and even show the actor a few tricks to use in his next flick—

"Foxx said you could be discreet."

Back to that, were they? Midas grunted.

"Tactful."

Ryker was going through the list again. Midas began to tap his left index finger against the arm of the chair. "Want to get to the point?"

"My daughter."

Just those two words. Nothing more. Seriously, it was like pulling teeth with Ryker Bellamy. But, Midas knew quite a bit about the woman in question. Before coming to this meet-and-greet, Midas had researched Ryker and his family. Not like he ever went into a situation unprepared. So he was well aware of the man's daughter. "Alina Bellamy." Her mother had been a Russian beauty who married Ryker after she met him in Paris. Her mother's second marriage. From all accounts, a happy one, too. Until Alina's mother had died in a skiing accident. One that occurred two days after Alina's eleventh birthday. *That must have wrecked her.* "Alina's the figure skater," Midas said, voice flat and emotionless. Because he could be emotionless whenever he wanted.

Ryker stiffened. "She's not *just* a figure skater. Alina will be a gold medal winner in the next

Olympics. She is the current world champion in women's figure skating. No one is better on the ice than she is. No one."

Okay, someone was clearly passionate about ice skating. "She got a stalker you're worried about? Some fan who is sending her crazy emails and letters?" He'd seen that plenty of times. People in the spotlight attracted attention. Good and bad attention.

He was the one typically called in to handle the bad attention. His forte.

"Something like that." Ryker sniffed. "I've tried to hire guards before. Alina hasn't liked them."

A laugh slid from Midas. "She's not gonna like me, either." Few people did. "Doesn't matter. I'm not in the business to be liked. I'm in the business of keeping my charges alive. Protecting them, for a hefty fee." He smiled. Best to just go ahead and get the fee business out of the way now.

Once more, Ryker tugged at his tie. "I don't think you fully understand."

Probably because someone was beating around the damn bush and not getting to the point.

"It's a necessity that Alina likes you."

Fine. Whatever. "Then I'll be on my best behavior." She'd still think he was an asshole. Because he was. Fact of life. But she'd come around when she saw that he was a good guard—no, a great guard.

"No, you ah...*discretion,* remember? Tact. And—"

"Jeez, don't go through the list again. You're boring me out of my mind." Midas unfurled from the chair and rose to his full height. A height that had him towering over Ryker. Midas generally towered over most people. Midas glanced at his watch and acted like he didn't see Ryker scuttle back. "Look, man, I've got places to be. Other potential clients waiting." Actually, no one else was waiting. Ryker was the only one on his schedule for the day. "If you're not hiring me for the gig, then I need to go and accept the next job." He turned to the side, as if he was, indeed, about to leave.

"Wait!"

Maybe I'll make my fee a wee bit higher. Because Ryker had sure sounded desperate. Desperate people tended to be willing to pay desperate amounts. Midas glanced back at him.

Another sniff from Ryker. "She can't know you're her bodyguard."

Midas laughed.

Ryker didn't.

"I must have misheard," Midas said. An unusual occurrence because he had exceptional hearing. "Thought you said Alina couldn't know I was guarding her."

A nod from Ryker. "That's...ah, yes, that's what I said."

Midas pursed his lips. Considered the situation. "Why, exactly, can't she know?"

"I don't want her to...worry."

"I believe she's an adult, not a child, so worrying is really part of the package." Like he needed to deal with some overprotective-dad BS.

A totally foreign situation to Midas. Considering just what his own father had done...*Twisted sonofabitch. I will not go back there.*

"I need Alina to stay focused on her ice skating. If her concentration is broken, if she fears that some—some deranged fan might just be watching her from the stands or following her when she's training, that worry could lead to mistakes. Alina cannot afford any mistakes."

Great. Just so they were clear—the dad wanted her staying in top form so she'd bring home the gold for him. Midas crossed his arms over his chest. "How do you propose I guard someone who doesn't know I'm her bodyguard? Getting close enough to protect her from threats will be rather hard."

"Oliver Foxx assured me you'd be up for any challenge."

His friend Oliver was starting to get on Midas's—

"I'll double your normal fee, of course. Seeing as how you will be working at a disadvantage and having to be undercover." A wince. "From your client."

Double your normal fee. He hadn't even told the guy his normal fee yet. "She's not the client," he said smoothly. "You are. She'll be my charge." And before they went ahead with this crazy case... "Is she aware of my reputation?"

Nice way of putting it.

Not like he was mega famous or anything. Actually, he was infamous. But only in certain circles. The circles that happened to follow murder and crime. Because for a while, his face had been blasted on the news.

But that was years ago. Most people had forgotten. Time had a way of blurring the jagged, ugly pieces of life. Still, it never hurt to find out just what a charge knew. Especially if he was going in pretending *not* to be her bodyguard.

"Alina never watches much TV. She doesn't have time for things like that. She's focused on training. She's on the ice six days a week, for up to five hours a day. And when she's not skating, she's working out. She has to stay in top form." A dismissive shake of his head. "She doesn't even handle her own social media. I have a person for that."

Fabulous for you. "So Alina is insulated." *And has zero idea that she has threats out there against her?* Hell, that was kinda like leading a lamb to slaughter.

"Alina does not know about your past. You'll be a complete stranger to her." Ryker seemed to hold his breath. "She...isn't involved with anyone. I was thinking that, uh, perhaps you could—" He flushed.

"Are you asking me to seduce your daughter?" Midas drawled deliberately. Then remembered, whoops, he was supposed to have tact. Had tact been his middle name? Or maybe it had been control?

"No! Absolutely not! No seduction. There is no need to go that far." The flush darkened Ryker's cheeks even more. "She has to stay focused on her skating."

Check. The skating. Like he could have missed it. Midas barely contained another eye roll. Was the gold medal going to be Alina's or Ryker's?

"But...my daughter doesn't date much. And I think she might be...flattered by your interest."

Instead of rolling his eyes, Midas narrowed them on Ryker.

"She's very shy. Reserved. Inexperienced with men."

Lamb to slaughter.

"But by pretending to be interested, it would be a way for you to get close to her. Just platonically, of course. No real seduction."

Check. The man did not want Midas fucking Alina. "Platonic is my middle name."

Ryker backed up a step. "I thought you said it was tact."

"Whatever." Then he tossed out a figure for the protection gig. Supposed to be double his usual rate, huh? *Go big or go home.* He loved that freaking saying. Mostly because he was very big.

Ryker didn't even blink. He just asked, "When can you start?"

Hell, yes. His gaze slid to the picture window. The setting sun turned the sky a brilliant gold splattered with dark red. "How about first thing in the morning?"

Ryker extended his hand to Midas. "Discretion. Tact."

Midas gripped the offered hand. "Total control. Don't worry, I've got this."

CHAPTER ONE

Her skates slid across the ice as she picked up speed. Silence surrounded her—silence except for the occasional slice of her blades when she would launch into the air and twist. *One turn, two.*

She landed. Pushed faster. Faster and faster. She didn't feel the cold. The moment she stepped onto the ice, the cold always vanished for her. No one else was at the training facility. Her day. Her time. She'd come in long before her coach was even scheduled to arrive, and she'd been skating for hours. The only illumination in the entire building were the lights that shone directly onto the ice. Darkness was everywhere else. Her choice because the only thing that could matter was the ice.

Hadn't she been told that all her life? The only thing that mattered—

Alina Bellany launched into a quadruple axel. The first rotation had her heart racing. The second had her breath catching. The third had her—

Her body slammed into the ice with bruising force. For a moment, she didn't move at all. Couldn't. The breath had been knocked from her.

"Fuck, that looked brutal."

A man's voice. Coming from the darkness. A voice that should not have been there.

Her hands pushed down against the white sheet of ice as she levered herself up. Her heart raced fast now, but not from the adrenaline of trying the most difficult ice skating move out there. No, the out-of-control pounding came from fear.

No one else should be here.

Certainly not...

Not the tall, muscled stranger who stood at the edge of the ice. He'd opened the small half-door that would allow him to access the rink. Darkness stretched behind him, but the light over the rink hit the front of his body.

Big. Too big.

He wore a black sweatshirt, but his bulging muscles seemed to strain the clothing. Faded jeans stretched over his powerful thighs. Tennis shoes covered his big feet.

Tennis shoes?

His hair was thick and streaked with bits of dark blond. His face...A close-cropped beard covered the bottom of his face. Made his hard, square jaw look even harder.

"You need help?" Grimacing, he put a tennis shoe onto the ice. "Hope I'm not about to bust my ass."

Bust his ass?

Then he stepped onto the ice, only sliding a little, and rushed toward her.

She pushed to her feet. Stood and angled her right toe down for balance. And gaped.

He was way bigger than she'd realized at first glance. A big, gorgeous bear of a man who hurtled toward her. Considering she stood at five-foot-three, most people were bigger than her, but this stranger...

Who in the world is he? Huge. Powerful. Drop-dead handsome. For a moment, she wondered if maybe she'd hit her head on the ice, and this was all some crazy hallucination. Because no way was a man this gorgeous rushing across the ice toward her.

He shouldn't be here. No one should be here but me. And this doesn't feel like a hallucination. It feels all too real. Her body still ached from the fall. And if everything was real...

Who is he?

Too late, she started to retreat. But he was—

"Gotcha." His hand closed around her right wrist just as she prepared to back away. And Alina was surprised because for the first time, she felt—

Heat.

Sliding up from where he touched her. Warming her skin. Her blood. A shot of electricity seemed to zip through her entire body. The shock of that heat had her mouth dropping open in surprise.

"That was one hell of a fall." His eyes—a warm, deep amber—swept over her. "You're standing okay, so I'm guessing nothing is broken?"

"I fall all the time," she blurted.

His amber eyes rose to lock on her face.

"I just get back up."

The faintest of smiles lifted his lips. "Of course, you do."

"You have to get back up. Staying sprawled on the ice isn't an option. You fall in a competition, you get back up, and you keep skating. You try to make up the points you lost. You never stay down." Alina was rambling and she knew it. What she didn't know? How to stop the rambling because she opened her mouth and said, "I fall in practice, too. You can never learn something new without falling first."

A slow nod. "I'll remember that." His fingers flexed a little against her.

More heat trickled through her. "You are...oddly hot."

He laughed.

And her face flamed. "I meant...your hand feels really warm against me." She tried to tug free.

He didn't let her go. He did lean down toward her. Up close, he was just...even bigger. Alina figured he had to be around six-foot-five, maybe even six-foot-six. The man swallowed her with his size.

Unease slithered through her.

"I feel warm because you are ice cold. It's freezing out here."

"Ice has to be cold."

Amusement danced in his eyes. "Yes, I am aware of that fun science fact. But *you* don't have to be freezing. Your body is shaking."

Not from the cold. From that strange awareness of him. And she knew exactly what it was. Sure, she might not have a ton of experience with the opposite sex, but when a look-alike Norse god stepped into your path, a woman recognized lust when it hit her.

Lust.

Instant attraction.

For a man who was way, way out of her league. "I'm not hurt. You can stop touching me." She needed to take control of this situation, ASAP. "Look, I don't know who you are or why you are here—"

He slowly withdrew his hand. "Midas."

"Excuse me?"

"My name. It's Midas."

She blinked. "Like the king who turned everything he touched into gold?"

"Sure, yeah. Like him. Only you didn't turn to gold, did you?"

No, but she could have sworn part of her was getting so hot she felt close to melting. All from standing in front of a stranger. Feeling him touch her wrist. Feeling his heat reach out and surround her.

She'd met plenty of good-looking men in her life. Plenty of physically fit men ice skated. But an ice skater's body and Midas's body...

Two entirely different things. "Why are you here?" she breathed. No, dang it. Being breathy and leaning toward this stranger was not the way to act. What was wrong with her? Her spine snapped straight. "This area is closed for my private practice. No one else should be in the building."

"Huh. The door was unlocked. I just walked right in."

No, no, she'd locked it after she'd entered. She always did that. Then her coach came in and unlocked it with his key and—

"As for why I'm here, I came for you, Alina."

Now a shiver darted down her spine, but it was one that had absolutely nothing to do with the ice. Unease had plagued her for days. The feeling that someone might be watching her. The feeling that she wasn't always alone when she should have been.

Just like I thought I was alone here. But I'm not. This big stranger is here. A stranger who was blocking her path. A stranger so much larger than she was. A stranger who knew exactly who she was.

"No." Flat. All amusement had vanished from his gaze. "You don't need to be afraid of me. Not ever. That's probably the first thing you should know about me. I would never hurt you."

Her breath heaved out. "Why would you say that?"

"Because fear filled your eyes. I don't want you being afraid of me." He shrugged his massive shoulders. "And because I would never hurt you. I was just stating a fact."

"Wh-why are you—"

Darkness. She didn't get to finish her stammered question because the lights above the rink had just turned off and the entire place plunged into complete and total darkness. A gasp spilled from her and, once more, she started to back up.

His big, warm hand curled around her wrist again. "It's okay." Growling. Rumbly. "I've got you."

But maybe that was the problem?

"I'm the new head of security for the training rink. I was just coming to introduce myself to you."

Her breath shuddered out in relief.

"And, sure I'm the new guy, but I don't think the lights are *supposed* to go off during a training session."

Instead of retreating, she pushed close to him. "No, they are not." A whisper. "They won't turn off unless someone *turns* them off."

"Well, that's just not good shit to hear."

No, it, um, wasn't good shit to hear. It was bad. Scary.

"I can't see worth a damn," Midas groused. "I have to turn on my light."

And he did. A small, pinprick of light shot up from his left hand. Automatically, she glanced down at the light. A flashlight. One of those penlight things.

"If someone is out there watching us, this light is going to show them exactly where we are," Midas warned her.

Why would someone be watching?

"So you stick to my side, got it? Step one is getting you off this ice. Step two is figuring out who the hell is in my rink."

His rink? Already possessive when he'd just started the job? But she wasn't about to complain. Because being alone in the dark was one thing. One terrifying thing. But being with the giant, muscled head of security for the rink? A world better.

They made it off the ice. She balanced on her skates because it was second nature to her. He kept his right hand curled around her wrist as if— as if holding her was somehow second nature to him.

"I want to check the perimeter." He'd lowered his head, and his breath blew along the edge of her ear. "But I am not leaving you alone. Ditch the skates, and we'll search together."

Ditching the skates would take a bit of effort. "I—"

The lights flashed on. Not just the lights over the rink, but every light in the building seemed to turn on all at once. Then footsteps rushed toward them.

Before she could even pull in another breath, Midas had pushed her behind his body. Being behind his body was pretty much like being behind a giant brick wall. She couldn't see whoever was approaching. She'd been completely concealed.

"Who the hell are you?" A familiar voice snarled. A Russian accent thickened the angry question. "And why are you in my rink?"

Familiar because it was her coach. Dimitri Sokolov. Former two-time gold medal Olympic figure skating champ. Absolute brilliance on the ice and an absolute monster of a demanding instructor in every other moment of his life. There was no room for anything less than perfection in Dimitri's orbit.

Before Midas could answer, Alina shifted her position and craned her head to the side so she could put her eyes on Dimitri. "He's with me."

Midas tensed.

"What?" Dimitri gaped at her. "You...you brought a *personal* friend to a practice?"

No, she never brought friends to practice. Mostly because she didn't have a lot of friends. Or any. She only had skating. It was what she'd done for years and years. Years of broken bones. Aching muscles. Falls onto the ice over and over.

But I get back up. You always have to get back up.

"Yep, she brought me. And were you the asshole playing games with the lights?" Midas demanded.

Her jaw almost hit the floor. As far as she knew, no one had ever called Dimitri an asshole. Well, not to his face, anyway.

And speaking of his face—it turned an unnatural red. More like reddish purple.

"She was on the ice when the lights went *off*," Midas continued, apparently not giving a damn about the odd color of Dimitri's face, "and she could have hurt herself. Even someone as talented as Alina can't skate in pitch darkness."

"I didn't turn anything off," Dimitri fired right back. "I came in and turned everything on. I would *never* do anything to jeopardize Alina! She's my prize skater."

"Really don't like the possessive *my*. Not when it comes to Alina," Midas drawled. "We'll revisit that one." He turned toward her. "Stay with the douche."

Her eyes widened. He had *not*—

"I'll check the perimeter and come back for you." His hand lifted and brushed over her cheek. "You are...quite something, Alina Bellamy."

Then he was off. Moving very swiftly for someone of his size. She gaped after him.

"*No.*" Dimitri moved into her path and blocked her view of Midas's determined figure striding away. "You are *not* to get involved with anyone."

She wasn't involved with Midas. They'd just met.

"Your attention is on the ice. One hundred percent on the ice."

Wasn't it always? While everyone else had normal lives. Normal relationships.

"He isn't for you, Alina. Now, get back on the ice. You have several hours of practice to go. You aren't nailing that quadruple axel."

Because most female figure skaters didn't nail it. There was a reason it was the rarest jump.

"On the ice," he snapped. "And into the air. You don't have time for anything else. This is your life."

Midas had vanished.

The ice waited.

She turned from her coach. Made her way back to the ice. Her skates slid forward, slowly at first but then faster and faster. Silence settled around her. Silence and the occasional slice of her blades.

No, she didn't feel the cold. She was on the ice again. She didn't feel the cold when she—

Maybe all I ever feel is cold. Maybe I feel it so much that I don't know when I'm freezing.

Maybe...maybe she only noticed when she wasn't cold.

When warmth touched her.

When...Midas touched her.

She launched into the air. One rotation. Two rotations. Three. Four—

She slammed onto the ice. So hard that her whole body quaked.

Her breath shuddered out.

"Up!" Dimitri thundered.

Alina got back to her feet and started skating again.

***

If Alina fell one more time, Midas was walking on that damn ice and carrying her off himself. And that prick coach? Barking instructions left and right. Talk about an asshole. His voice grated with every order that he threw at Alina. And the possessive way he talked about her? The way he ordered her?

A growl built in Midas's throat. He'd checked every inch of the facility. Hadn't found any sign that someone else had been there. He had no clue why the lights had gone off, but he damn well didn't like the situation.

Ryker had given him the barest of details on her case the night before. Someone had been sending threatening emails. Letters. There had been some threats made on social media. Her father had made sure those threats hadn't actually been read by Alina. None of the threats had been traced back to the perpetrator—or perpetrators. But with the Olympic competition season heating up, Ryker had wanted to make sure a guard was close to Alina.

Her undercover protector.

So, here he was. Watching her skate. Feeling a strange rage snake through him each time that dick of a coach ordered her to complete a different maneuver. Alina had been skating for hours. She needed a break. Sweat gleamed on her face, shining a little on her forehead and her curving cheekbones. Her hair still remained pulled back in its tight bun, though a few tendrils had escaped to dance around her face. Classical music played from the speakers as she streaked across the ice, and when she began to spin—over and over—her delicate body became a wild blur that was really damn impressive to see.

She kept spinning and spinning. He could not take his eyes off her and then—

The music stopped.

So did she. With her back arched, her chest heaving, and her hands in the air.

Perfect.

He clapped.

Her head whipped toward him. Surprise flashed in her eyes. Amazing eyes. Dark and deep eyes. A quick smile curved her lips. No dimples from Alina. But she didn't need dimples. That smile of hers was absolutely gorgeous.

"You will not be here tomorrow," Dimitri informed him. His Russian accent grated hard in the words. No "W" sounds there. Just a hard "V."

"Oh, I absolutely will be here." Midas turned his head and looked down at the much smaller man. *I can break you with barely a thought, asshole.* "I'll be here tomorrow and the day after that and the day after that. Pretty much as long as I'm needed, I'll be here."

"You are *not* needed."

"Um, well, see, her father—you remember him, right? The man who pays you? Who built this lovely facility? He hired me. He wants me to keep an eye on things. Ryker wants me to ensure that the building is secure for Alina and the other skaters. Be assured, I take my job very seriously." He did. A charge had never been hurt during his watch.

"You can watch from a distance," Dimitri bit out. "You will *not* distract Alina." He whirled toward her as she skated to join them. "Adequate performance. Add an extra hour for tomorrow. You'll need it." Then he marched away.

"Adequate, my ass," Midas informed her. Loudly. He wanted the dick to hear him. "That was amazing. Never seen anyone skate like you. You are phenomenal."

Her head dipped forward as a faint pink tinted her cheeks. "Thank you."

His hand lifted and curled under her chin. He tilted her face up because he wanted to look into those incredible eyes of hers again.

Wow. Slow your roll, man. You're playing the role of interested suitor. This is not the real deal. He had one big rule that he usually told his charges...*Don't go falling for me.* Yeah, probably a BS warning that they didn't need but he gave the warning because he never, ever allowed emotional ties. Those ties would always get in the way of a job.

"Adequate is actually a really big compliment from Dimitri," she murmured. "You should hear what he says when he isn't impressed."

"No, I don't think I should hear that." It would just piss him off, and Midas already didn't like the jerk. His thumb slid over her lower lip.

Her breath caught.

What the fuck am I doing? The caressing movement of his thumb had been instinctive. She had gorgeous lips. Full. Bow-shaped. Kissable.

And he needed to back the hell off. She was the reserved one. The shy one. The one her own father had said didn't have a lot of experience with men. If he came on too strong, she'd bolt.

He dropped his hand and stepped back.

She made her way to the bench and began to remove her skates.

Damn but she was small. He looked at his hands. Freaking bear claws. He towered over her. The woman was built along ballerina-like lines. Was that a figure skater thing? Did they have to be small in order to do all that crazy shit in the air? Kinda like a gymnast or something? Wait, he did remember reading that she'd competed in gymnastics for a time, before she'd switched fully to figure skating.

"Did you figure out why the lights went off?" She laced up her tennis shoes. She'd been skating in a pair of what looked like black yoga pants and a form-fitting black top. A top that stretched over her small but round breasts. And, yes, dammit, his gaze had dipped to those breasts a time or two.

Or ten.

He cleared his throat. Her pants *weren't* yoga pants. He was sure there was some sort of special skating name for them. Midas just had zero clue what that name might be. As he watched, Alina shouldered into a white, puffy coat and zipped it up.

Then she rose to stand in front of him.

"Shit," he exclaimed. "You're even smaller than I thought."

A shake of her head. "I'm the same size. Just not standing on blades any longer." She lifted her hand and pulled her hair free of the bun. The silky mass tumbled over her shoulders as a long sigh slipped from her. "Oh, so much better."

He swallowed.

"So, did you figure out why the lights went off?" Alina asked again.

"Got a crew investigating the electrical panel right now. Lead maintenance fellow thinks it could have been a short." One possibility, certainly. But there were a few things about the situation that bothered him.

One...the door to the facility *had* been unlocked when he arrived.

Two...the lights had all come on easily enough when Dimitri had flipped the switches. And, of course, when Midas had questioned him, Dimitri hadn't been able to say if the lights over the rink had been turned *off* before he started flipping things. The Russian coach had no idea what he'd turned on and what he hadn't.

Three...*I don't like her training alone.* "You should have someone with you when you train in the mornings."

Her mouth kicked into a half-smile. An oddly sexy one. "It's my *alone* time. My time to glide across the ice without Dimitri growling at me."

Yeah, he could get wanting to be away from the prick, but... "I'll be here in the mornings before you arrive from now on."

Her brows climbed. "The last head of security didn't arrive that early."

"Then he wasn't doing the job right. I'll be here with you. There won't be any other instances of you skating alone in the dark." The idea of saying he was the new head of security at the rink? Totally his. Midas liked to keep his truth and his lies as close as possible. Ryker *had* needed someone, and Midas was the most qualified. He'd watch over the facility and take extra care to watch Alina.

Alina nibbled on her lower lip.

"Got a problem?" he queried. He was sure she was gonna tell him that she wanted her "alone time" in the morning for skating, and that was just gonna be too damn bad because he was there to protect her. He'd get the job done, no matter what. He would—

"Would you like to go out with me? Like, on a date?"

Midas blinked.

"Or is it weird because my father hired you to work here?" She retreated a quick step. "Or maybe it's weird because you're not interested, and I shouldn't have said anything at all. Forget it." She spun away. Her hair fluttered in her wake.

It took him about two seconds to break out of his stunned stupor. Then he lunged and curled his hand around her shoulder. "Wait!"

She looked back at him. Back first at his hand, then her dark gaze rose to meet his.

Fuck. There was something about her dark eyes…

"I am *very* interested." Another truth. Something he hadn't expected. Okay, fine, he'd expected some interest. Alina was a beautiful woman. Interest would be normal.

He typically dated women who were tall, stacked—with curves for days.

But Alina…small, delicate…

Those eyes…

The instant he'd touched her for the first time, a blast of lust had burned straight through him. *Had not expected that kick.* And the more he'd watched her, as she'd kept pushing herself over and over, never once complaining or giving up…beauty, grace, strength…

She licked her lips.

Sexiness.

He could have a problem on his hands.

"Would you like to have dinner with me?" she asked.

Dinner, dessert—anything and everything. Nope. Not supposed to say that or think that. He was gonna be the platonic boyfriend who toed the line.

Like he'd ever toed a line in his life.

"I know this probably seems crazy, especially seeing as how we just met," Alina continued with nerves shaking in her husky voice.

He didn't speak. Too busy trying to figure out what the hell to say. Yes, she'd just made things way easier on him. He'd been searching for a way to move to the next level so he could stay close to her, and she—

She was offering him that way on a silver platter.

"When you touch me, I feel something," Alina confessed softly.

Her honesty rocked straight through him.

"Heat goes through my whole body."

No woman had *ever* said this—

"Physical attraction, right?" She turned to fully face him. "I'm sure a man as gorgeous as you gets hit on all the time. You probably attract and *get* attracted to people all the time."

He wasn't blushing, was he? He damn well better not be.

"But this doesn't happen with me." A wince. "Not that I exactly get out a lot." She waved a hand to indicate the rink. "Not like there are a ton of people you can meet here. And...I'm rambling. I do that. Probably because I don't have very good people skills."

"Your skills..." He sounded too growly. A side-effect of having a deep, rumbling voice. But he tried to clear his throat and speak a little softer, for her. "Your people skills seem just fine to me."

Her smile beamed at him.

His chest ached.

"So I'm not being too forward?"

She didn't get it. Often, people *ran* from him. His size alone was intimidating as shit. But when people learned about his past...

She doesn't know. She doesn't know a damn thing about me, except that when we touch, heat goes through her whole body. She'd said that. The sexiest admission he'd ever heard.

This was more than a problem. He was starting to venture into clusterfuck mode.

He didn't cross the line on his cases. Never, ever got personally involved.

"I just didn't want to lose the opportunity, you know? To see what might happen?" Her hair slid over her shoulder as she studied him. "Sometimes, something special can be right in front of you, but you miss it because you don't take a chance." A wince. "I don't take a lot of chances in my life. Quite the opposite, in fact."

"You're taking a chance with me." She didn't know him. Not a damn thing about him. *If she did, would she run?* He doubted the sweet little ice skater would be asking him for a date.

Not if she knew all his dark secrets.

His phone vibrated in the front pocket of his jeans. He ignored the vibration. Right then, nothing was more important than the woman before him.

A bob of her head. "A chance...a date. If you want one."

"I fucking want it." He did. Moreover, he wanted her.

Clusterfuck or not.

"Then dinner, tonight?" Hope lit her dark eyes. Eagerness.

"Dinner. Tonight."

"There's a great barbecue joint not too far away. Nice and casual."

Barbecue? Be still his heart.

"I could meet you there, say at eight o'clock?" Alina rattled off the name of the restaurant.

He nodded. "Meet you there."

She did a quick bounce. Freaking adorable. Then Alina bestowed him with her wide smile once more. The smile was a weapon, one she might not even realize she possessed. It made a man want to do crazy things.

Made him want to do anything to see the smile again.

Oh, hell. He inhaled.

"It was great meeting you," Alina told him. "Scary, at first, but I'm glad you walked into my rink."

"Same," he told her. Too gruff, but she didn't seem to mind. "Great meeting you." *Guarding you. I am supposed to be guarding you.* And he would guard her. On their date. Pretend boyfriend, reporting for duty. It was really too easy.

So why did he feel like shit?

With a quick wave, she headed to the locker room area. He waited until she disappeared.

Scary, at first. Most people said he was always scary. Always intimidating. But, not Alina.

His phone vibrated again. Jaw locking, he pulled it out of his pocket. Once glance at the screen, and every muscle in his body tensed.

He's asking to see you again. Says it's important.

Midas recognized the text sender's name. Would have been damn impossible for Midas not to know the name of his dear old, twisted, piece of shit father's new lawyer.

It was the fourth time within the last week that he'd gotten the message. And, just like before, Midas's reply was the same.

When hell freezes over.

Because he had no intention of ever talking to his father again. When your dear old dad framed you for murder—and turned out to be one of the most twisted serial killers in existence—it tended to make you want to cut ties.

Especially when there were too many folks out there who kept thinking that you were a chip off the old sadistic block.

Once more, Alina's voice drifted through his head. *It was great meeting you. Scary, at first, but I'm glad you walked into my rink.*

Just how long would she stay glad? He glanced at the ice.

He fucking hated the cold.

***

Ryker Bellamy stared at the photo on his desk. A photo that had been in his car, waiting for him, a week ago.

A photo of his daughter. One taken while she was mid-spin on the ice. Not a promotional image. Not something taken by one of the photographers he hired. Not even the usual press people.

Alina wore her workout uniform. No makeup.

A red X had been drawn over her body.

Swallowing, he flipped over the photo and reread the message he'd already studied at least a hundred times.

You can't escape the past.

Then, beneath those scrawled words...

How much is she worth to you?

Everything. Alina was everything. And she would be safe. She *had* to be safe. Midas Monroe was supposed to be the best. Sure, he hadn't told Midas everything, but there was no need. Midas would protect her. He'd stay close. He'd be her bodyguard.

No one needs to know what's happening. Because if the full truth came out, Ryker's life could be destroyed.

Slowly, deliberately, he tore up the photo. Tore it into as many tiny pieces as he could.

No one threatened him. Or his daughter.

Alina would be safe.

There was no other alternative. He wouldn't lose her. He'd lost her mother. He would not lose his Alina.

Midas Monroe had one job.

Keep her safe.

He'd better fucking do his job.

CHAPTER TWO

"No, no, no, no...*no*." Alina shook her head and tried turning the key in the ignition one more, desperate time. The engine sputtered, and she *thought* that she was going to get the vehicle to crank. Hope had her heart racing but—

The sputtering died away. The brief flare of her headlights also died away, and she was thrown into darkness on the long, lonely road.

"Dammit." Things had been perfect until five minutes ago. When her engine had started making a weird, grinding sound. When her speed had suddenly decreased. When she'd barely made it to the side of the road before the car died.

A car that was barely a year old. Excellent condition.

This should not have happened.

But it had. Now she was going to be late for her date with the mysterious Midas, if she made it to the date at all. Alina grabbed for her purse, and her hand fumbled inside until she pulled out her phone.

Then she realized that she didn't have his number. She didn't even have the man's last name. How weird was that?

But she did have the number for a tow truck. She kept a local tow truck number programmed in her phone, just in case of emergencies. She'd get a tow truck out and she'd be on her way, and she'd call the restaurant and ask that someone there please tell Midas what was happening. No way did she want him thinking that she'd stood him up and—

Headlights. Bright lights. In her rear-view mirror. They flashed and blinded her for an instant, and her left hand instinctively rose to shield her eyes. She waited for the vehicle to pass her.

Only it didn't.

It pulled in directly behind her. The too-bright lights illuminated every inch of her vehicle. She turned back, but there was no making out anything about the driver. Her eyes narrowed against the glare.

Then the light was gone. Darkness once again.

Darkness, just like on the rink this morning. Unease slithered through her. How could it not? She was a woman alone, on a dark road, with a car that wouldn't start. And, maybe, maybe that was some good Samaritan who'd just stopped to see if she was all right. There were good people in the world. She didn't need to let her imagination run wild. She wasn't being attacked or stalked or—

Knuckles tapped on her driver's side window, and Alina jumped. She hadn't even heard the driver approaching.

He rapped against the window again. She hit the button to lower the window, but nothing happened. *No power.* She'd have to open the door and if she did that—

"Alina!" Loud. The person on the other side leaned down. He was a big, heavy shadow.

Her eyes narrowed.

"You're supposed to be heading for a date with me. Not stopping on the side of the road to see the sights."

Her breath shuddered out.

She pushed open the door and practically leapt at the man. Oh, there was no practically to it. Alina threw her arms around Midas and hugged him tightly.

"Is this you getting cold feet about our date?" Midas asked. "You pulling over to rethink the plans for the night?"

She shivered. For a moment there, she'd been afraid. "Not cold feet. My car broke down." She tilted her head up to peer at him. "How are you here right now?"

A moment passed before he responded, "Lucky timing. I was heading this way to meet you at the restaurant. Spotted your car on the side of the road—knew it was you because I saw the vehicle at the rink's lot when you were leaving. Noticed your hiking sticker on the back."

Her sticker. Right. Because sometimes, she just had to escape and clear her head. Hiking had always been a great escape for Alina.

"It just died," she told him and realized that her arms were still around him. She held him too tightly and should probably step back.

Only—

There was no stepping back. He'd suddenly lifted her into his arms and was carrying her away from her vehicle and to the passenger side of his SUV.

"Uh." She cleared her throat. "What are you doing?"

He opened the door and deposited her inside. "Getting you safe. If cars come zipping by, no damn way I want you on the side of the road."

There were no other cars zipping by. It was just them.

She realized that his emergency blinkers were flashing. A good thing since her car hadn't been able to flash any signal to alert anyone else. "My bag is in my car."

"I'll get it. And your keys. *Stay here.*" He started to slam the door shut. Then seemed to catch himself. Half-turned toward her, Midas gritted, "Please."

Her brows climbed. "I'll be here."

She watched as he stalked to her car. He lifted the hood. Poked around inside. She leaned forward, trying to see more. But there wasn't much to see.

The hood slammed closed. He snagged her bag. Presumably her keys, too. His stride was fast and hard when he came back to her.

Midas climbed into the driver's seat. "Tell me what happened." He put her bag on the floorboard near her leg. His hand brushed over her thigh.

A surge of awareness slid over her. "I...it just stopped. Sputtered. Slowed down. I barely made it fully onto the shoulder before it died. I tried cranking it—a lot," she confessed. "Maybe I flooded the engine." That was a thing, wasn't it? Cars weren't exactly her specialty. "At the end, everything just turned off. The lights. Radio. I couldn't even get my windows to lower."

"You didn't flood the engine." He cranked his vehicle. Heat blasted from the vents.

"Well, that's good to know." She reached into her bag. Her phone was inside. She didn't even remember dropping it back inside, but she must have done it before opening the door for him. "I'll call a tow truck."

"I'll handle it." Flat.

And, again, her brows rose.

"I have an acquaintance who specializes in auto repair. He can find out what happened to the car. Tow the ride. Get you repaired. No problem." He hauled out his own phone and made a quick phone call.

"That's nice of you," she murmured. "Thank you."

Headlights filled the interior of the SUV. Automatically, she looked back.

And heard the fierce growl of an engine. Not someone who was stopping to help. This vehicle hurtled past them as the engine seemed to suddenly roar.

"Sonofabitch," Midas snarled.

Yep, very good thing she hadn't been standing on the edge of the road by her vehicle.

"Ron, I need a pickup," Midas said into his phone. "An Audi shut down on a friend of mine. Yeah, I can give you a location." He did. A very specific one. "Let me know what the hell caused it to stop running, got me? ASAP on this." He ended the call. Stared out after the vehicle that had just blasted past them. "He sure was in a hurry." His head turned toward her. "You're all right?"

A knot twisted in her stomach. "My car just broke down. No big deal."

Illumination from the dash spilled onto him. His face seemed extra intent. Extra hard. "You were scared when I arrived."

Why lie? She had been afraid. "For a moment, I didn't know if you were the good guy or someone who might want to harm me." Wasn't that a worry everyone faced? In the night, stranded with a broken-down vehicle...

Was someone coming to help?

Or to hurt?

"I was calling for help," she rushed to add. "Right before you arrived." Though she just had to shake her head over his arrival. "Talk about perfect timing. For the second time today, you've been right there when I needed someone." She tried to lighten her tone. "If I didn't know better, I'd say you just might be my guardian angel."

"Oh, baby, no, I am no angel. Do not make that mistake." He sounded so horrified that she had to laugh.

But he didn't laugh with her.

"That's not who I am," he assured her and there was no humor in his voice. Only what seemed like a grim warning. "Not by a long shot. I'm more like the devil than anything else."

But she shook her head. "Not to me." Her hand lifted and curled around his fingers as he still gripped his phone. "To me, you look like a hero."

He glanced down at her hand. She smiled as he said—

"Fuck."

***

"Would you like to dance?" Alina's question came out hesitantly even as her gaze flickered toward the small dance floor. Because the barbecue restaurant she'd picked? Just so happened there was a guy playing guitar there that night. Strumming along as a few couples moved slowly on a faded, wooden dance floor.

Dinner and a dance…and a side dose of danger. Because Midas had sure as shit felt dangerous when he'd followed Alina and saw her car pull over to the edge of the dark road.

Good thing I was on her trail. The car was dead. She would have been stuck there, all alone.

Two suspicious incidents in one day. Every instinct he had was on high alert.

"But we don't have to dance," Alina hurried to say.

Hurried because he'd been glaring at the guitarist. Not deliberate. He'd just been thinking about the damn *incidents* in her life. To him, they looked like attacks that had been designed to terrify her.

He didn't want Alina terrified.

His gaze swung back to her. His buddy Ron had picked up her car, and Midas had taken Alina to dinner. The woman had to eat, didn't she? No sense in canceling their plans. Especially since he needed to stay close to her.

Dancing with her would put him extremely close.

Temptingly close.

His right hand flattened on the tabletop. "I'm not a very good dancer."

"I don't think you have to be," she assured him. "The other three couples are pretty much just swaying back and forth." That bright smile of hers came again. The one that disarmed him and also made him want to go out and freaking slay a dragon for her or some stupid shit like that.

"This is not me," he growled.

She blinked. "Oh, I'm sorry. That's fine." Her smile dimmed, then blossomed again. "We absolutely don't have to dance. Why don't you, um, why don't you tell me about yourself? Your life? Your family?"

*This is not me...*He hadn't meant the dancing. Though, yeah, he was a horrible dancer. He basically lumbered along and didn't follow a beat at all. When you were his size, grace didn't tend to be your strong suit. Brute strength? He had that one covered.

*This is not me...*He'd meant the wanting to slay dragons BS. He wasn't a knight or some guardian angel. He was a bodyguard who was doing his job.

So guard that sexy body of hers. "Let's dance." He shoved back his chair and stood. Dancing was far better than the alternative. The alternative in question?

Telling her about his life. His family.

Hi. I'm Midas Monroe, the son of a serial killer. My dear old dad is currently rotting away in a maximum-security facility. Who did he kill? Multiple women. He broke their necks. Oh, and for extra fun, he would stab them in the heart after he broke their necks. See, a broken neck doesn't always kill the victim. Guess my dad learned that lesson early on. So he evolved as twisted killers do.

And he also tried to frame me for his crimes. No big deal.

Alina peered up at him. "Are you sure? I don't want to make you uncomfortable. If dancing isn't your thing, we can skip it."

She was so freaking *nice*. His hand extended toward her. "There is nothing more I want right now than to dance with you."

Delight lit her features. She hopped to her feet and put her hand in his. Of course, his hand swallowed hers, but he was sure to use care. Not to grip her fingers too hard. Not to squeeze too tightly.

He led them onto the dance floor, and when he caught another jerk staring at Alina's ass, Midas sent the guy a go-to-hell glare.

The man whipped his stare away from Alina.

The woman *did* look extra good. No ice princess tonight. Instead, she wore a pair of jeans that hugged her tight ass, low black boots, and a dark sweater. Her hair tumbled down her shoulders and back. It curled. One of those long, twisting curl things that women could do with their hair that just confused and impressed the hell out of men.

Soft red lipstick covered her lips. Smoky shadow made her eyes seem even darker.

He stopped in the middle of the dance floor and pulled her against him.

So delicate. He was still having trouble getting used to her size. When she was on the ice, she'd seemed bigger. Stronger.

Off the ice, she felt too breakable.

Her hands curled around his waist.

His...hell, he put his hands on her. Enjoyed the feel of her far too much. When he inhaled, he caught her scent. Vanilla cream? Something that sure smelled good enough to eat.

He realized that Alina had started to sway in time with the strumming guitar while he was standing still. He lumbered to the left. Then the right.

"You're incredibly light on your feet," Alina murmured.

A quick bark of laughter burst from him. "You're a shit liar."

Her head tilted back as she gazed up at him. "You have a great laugh."

"And you have the sexiest mouth I've ever seen." Whoops. Okay, that was not the way to head down platonic boulevard. But, having her body pressed to his and his hands curled around her—that probably wasn't the way to platonic boulevard, either.

Dancing had clearly been a mistake.

Mentioning her mouth had been his second mistake. Because now his gaze had locked to her lips. For one moment, he imagined curling his hands around her waist, lifting her up against him, and taking that hot mouth of hers.

One kiss...

And that would start me down the road to hell.

He whipped away from her. Pulled his hands from her as if he'd been burned. This undercover assignment was stupid. Her dad should just tell the woman she was in danger. It would sure make Midas's life a whole lot simpler. Then he could put his normal rules in place.

They could establish clear boundaries.

"Is something wrong?" A little furrow appeared between her brows.

Oh, nothing. He just wanted to rip off her clothes and fuck her right then and there. His dick shoved too hard against the front of his jeans, and he was thinking about how to get his charge into bed.

Okay, fine, that qualified as *wrong*. Because his number one rule with a charge? *No attachments.*

"We should go," he rumbled. "It's getting late. You have to be at the rink early tomorrow." Did ten p.m. count as late? Probably not. Screw it. "I have to be there early, too." Like she'd be alone in that place again. Not happening.

"All right." She tucked a lock of hair behind her ear. "I just need to run to the restroom first real fast. Be right back." She hurried away.

Hell, had that been a flash of pain in her eyes? He had yanked away like he didn't want to touch her. Not exactly a smooth move. But...*I don't want to touch her. Because touching her feels too good.* As for kissing her, he was sure that would feel utterly fantastic.

He ambled off the small excuse for a dance floor. His check had been left on their table, so Midas scooped it up and made his way to the bar. He'd settle the tab and get them the hell out of there. But as he approached the bar, he saw that the bartender and two waitresses were huddled around the flat-screen TV that perched on the wall nearby.

"That's terrible," he heard one of the waitresses softly exclaim. "Missing all this time, only to find out that she'd been murdered? Broken neck. Stabbed in the heart. God. What a terrible way to go."

Midas froze.

"Who would do something like that?"

His gaze flew to the screen. The volume was turned down low—probably so it wouldn't blast out that strumming guitar—but the closed caption option was on, and he read the words flying beneath the reporter's image.

The autopsy report has just been released, and although socialite Maureen O'Sullivan had several fractures to her cervical vertebrae, the medical examiner has determined that her actual cause of death was due to the knife wound in her heart that—

"Midas?"

He whipped around.

Alina frowned at him. "Is something wrong?"

Yes. Very. *No, no, it's just a coincidence.* A terrible, twisted coincidence.

And since when did he believe in those?

"You look like you've just seen a ghost." Her hand rose to press against his chest. "What is it?"

Not a ghost. The devil. *Had to be a coincidence.* His dear old dad was still locked away. He couldn't hurt anyone. Not ever again. "I need to get you home. Now."

She stared at him as if—as if she cared about how he felt. As if she truly worried about him. They'd just met that day. No way did she care. No way did he care.

This was all fucked.

Midas glanced back at the TV. A different reporter filled the screen. A different story. The waitresses had moved away. He tossed down his cash and the tip and caught Alina beneath the elbow. "Let's go."

Coincidence. Had to be. But at the earliest opportunity, he would be calling in some friends because he just needed some clarification. No, what he needed was for his guts to unknot.

In moments, he had Alina back in his ride. As soon as her seatbelt was hooked, he shot into reverse and got them the hell out of there. Midas knew he should probably make some small talk. Ease the tension filling up the interior of the vehicle, but he didn't know what to say. Mostly because that news report kept blasting through his head.

It wouldn't be the first time a copycat had tried to follow in the twisted footsteps of Midas's father. Hell, about four years ago, there had even been one guy who deliberately tried to stage his wife's death in the same manner because he'd hoped the cops wouldn't realize that the man had killed his own wife in a jealous fury.

No, not the first time but...

But I still hate it. Hate it for the vic. Hate for the past to rush forward.

So he didn't have any words to give Alina.

And the tension grew thicker.

***

She'd done something wrong.

Alina twisted her hands in her lap as Midas brought the vehicle to a stop in her driveway. She lived in a small house not too far from the rink. Having her own place was important to her. Her father had protested like crazy when she'd first told him she was moving out of the family estate.

She hadn't given in, though.

Everyone needed space.

I wanted my own life.

He killed the engine. Tapped his fingers against the steering wheel. And a belated question sprang to her mind. "How did you know where I lived?" The first question she'd asked during the too-silent ride home. She didn't have a ton of experience with men, but when your date went stone-cold silent on you, that was a bad sign.

Sure, the night hadn't gotten off to the most stellar start—not with the whole broken-down-car situation. But he'd seemed to be having fun with her at the restaurant. Right up until the dance. When she'd come back from the bathroom—she'd only gone there so the terrible flush in her cheeks could die down after he'd backed away from her—he'd seemed like a completely different person. His amber eyes had blazed and his whole expression had hardened as if it had been cut from stone.

At her question, his fingers stopped tapping. "Saw it in a file while I was reviewing notes at the rink earlier. Remembered it because it's close to my own place."

It was?

"That's why I was on the same road tonight," he added smoothly. "Both heading the same way."

"Where do you live?"

"Two blocks away."

Oh. That was close. "It's a great area. Quiet." And she was rambling again. The man was *not* interested. Time for her to go.

Too bad. She'd been so excited at the sensual promise that seemed to flicker between them. After waiting forever to finally *feel* that promise with someone, the night was sure settling into a heavy disappointment. She reached for the door.

"I'm coming inside."

Her head snapped back toward him. "I...don't remember inviting you inside." The man could not keep running hot and cold on her.

"I—"

"Look, either you're interested or you're not. I'm not into playing games. Mostly because I do not know how to play them." Her dating history was abysmal. Not like she'd gained the knowledge to confidently play a game with anyone.

"Fuck. You are so honest."

"What am I supposed to do? Lie?" A shake of her head. Her hand pressed to the handle on the side of the door. "You backed away on the dance floor." Backed away like she'd burned the man.

"You've been acting like you couldn't wait to drop me off. *Now* you want to come inside?" *Make up your mind, Midas.*

"I want to make sure no one is waiting in there."

Her mouth opened. No words emerged. How was she supposed to respond to that? Finally, she managed, "Who would be waiting?"

His head turned, and he glanced back at her house. Her dark house. "I have this thing…I believe in seeing my date safely to her door."

"Fine. Walk me to the door." She exited the car. Made sure to haul her bag with her. Midas followed right at her heels. For someone so big, he could certainly move fast.

At her door, she fumbled with her bag and took out her key. But she didn't put the key in the lock. Not yet. "Job done," she assured him. "I am safely at my door. You do *not* need to come inside."

"I fucked up."

She slanted him a glance from beneath her lashes.

"I don't know how I'm supposed to react to you." His hands were loose at his sides, his voice oddly hesitant. "I don't usually get involved with people I work with. In fact, I have a rule about that very thing."

Alina wet her lips. "We don't really work together. More like I visit the place you work at." A clarification.

He shook his head. "Why the hell would you even want to be involved with someone like me?

Shouldn't you be dating some movie star or tech billionaire or something?"

The question floored her. "Why would I be doing that?"

"You should be with someone who moves in your circles."

A laugh sputtered from her. "My circles? Ice skating circles? There aren't a lot of movie stars in them. Or tech billionaires. There are demanding coaches. Competitors who will slit your throat in order to take you out of the game."

He surged toward her. "What?"

"Figure of speech. Let's just say they are really cutthroat. It's the nature of the beast."

He didn't look reassured as he stood beneath the light on her porch. His gaze traced over her face. No, definitely not reassured. But...

Hungry?

Had that been longing that just flashed on his face?

Tension snaked through her. "Why did you agree to go out with me?" She'd been the one to ask for the date. Had he been able to tell that her knees were practically knocking together as she'd dared to ask him to dinner?

"You're beautiful. Gorgeous. And no matter how many times you fell in practice, you always got up."

Her lashes fluttered.

"You're a fighter, aren't you, Alina?"

"If you want to win gold, you have to be. No one hands you an Olympic medal just for showing up."

He smiled at her. Her breath caught because that smile of his sure did pack a powerful punch. One that she seemed to feel throughout her entire body. And, almost against her will, she felt herself leaning toward him.

His hand came up, and his fingers curled under her chin. "You'll regret being with me."

Maybe. "I'd rather regret doing something than regret not taking the chance and missing something great."

His eyes narrowed. "I'm not the man you want."

"Really? Huh. So strange. Because I think you're the only one I need." Her tongue swiped over her lower lip. "But you can't run hot and cold on me. No stepping back just because you get scared."

His head lowered toward her. "I don't get scared. Not of anything."

No? "Then you didn't back away on the dance floor because you were scared?"

The sound that rumbled from him seemed to be a cross between a rough laugh and a growl. "I backed away because I wanted to fuck you right then and there."

Okay. She had zero comeback for that response.

"Figured you wouldn't appreciate that," Midas rasped. "Seeing as how we had an audience, and it was our first date. Thought I'd be a gentleman."

Had anyone ever wanted to fuck her *right then and there?* Those words were hot. He was hot. But... "You haven't even kissed me yet."

"True."

"How can you already want to fuck me without kissing me?"

Laughter. This time, his response was definitely a laugh.

"Oh, baby…"

Her shoulders stiffened.

"I wanted you the first time I saw you spiraling across the ice. That was seconds before you fell, by the way." A pause. "I don't like it when you fall."

He seemed way too concerned with her falls.

"I'd have to be careful with you." His head dipped even closer. But his hand moved away from her chin. Dropped back to his side. "Keep all my control."

Her breath came a little faster. Her heart raced a little more. He was going to kiss her. She was sure of it. He was—

Stepping back. "Really wish you'd let me come inside."

"No." Alina shook her head. "This was our first date. You don't get to come inside yet."

His jaw hardened. "Not come in to fuck you. I want to come inside and make sure the place is safe." His head turned toward the closed door. "You can stay right near the entrance while I search."

"You are really taking this protection bit seriously, aren't you?"

A muscle flexed along his clenched jaw. "Yes. I am."

"Do you always search the houses of your dates? That's a normal thing for you?" Just so she understood. Because he'd said something before about always seeing his dates to the door.

"The full-house search is just a normal thing with you."

That *was* protective. And weird. Both?

"The lights shouldn't have gone off at the rink. The maintenance guy says nothing was wrong with the electrical system. I think someone turned them off. And I don't like that your car just randomly stopped while you were driving down a long, lonely stretch of the road."

Goose bumps rose on her arms.

"You're a beautiful woman in the public eye. I'm a guy used to working security. I see red flags flying around you right now. I don't like them."

She lifted her key toward the lock. Her fingers shook so it took three tries to actually get the key in the lock successfully. Once the door was open, she disengaged her security system, but she remained near the front door. With one hand, she waved for him to enter. "Take a quick search. Have at it."

He stepped over the threshold.

"You've scared me, so I won't be able to sleep tonight without a search." A rough exhale. "Search away."

And he did. Fast and thorough while she stood near the doorway gripping her purse. The man searched her house as she tried not to think about red flags and just how very terrified she'd been when the lights went out on her at the rink.

He returned to stand in front of her. Big, bold, and taking up so much space. "It's clear."

"Excellent to know."

That muscle flexed along his jaw again. "You think I'm overprotective."

That was one word that could be used to describe him.

"I've seen bad things in my life, Alina. I just don't want to take chances."

Her hands tightened on the strap of her purse.

"Not with someone as important as you."

All of the moisture seemed to dry from her mouth.

He inclined his head. "Good night, Alina. Lock the door behind me."

No, she'd just leave it unlocked for fun. He opened the door, and the man crossed the threshold. "That's it?" Alina's voice rose.

He froze.

"You tell me I'm important, you insist on searching my house, and you're walking away without even kissing me good night?"

Very slowly, he turned to face her. "I don't think a kiss is a good idea."

Her temper began to stir. "What is it with you? I just can't understand you. One minute, I think you like me. The next, you keep backing away."

"I'm trying to keep up the gentleman act with you, Alina. Kissing you would blow that act to hell and back. Let me be the good guy for you. At least for a while."

Not like she was going to beg the man for a kiss. She'd already been forward enough.

"Dammit. Don't look at me that way." His brow furrowed.

What way?

"Don't be hurt. I'm trying to do the right thing here." He inched closer. "I'm trying to—fuck it."

Fuck—what?

"Hell and back," he breathed. "Hope we're both ready for this."

His hands went to her waist. She didn't get a chance to say another word because he lifted her up—and his mouth plunged down to claim hers.

***

Henry Monroe sat in his prison cell and peered out at the sliver of the moon. Such a small window. A real annoyance. He wanted a bigger window. A bigger cell. Better food.

No, what he really wanted was to be free. To be on the outside again.

Hunting.

God, he missed the thrill of the hunt. The sweet scent of his prey.

He looked down at his hands. Big hands. Hands that had so easily captured the women he wanted. Hands that had curled around their necks.

Snapped them.

His son was still refusing to see him. His golden boy. That would be changing. Midas couldn't ignore him forever.

Not now.

Now when a new game was at play.

So he stared at the moon. That little sliver. And Henry began to dream of all the fun he'd have...

Once he was set free.
He wondered...had Midas already met Alina? Oh, but he hoped so. He'd gone to such lengths to bring the two of them together.

CHAPTER THREE

Sometimes, you knew something was a mistake, but it just didn't fucking matter.

In that moment, nothing else mattered to Midas. Nothing but kissing Alina. Tasting her. He'd screwed up this date. Yes, clearly. And kissing her was probably going to screw things up even more.

But why not go down in a blaze of glory? Better to be damned for the things he did than for the things he didn't do.

Like when I nearly got sent to prison for murders I never committed.

His hands circled her waist as he lifted her up against him. His mouth crashed onto hers, and her lips parted for him. Eagerly, feverishly, she kissed him back. No controlled or cautious kiss from Alina. She kissed him with enough heat to absolutely burn him alive.

Growling, he turned with her in his arms. He kicked the door shut. One hand reached out and flipped the lock, then he pinned her between his body and the wood of the door. He didn't free her mouth. Couldn't. He just kissed her deeper.

Harder. The moan that rumbled in her throat drove the desire he felt for her even higher.

Her legs wrapped around his hips. Her hands grabbed onto his shoulders as she held him tightly.

He'd wondered what it would be like to kiss her.

Thought it would be good. How could it not be good?

Her tongue slid against his. His whole body shuddered. His eager dick thrust against her.

And he realized this kiss wasn't good. It was great. It was phenomenal.

And I am lying to her. Fuck. Fuck.

Fuck.

He tore his mouth from hers. Lifted his head. Stared down into her eyes—eyes even darker and more turbulent than they'd been before.

If kissing her is this fantastic, I will lose my mind when I fuck her. No, no. He was not doing that. The job was to watch her. Guard her.

Pretend to be interested.

Screw pretending. I am one hundred percent onboard with real interest.

"That was the best kiss of my life," she whispered.

His chest burned. "Same." He'd give her as much honesty as he could.

And hope she didn't hate his guts later.

"So why did you stop?"

"Because I want more than a kiss." His hands slowly lowered her down until her feet touched the floor again. Then he let her go. "And you're not ready for that."

"First date," she breathed. "No, not ready." A swallow.

"I want another date." Was he really continuing this dumbass ruse? But, it didn't feel like a ruse. He wanted to be with her.

"So do I."

"Tomorrow night?" It would give him a reason to be close to her again. A perfect excuse. Only it was about more than being an excuse.

Her high-voltage smile flashed. "Sounds great to me."

"Lock the door behind me."

"Absolutely."

He still lingered. "You...you'll need a ride to the rink tomorrow. I'll come by first thing."

Her eyebrows arched. "I get to the rink at four a.m."

"I'll come by and get you."

"That early? You sure?"

"I'll be here." He made himself step to the side. She was technically between him and the door since he'd lifted her up and pinned her there. But when he moved, she slipped away. Her heady and sweet scent teased him. He drank it in then made himself leave.

A job. She's a job. A charge. You're supposed to treat her the way you treat every other charge.

Only she wasn't just like the others. And not just because she had zero clue that he was actually her bodyguard. He felt something different with her. Something he had never felt with anyone else.

A ferocious hard-on? Check. But he'd had those before. Plenty of them. Sex was natural, fun, and a vital part of his life.

But the consuming desire he felt for her? The flare of possessiveness that had begun to beat beneath his skin? *Trouble.*

He stood on the porch until he heard the click of her lock. Then, nodding and flipping up his collar against the bite in the air, he headed back to his ride. After climbing inside, he glanced at her house. In case she was watching from behind the blinds, he drove away. But he didn't drive far, and when he came back, he parked down the street and killed his lights.

On a normal bodyguard case, he'd be in that house with her. Hunkered down on the couch. Within shouting distance. Locking his jaw, he yanked his phone up to his ear and called Ryker.

"Is my daughter safe?" That was how the man answered the phone. With a tight edge in his voice.

"Checked her house, every room. No intruders. When I left, I made sure she locked the door behind me." Had she reset her alarm? Surely, she had.

A relieved sigh whispered over the line. "When I received your text about her car breaking down, I got worried."

A text he'd sent right before entering the restaurant with Alina.

"But you assured me she was safe," Ryker added roughly.

"She was safe. She was with me, and when she's with me, she's always gonna be safe." His eyes remained on her house. "But you're tying my hands, and this shit has to stop. There were two incidents today. Two incidents on day one of my employment."

"The...the lights at the rink could have been anything—"

"I don't buy it. I don't like it. I don't like the deal with her car, either."

"But you don't have any proof—"

"My buddy is doing a thorough scan on her car first thing tomorrow. We'll see if he thinks someone sabotaged the ride or not."

Silence.

"She needs to know. You felt like the threat to her was so big that she needed a bodyguard. We have to tell her the truth. *I* need full access."

"Alina doesn't like bodyguards. I told you that before. She gets rid of them. Refuses to work with them—"

"Yeah, yeah, yeah. Look, I might have bought that story *before* I met the woman. She's no spoiled debutante who can't understand reason. She's smart and funny and—" Wow. He needed to be careful. "Logical. Clear-headed. We tell her what's happening, and she'll understand." All of the lights were out in the front of the house. Was Alina showering? Getting ready for bed? "Something else is at play. I want to know the real reason you don't want your daughter knowing she has a bodyguard."

"I *don't* want her frightened. She has to remain focused on the competition. Knowing there is danger surrounding her will undermine her confidence. She won't be able to perform at the top of her ability."

"Screw the competition."

A gasp from Ryker.

"Isn't her life more important than a competition?"

"That's why I hired you. I don't want Alina to lose her dream. She's lost enough. We can keep her safe. You do your job. Stay close to her—"

"I'm freaking down the street in a dark car, spying while I talk to you right now. If a neighbor spots me, my ass will be hauled to jail because someone will think I'm a freaking Peeping Tom. Being *outside* doesn't give me the access I need."

Silence. Then, "I don't expect you to stay there all night. That was never part of the deal."

No, it hadn't been. But it should be. All-night surveillance. But not outside. He wanted to be in that house making certain Alina was protected.

"You said she was home," Ryker continued crisply. "I have personally overseen the installation of a top-of-the-line security system at her house. Alina is secure for the night. You can leave. But you have to be back first thing in the morning."

Yeah, he *could* leave. The problem was that he didn't *want* to leave her. "What aren't you telling me?"

"Excuse me?"

"You're holding back on me. You think I don't realize it? If you've had a direct threat, if you've got material I need to see—*show it to me.* I can't work blind." He'd been told about threatening emails and letters, but he hadn't seen them. So far, he'd seen jack.

He heard Ryker inhale and then Ryker said, "All you have to do is keep an eye on my daughter.

Make sure she is safe at her practices and at any public events. The day is over for you. She's home, secure. You're done. Go get some rest so you'll be fresh tomorrow."

He didn't feel done. "I need to be in that house with her."

"As I've told you, the house is secure. Her security system is top-of-the-line. Her home would be harder to get in than Fort Knox."

He doubted that. "What aren't you telling me?" Midas went right back to his question.

"You were hired to protect my daughter. To remain undercover. If you can't do these things, then maybe I need to find someone else, recommendation from the FBI be damned."

Let someone else get close to Alina? "I took the case. She's mine." Hell. He needed to dial things back. "My charge."

"Then get some rest. Alina's day starts early. You have to be ready for it." Ryker hung up.

"I know her day starts freaking early," he rumbled. He didn't drive away. Not yet. Eyes still on the house, Midas made a second phone call. Because something else kept knotting his stomach...

And he reached out to someone that he really, really did not expect to be contacting. But he needed fast intel and Oliver was still honeymooning so...

"Yo," Memphis Camden answered. "Tell me that my caller ID isn't deceiving me. Tell me that I am talking to the one and only—"

"Don't be a dick," Midas growled. "I need help." Like that wasn't hard to admit to the former bounty hunter turned cold case solver extraordinaire.

Memphis Camden. Trouble with a southern drawl. A damn good hunter. Probably the best. And now that he and the other *Ice Breakers*—a crazily efficient cold case crew—were being bankrolled by billionaire Archer Radcliffe, Memphis's reach was pretty limitless. So, when you needed help, why not turn to the big guns?

"Tell me what you need."

A fast response that Midas hadn't quite anticipated. "You're not gonna ask me to make some deal? Promise you my first-born child or something?"

"Who the hell am I? Rumpelstiltskin?"

Midas's brow furrowed.

"Tell me," Memphis ordered. "You've got about two minutes before my beautiful wife gets out of the shower, so you need to make it fast."

He could do fast. "There was a missing socialite in Colorado Springs. I caught a news story tonight saying that an autopsy had been conducted on her recovered body."

"Maureen O'Sullivan. I'm aware of her." Tension tightened Memphis's voice. "She'd been missing a few weeks. Her brother actually reached out to us, but the local cops and Feds were swarming so we couldn't get close to investigate. I hate this is the ending she received."

"Broken neck and a knife to the heart." A brutal ending, indeed. Midas exhaled. "That's a very specific way to murder someone."

"A familiar way, too, isn't it?"

Clearly, Memphis wasn't going to pretend he didn't know where this chat was going.

"I'm in Colorado Springs right now," Midas informed him. "Been here a while. Just wrapped up a case with an action star in the area and signed on for a new job last night. Rather an interesting coincidence that this O'Sullivan woman was taken and killed—*this way*—while I'm in town."

"The MO is the same as your father's."

"Copycat," Midas returned. "Has to be, right?"

"Unless I missed a news story about your old man escaping a prison cell." Grim. "That escape shit happens, you know. Look at that prick Lane."

Lane Lawson. Midas was very familiar with the name—and the man. "Lane was innocent." He'd just worked that case with Oliver Foxx. In fact, Oliver was out honeymooning *with* Lane Lawson's sister. Oliver had married her as quickly as he could. "He escaped because it was either escape or die behind bars. You're just mad because Lane got the drop on you."

"He locked me in a freezer."

True. "Aren't you guys like...working together now?"

"*Trial basis.*"

Midas took that as a yes. They were. Back to the matter at hand. His two minutes had to be nearly up. "I called to see if you or the other Ice Breakers knew anything about Maureen's killer. Anything that would..." But he trailed away because he didn't know what to say.

"Anything that might help you sleep at night?"

He didn't sleep most nights. Nothing helped with that.

"We're just starting to look into things. I told you, her brother came to us, but the locals locked us out. The case was still—it was still *fresh*, so you know it's not exactly our wheelhouse."

No, the Ice Breakers usually only worked the cases that had been unsolved for years. The ones that the cops and Feds had given up on solving. "So you don't have anything to give me." The call had been a mistake.

"Slow your roll, man. I said we were just *starting*. Starting doesn't mean we have nothing. The team learned there was another abduction not too long ago. A few months before Maureen went missing. It was in Cherry Hills Village. That's only about an hour away from Colorado Springs so it caught our attention. That vic was gone for a week before she made it home."

"She came back?" Good news. Surprising news. In most of these stories, the vics never came home.

"Yes. She came home. The family won't talk to us. And, again, local authorities are telling us that we are *not* welcome on the investigation. They want us to stop digging. But I happen to be really good with a shovel."

One of the things Midas admired about the guy. Not that he'd confess that to Memphis.

"You've got proximity with the case locations," Memphis said. "You've got two women from wealthy backgrounds. You've got a situation that sets off my alarms."

Midas's, too.

"If I learn more, I'll let you know. Now, look, the bathroom door is opening so—"

"Thanks for the intel." Midas started to end the call.

"Who's the new client?"

His eyes were on her house. "Not at liberty to say." Ryker wanted things confidential. They'd stay that way, for now.

"I get that you like to think of yourself as a one-man army and all that uber cool stuff."

Midas grunted.

"But even you can need backup." Memphis's voice was dead serious. "You see that you need backup, then you call me again, got it?"

"Thanks." He hung up the phone and hoped that he wouldn't have to take Memphis up on his offer.

Then he made himself comfortable in the vehicle. Two abductions. One woman returned. One dead. Wealthy women. Women linked by fairly close proximity.

Someone was clearly hunting in Colorado.

He had no intention of just driving away. He wanted to keep an eye on Alina.

I should be in the house with her.

***

Her eyes flew open, and her heart raced in Alina's chest as a sudden and startling realization filled her head. *Someone is in the house with me.*

She'd been sleeping one moment, dreaming about Midas and what could have been, but then the faintest sound had ripped her to consciousness. That sound had been—

The creak of her bedroom door opening.

A door that should have stayed closed.

Someone is in the house with me. In that terrifying instant, she didn't know if she should pretend to be asleep, if maybe this was just a thief who'd steal something and leave and not harm her if she *just did not move.* Or if—or if—

"Get her," she heard someone snarl.

She screamed as loud and as hard as she could. Alina leapt from the bed and her hands flew out toward her nightstand. Total darkness filled the room, but her hands found the lamp. She intended to throw it at her attackers, but hard arms grabbed her. Yanked her back.

Her fingers slid up the base of the lamp.

It turned on. A flood of illumination filled the room.

"Turn that shit off!"

She heaved the lamp at her attackers. One swore when it hit him, but it must have bounced off because she heard a thud as it hit the floor.

And the light vanished.

She hadn't seen their faces in that instant, but she knew there were two people in the room with her. Both covered in black. Hands grabbed at her and tossed her back onto the bed, and she tried to scream again.

A hand slapped over her mouth. "Can we shut this bitch up already?"

No, no, no. Her body heaved.

"She's like five-foot-nothing. Can't you handle her?" A mocking rumble.

She kicked out. Caught someone hard and heard a grunt.

"Knock the bitch out." A snarl.

She twisted and clawed and—

"She fucking bit me!"

Yes, she had, and she was free, for a second. With all of her strength, she heaved to the left. A hand grabbed for her, and she heard her shirt tear, but she got away and fell to the floor. The impact had pain shooting through her left knee, but she didn't slow. She leapt up, ignored the pain, and hurtled toward the direction of her bedroom door.

"Get her!"

Laughter. "She's gonna be unconscious in like five seconds. I will make her so sorry—"

"We're not supposed to hurt her. Well, not much. *Get her*. She can't reach the front door!"

Her bare feet slipped, but she didn't fall as she raced through the hallway and toward the front of her house. Her eyes had adjusted to the darkness. She could see the looming front door. Her hands flew out for it.

"That asshole is out front! He's watching the house. If she gets to him—"

Who was watching her house? "Help!" Alina cried.

A hard hand caught the back of her head and slammed her into the door. Her forehead hit, brutally hard, stunning her, and as she swayed, someone caught her wrists and jerked them behind her body. Something sharp and plastic—

zip ties, I think those are zip ties—bound her wrists. She tried to scream, but what felt like a long, twisting scarf was shoved between her lips. Her attacker tied it behind her head. She could feel the knot pulling at her hair.

She spun and kicked at him because at least her legs were still free.

He drove his fist toward her jaw.

No one had ever hit her like that before. The shock and pain left her weaving. But she didn't fall. Her attacker caught her and tossed her over his shoulder. Nausea rose in her throat, and she tried to choke it down. If she vomited, with the gag between her lips, would she just choke? Tears stung her eyes.

"Let's get the hell out of here." The voice belonged to the second intruder. Not the one who'd hit her. "The last thing I want is to tangle with that big bruiser outside."

***

Midas jerked upright in the driver's seat. Had a light just flashed on in Alina's bedroom? His eyes were gritty, his mind a little too slow, dammit, but he'd been sure that he saw illumination fill that third window.

Only for the room to plunge right back into darkness.

Could be nothing. Maybe Alina turned on a light for a moment to check her clock. Maybe she turned the light off and went back to sleep.

But…

But his heart pounded, and he found himself shoving open the door to his SUV. He stepped out into the night. Quiet. Still. His gaze shifted to the left. To the right. No sign of any new cars on the street. There'd been no sign of any of her neighbors. He hadn't been chased off by worried people who wanted to know what the hell he was doing stalking Alina.

Alina.

If he rushed to her front door and pounded and she appeared and nothing was wrong, he'd have one hell of a time explaining himself.

That's why you should never accept a stupid undercover job.

The light was off. Off.

And yet he was running toward her front door. *Screw the cover.* There had been two attacks already on day one. *Day freaking one.* If everything was okay, he'd come up with some excuse for pounding on her door in the middle of the night. Hell, maybe he'd just say that he hadn't been able to get her out of his head.

Truth.

That he wanted more of her.

Another truth.

That leaving her and playing the gentleman had been a dumbass mistake.

Absolute total truth.

He pounded on the door.

Nothing.

The tension in the base of his neck grew. He pounded again, driving his fist into the wood. No lights turned on. No footsteps rushed toward the door.

Was Alina just the heaviest sleeper in the world?

I fucking doubt it. Okay, he was probably going to scare the hell out of her but—

He broke down her front door. A hard kick against the lock and the door flew inward. The first thing he noticed? No alarm blared.

The second thing? There was no terrified cry from Alina. There was no sound at all in the house. He ran to her bedroom. Hit the light switch near the door.

Empty bed.
Tangled sheets.
Broken lamp on the floor. And what looked like—was that part of a torn shirt? A piece of silk fluttered on the floor. Like a pajama top. Bright blue.

Fury and fear barreled through him, but he didn't hesitate. He'd gone through the front door. Whoever had taken Alina—*She was taken. She's gone*—the abductors must have gone out the back. He raced out the back. Had his light shining on the ground so he could try and figure out where the hell she'd gone. He snaked through the yard. Behind the trees. Heard the growl of a motor as he shoved through the shrubs and came out on another street—

There were no lights to warn him of the vehicle. Just the growl of the angry engine. He turned and saw the vehicle lunge out of the dark. It rushed straight toward him.

In that instant, Midas knew there were two options.

Option one—get the hell out of the way.

Or option two—
Option two, fuck me, but this will hurt.
He bunched his muscles and got ready for impact.

CHAPTER FOUR

The car hit him. Or maybe he hit the car. Really damn hard to say because all Midas knew was that his body was suddenly screaming in pain, and he was on the freaking hood of a black SUV. His hands spread wide as he tried to hold the hell on. He looked up and strained to see into the interior of the ride.

The driver yanked the steering wheel to the left, and Midas nearly flew off. With all of his strength, Midas heaved up to a more secure spot on the hood. *Like there is a secure spot on a moving vehicle!* He caught the upper edge of the hood—the part right next to the bottom of the windshield wipers. His fingers curled around that edge. The edge gave him a perch to hold. Locking his teeth, he kept that grip.

The car swerved to the right. A jerking, vicious swerve. One of his hands flew loose, his whole body almost propelled into the darkness, but he steadied himself. Mostly. His hand went into his coat pocket. He tried to grab for the—

Another swerve. Harder. The damn car was twisting back and forth like a snake.

Both of his hands clamped around the hood's upper edge again. He didn't see Alina, but she had to be in the car. "Mistake!" Midas roared at the driver. "You made the worst fucking mistake of your life!"

***

"He's crazy," the man beside Alina whispered. They were in the back seat. Her ankles were bound with zip ties that bit into her skin. Her wrists still twisted and secured behind her. And the thick scarf cut into the sides of her mouth as it pulled against her lips. "That bastard is *crazy!*"

She strained to see through the space between the two front seats. Everything was so dark—in and out of the car. She couldn't make out anything.

"Told you he was trouble the minute I saw him sniffing around her," the guy added as he leaned forward. "Fucker is on the car! Get him off!"

On the car? She craned her head again. Narrowed her eyes and saw—wait, someone was on the hood? Someone coming to help her?

The car swerved left. Right. She slammed into the jerk next to her.

He shoved her away. "Your stalker boyfriend is *dead!* Dead, got me?"

Stalker boyfriend? But—

The abductor next to her yanked a seatbelt over her squirming body. Clicked it into place. Then pulled on his own seatbelt.

"Slam on the brakes!" he ordered the driver. "Throw that big bastard off the car!"

And she knew—she knew he meant Midas. Big bastard? Stalker boyfriend? Had to be Midas. Her abductors must have seen her with Midas, and they thought he was her boyfriend. *And now they think they are going to kill him.* "No!" Alina tried to scream but couldn't. She could only grunt behind the heavy scarf.

The driver slammed on the brakes. A loud screech filled the air.

Silence. Silence except for the heavy, panting breaths that came from the man beside her and from the driver.

"That took care of the SOB," the driver said, sounding pleased.

She stretched her neck to see in front of them. *Midas. Midas!*

The driver flashed on his lights. And in the beam of those headlights, she saw the slumped figure of a man as he lay sprawled on the road.

The abductor beside her started laughing. Deep, bellowing laughs.

But that laughter stopped when Midas began to rise.

"Holy fucking shit," he gasped as the laughter died. "Who the hell is your boyfriend?"

Midas rolled back his shoulders. And started walking toward the vehicle. The bright headlights illuminated him fully, and as she took in his determined march, wild hope blossomed in Alina. Midas was okay. He could help her.

"Hit him again!" the man next to her yelled.

"What if he jumps on my fucking ride again?"

Ah...he'd done that?

"Screw this," the driver snarled. The car whipped into reverse, then it spun around and took off in the opposite direction, leaving Midas behind them. She turned her head and tried to see him.

Darkness.

Getting thicker and thicker in their wake. But she could have sworn that—*is Midas running after me?*

Laughter came once again. "Yeah, bastard, you try running," the man beside her muttered. "Don't think you can keep up with a freaking car."

Tears trickled down her cheeks.

He grabbed her chin. "He won't find you. No one will."

The car turned left, and the engine howled as it raced away.

***

"Sonofabitch." The headlights had vanished. Midas stood in the middle of the dark road. Every muscle in his body screamed with pain. His breath heaved in and out. Alina had been taken. On *his* watch. Oh, the hell, no. That shit should never, ever have happened.

He yanked out his phone. A long crack ran the length of the screen.

Alina has to be scared. Screw that. She would be terrified. And if she'd been hurt...

His nostrils flared and he ground his teeth together as he waited for the damn phone call to be answered. *Pick up, you bastard. Pick—*

"I told you already that your work for the night was done," Ryker snapped. "Why are you calling—"

"Someone just abducted your daughter, that's what I'm calling about," he snarled right back.

Ryker sucked in a shocked breath. "Wh-what?"

"Abducted your daughter." He turned away from the dark street and raced back for his own ride. "Two men. Black Mercedes SUV. They went into her home. Took her out of the back door. *They took her.* I'm giving chase, and I'm going to need you to call the police." Hell, he could call the police while he chased the SOBs. But he'd felt like the dad needed a freaking heads-up.

Heads-up. Two soon-to-be-dead pieces of shit took Alina. But I have a plan.

"No police!" A fast and hard denial from Ryker.

Midas's steps stumbled. "What? You are not serious right now." Maybe the man was in shock. Midas double-timed his already fast pace. "Alina was taken. We need the cops. We need—"

"Are you going after them?"

Midas didn't go back into her house. Just rushed around it in order to get to his car.

"Can you get her back? *Please?* I am begging you...*can you get her back?*"

Nothing in this world would stop him from getting her back.

"I will pay you any price. Get her. Take them out. *Bring my daughter home.*"

Midas jumped into his vehicle. "Why aren't you calling the police?" He ignored the part where

Ryker had just asked him to kill her abductors. Ignored it, for now.

Most people think I'm a killer. Just like my old man. Was that why Ryker had hired him? The real reason?

"I...can't call the police. I-I think...I think Alina will be dead if I do."

"Why the hell would you think that?"

"Do you have eyes on my daughter?"

"The men who took her just tried to run me down with their car. We aren't dealing with people who are going to play nicely here. We need the cops." How many times did he have to say that shit?

"I know it's them...I was so afraid...*If you go to the cops, she's dead. Please, don't kill my daughter.*"

What. The. Fuck?

"Any price," Ryker said quickly. "You're the best. You must still have eyes on her—get her back. Take them out."

"I don't have eyes on her." This conversation was over. He had to focus on what mattered. *Alina.* "I have something better. I tagged their vehicle." When he'd been hanging tightly to the hood, he'd yanked a tag from his pocket. In his line of work, it paid to keep one at the ready. "Shoved it under the hood." He didn't think they'd realized what he'd done. And if they didn't know, then they couldn't search for the tag.

"You...you can track them?"

His fingers swiped over the screen of his phone as he pulled up the app. "I *am* tracking them." And they were definitely hauling ass. So he had to get moving, too.

"Thank Christ. Thank *Christ*."

"You knew they were going to take your daughter?"

"I-I feared—" Ryker broke off.

"And you ordered me away from her home?" Just so he understood.

"I thought she was safe there! I have top-of-the-line security."

He shifted into drive and pushed the pedal down to the floorboard. "Your top-of-the-line security was shit." The alarm had been disabled because it hadn't so much as beeped when he kicked in Alina's front door. "They got to her. If I hadn't been outside, she would be gone, and no one would know." *Gone. Terrified. Hurt.*

The rage flared hotter and darker within Midas.

"You're going to get her back?" From Ryker.

"I'm getting her back," he vowed.

Blood dripped into his right eye. He swiped it away.

"I'll pay you anything you want. *Anything*. But just—no cops. The cops can't be involved, understand? Make the bastards pay. End them...and bring my daughter home."

***

They carried her from the vehicle. Alina didn't fight, not yet. She was saving her strength and trying to figure out just where the hell she was.

How long had they driven? An hour? They'd gone away from the city and taken twisting, winding paths that led them up and down the mountain and deeper into the woods.

She was slung over the shoulder of one abductor. Both wore masks, and she tried to tell herself that was a good thing. If they didn't want her seeing their faces, then that meant they didn't want her to be able to identify them...like when she was free and she was talking to the cops later. If she never saw their faces, the men might think they had a better chance of getting away with their crime.

If they were going to kill me, they wouldn't hide their faces.

She levered up to look back at the vehicle. Big, black.

Snow covered the ground. *We went up a lot higher than I realized.* And farther from Colorado Springs. Because it hadn't been snowing at her house. No snow at all for days.

But snow crunched beneath the boots of the man who carried her. Black boots. Jeans.

And...

They were going up old, wooden steps. Her body began to shiver. Not from the cold. Mostly just from the absolute, stark terror that filled her. She squirmed and tried to see where they were taking her.

Then the lights flipped on.

A cabin. She was inside a small cabin. Two overstuffed chairs. A table. A little kitchen.

"Lock her in the closet."

Wait—*what?* Now she squirmed hard—so hard that the guy's hold slackened on her. Alina thought she was going to break free.

But he just tossed her into a closet. She landed on her ass, and one of her bound hands rammed into the wall behind her. She tried to scramble to her feet.

He slammed the door shut on her. Once more, she was plunged back into darkness. *No, no.* She turned around and backed toward the door. Her hand flew out and curled around the knob. She tried to twist and open the door.

Locked.

Tears leaked down her cheeks. She maneuvered sideways—taking mincing steps because her ankles were still bound together—and rammed her shoulder into the door. Once. Twice. Three times. They couldn't do this. Not trap her in some tiny closet that was like a coffin.

A coffin. I'm going to die here. No one knows where I am. No one knows—

The door flew open. "Do you *want* me to hurt you?"

Light. So much light. She blinked quickly and saw the knife in his hand.

"You're a pretty woman, and it would be such a shame..." The knife lifted and the tip pressed lightly to her cheek. "If I had to slice your face open."

She wasn't breathing.

"No more noises from you," he told her. The mask moved in and out with his words.

No accent in his voice. He's tall. Not nearly as big as Midas. Maybe about six-foot or six-foot-one. He's strong, but lean.

"If I have to come in this closet again, I'll slice you. I'll start with your right cheek."

"You're not supposed to hurt her," the man behind him rasped. "At least, not until we hear from the boss."

"Yeah, well, she's not supposed to be a pain in my ass, either." The tip of the knife skated down her cheek. He didn't press hard enough to cut the skin. A light warning. "Not a sound."

She was too scared to nod.

He lifted the knife.

And slowly shut the door.

But right before it shut, she looked over his shoulder. Her gaze locked on the other man—the driver of the car. He was lifting the mask off his head as he bent to start a fire in the fireplace.

She saw thick, red hair.

The door closed.

Alina retreated until she hit the rear of the closet. Five steps. That was all the room she had. But it wasn't completely dark. She'd been wrong before. A little light came from the bottom of the closet. There was a faint space between the bottom of the closet door and the floor. A small beam of light.

Click.

That sound seemed deafening to her ears.

He'd locked her in again.

Her weak knees gave way and she slumped onto the floor. Her head snaked down. Alina tried to peer beneath that little crack. She could just see the bottom of a chair. A booted foot walking. She could—

"When do we get paid?" Alina recognized the voice. It came from the man who'd threatened her with the knife.

"As soon as the boss arrives."

"Man, did you see that freak who came after her? He got *up* after you hit him. That was one scary fucker."

Midas? How badly had he been hurt?

"He's not going to be a problem."

Her heart squeezed in her chest.

And…the booted foot she could see suddenly turned toward the closet. Toward her. The foot rushed closer. Closer.

It slammed into the door.

She scrambled back as he laughed.

Alina hated the sound of his laughter.

***

Midas peered at the cabin from his perch in the woods. The bastards had made so many mistakes.

Mistake one? Leaving his ass alive. *You just pissed me off. And that makes me an even worse enemy to have.*

Mistake two? They'd let him track them. Too easy.

Mistake three? The idiots had a fire going. A cabin tucked away in the woods…with smoke spilling from the chimney. They might as well have waved a red flag for Midas.

They were inside, getting comfortable, while he was just waiting for his moment to strike. And that moment was—

The door to the cabin flew open. One man came rushing out. Followed immediately by the second. Light spilled from the open doorway and hit the men.

One was a redhead. One had dark hair. Brown. Both looked young. Early twenties.

The redhead yanked the door closed behind him. Hurried down the steps. The men went straight to the vehicle.

Midas had already looked inside the Benz. Empty. He'd even quietly popped the trunk, just to make sure they hadn't left Alina in the back.

There'd been no trace of her. What he *had* seen in the rear of the Benz? Zip ties. Duct tape. Rope. Two knives.

He'd taken the knives and the zip ties.

The men paced around the car.

"You shouldn't have threatened to slice her face," one said.

Midas stiffened.

"The bitch was trying to break down the door." The jerk lit a cigarette.

"Yeah, but *we're* not supposed to cut her up. You know the rules."

A long puff of smoke drifted into the cold night. "Fuck his rules."

The other man took a half-step back. "You...you aren't serious. He *pays* us."

"And he takes a whole lot more. Maybe—maybe we should be getting a bigger cut, you ever think of that?"

Midas eased closer. Were these two bozos the grunt workers? Someone else was pulling the strings?

"I think..." A shaking hand ran through the redhead's hair. "I think he scares me. You don't know what he can do."

Another exhale of smoke. "So he killed a woman, so—"

Snap.

Fuck. Midas glanced down. Had he really just made that amateur-level mistake? Yep, he had. The snow had covered an old twig, and he'd snapped it when he inched forward. But maybe these two jerks would just think an animal had made that sound.

The one smoking whipped toward Midas's location. "Someone's here," he said instantly.

The other guy laughed. "No way, man! We are in the middle of the woods. You just heard an animal. Maybe a rabbit. A raccoon." He shuddered. "It's cold as fuck out here. Let's go back inside."

"She can hear us inside. You wouldn't let me knock her out."

Midas's hands fisted.

The smoking man took a step toward Midas. His gaze seemed to push through the dark and the trees and lock on Midas. *Just seems to. I don't think the SOB really sees me. Yet.*

"How many times do I have to tell you?" A sigh. "We are not supposed to hurt her. You know he likes them undamaged. You shouldn't have hit her back at her house."

He'd hit Alina?

"Bitch was almost outside. Running to that freaky-ass stalker boyfriend in his car. Couldn't let her reach him."

You are going to suffer.

"You like this too much. You liked scaring her at the rink. Then messing with her car—"

"Stop your freaking preaching at me." The man tossed down his cigarette. "I'm going to check the woods."

"Fine. Go freeze your ass off. I'm heading back inside until the boss arrives. Shouldn't be too long now."

The boss was coming? Would he be bringing others? Right now, the odds were two against one, and Midas damn well liked those odds. But if more people came, then he'd be dealing with an even more unstable situation. Better to take control now.

The other guy had already run up the steps. Disappeared into the cabin. But the one who'd hit Alina was still there. Edging closer. Far too cautious.

The man clearly needed a bit of bait so that he'd come running. Deliberately, Midas pressed down on the twig beneath his shoe. *Snap.* That had the bastard springing into motion. He came running for Midas and the prick yanked out a knife as he headed into the woods.

And straight at Midas.

CHAPTER FIVE

The cabin's front door shut. A blast of cold air slid underneath the closet door. Alina shuddered. The two men had gone out moments before. But now, someone had returned.

She'd hoped they'd get in their car and drive away. If they left, she might have a chance to escape. Her wrists were raw and bloody because she'd been straining against the zip ties. So far, they hadn't broken, but she wasn't giving up.

She couldn't give up.

The floorboards squeaked with her abductor's footsteps. Closer and closer. The squeaks and creaks grew louder because he was closing in on her. Just one man. She only heard one set of steps. The other man must still be outside.

Alina scuttled back until her shoulders hit the wall. She wore a pair of blue silk pajama pants and a torn top. Goose bumps covered her body and the cold kept making her shudder. She had zero weapons and enough fear to choke her.

A hand rapped against the door. Then... "You've got to calm down."

He couldn't be serious.

"I don't want you hurt. But my partner doesn't feel the same. He's coming back in soon, and just…don't make him mad, understand? Don't do anything to set him off. If you fight again or if you try to escape…" The words trailed away, and her stomach knotted even more. He cleared his throat. "Look, be good and you might get home. The last one, though, she didn't."

The last one?

"But there have been others, and it doesn't always have to end that way. But, just…*be good*. If you think my partner is bad, wait until you meet the boss."

Alina shook her head frantically even though he couldn't see her. She didn't want to meet the boss. She wanted to wake up and have this whole scene just be some terrible nightmare. *Please, please let it be a nightmare.*

She'd kissed Midas. Felt heat pour through her body. Felt need and desire and passion and…

Then she'd woken to ice cold terror. Fear that numbed her. And a terrible, growing certainty spread through her that…

She wasn't going to make it through this.

Please, please be a nightmare.

"If your dad follows the rules, there's a chance you'll make it."

Her dad? Was this—was this some kind of ransom thing?

"But the boss…" His voice lowered. "He's like my partner. I think—I think he likes hurting people."

Her stomach heaved.

"I think he likes killing people." A pause. "And I work for him, so what the hell does that say about me?"

Her eyes squeezed closed.

The floor creaked as he walked away.

***

The bastard barreled into the woods louder than a charging bear. He gripped his knife tightly and ran in. Midas had just ducked behind a bigger tree, and when the fool prepared to run right past him, Midas threw up his arm and caught the guy right around the neck. The knife flew from the man's fingers even as his body whipped back at the sudden clothesline attack. The prick slammed into the ground, but Midas gave him credit, he jumped back up fast, even if he was wheezing.

"Who the fuck—what the—"

Midas drove his fist into the SOB's jaw as hard as he could. A fast and brutal hit. He heard bones crunch. Fine. *That's what happens when you hit a woman, you piece of shit. Prepare for someone else to hit you back, even harder.*

When the asshole hit the ground this time, he didn't jump back up. He couldn't. He was out cold. Midas pulled his phone from his pocket and put it over the man's face. He snapped a quick pic. *I want to know who the hell you are and who hired you.* Then, because he'd planned ahead like the good freaking Boy Scout he was, Midas pulled some zip ties from his back pocket. He secured the man's wrists and ankles and rolled his ass even deeper into the woods.

One down.

Midas glanced toward the cabin.

One waiting inside.

Midas sucked in a deep breath and headed straight for the cabin.

Someone else is coming. Could be multiple someones. You need to move fast. Get her out. Get her to safety. Alina is the priority. His only priority.

More blood trickled into Midas's right eye. The damn cut hadn't stopped bleeding yet. Hell, that was just one of many cuts still bleeding. He'd taken just enough stock of his injuries to know he wasn't in mortal danger. He could handle pain. What he couldn't handle?

Anyone hurting Alina.

He figured there were a couple of ways he could play the scene. He could slip around the cabin, see if there was a back entrance, and try to ease inside without being spotted.

But he was a big guy and easing anywhere was never easy.

So...

He could try another option. Midas bounded up the steps. He'd try the option where he just went straight to the door. Because the fool who'd gone inside moments before expected his partner to follow suit. Midas was willing to bet the guy hadn't even locked the door behind him.

Why would he? The man clearly didn't expect a threat to come to the cabin. No, he expected backup to be arriving any moment.

Midas reached for the doorknob. It twisted easily in his grasp. He opened the door and slipped inside.

The redhead stood a few feet away from a closed door—maybe a closet or a bedroom—with his hands on his hips. He didn't even look back when the front door hinges groaned with its opening.

"Didn't see anything, did you?" the redhead muttered. "We're in the freaking middle of nowhere. Only animals are running around in the cold."

Midas advanced on him with a rush of footsteps. "Not just animals," he rasped.

Too late, the redhead spun toward him. Or, tried to. *Far too late.* Midas caught him and locked an arm around the man's neck. The redhead barely grunted, but his fingers clawed at Midas's grip.

You'll need to do better than that.

Without hesitation, Midas applied pressure to the carotid arteries on either side of the SOB's neck. All it took was a few seconds. And Midas counted in his head. *One, two, three, four...*

The man's struggles weakened. He stopped clawing at Midas as his body went limp. He sagged in Midas's hold, and Midas lowered the kidnapper to the floor.

The guy sprawled, seemingly boneless. Midas put his hand to the jerk's throat. Felt the pulse. *Still alive.* It took only moments to zip-tie the bastard's hands. Midas hadn't gotten enough ties for the creep's feet, though. *But he's not moving right now.* Midas snapped a quick pic of the unconscious man's face. He would be ID'ing both these bastards.

Midas rose and looked at the nearby closed door. Yeah, he knew there was a reason why the redhead had been focused on it. When he saw the lock on the outside of the door, the fury within him burned to a molten degree. Locking his jaw, Midas reached for that lock.

***

Someone else had come inside the cabin. The one who wanted to hurt her? Was he back? She'd heard the words from the man who'd warned her moments before. He'd asked a question, then said animals were running around outside. But, no one had responded to him. Or if someone had spoken, the response had been too low for her to hear.

Then there'd just been silence. A thick, scary silence.

Maybe it hadn't been his partner returning. Maybe it had been someone else. The mysterious boss? The man who already terrified Alina straight to her soul?

She curled in on herself as much as she could as the floorboards just beyond her prison groaned and creaked. Whoever it was—he was coming toward her.

The lock disengaged. The door began to open. She closed her eyes because if this was the boss, she didn't want to see him. If he didn't have a mask on—like the other men—then...then it would mean he was going to kill her. Hurt her, because that was what he liked to do. Hurt her, then kill her.

She held herself perfectly still. If she didn't move, maybe he wouldn't hurt her. Maybe…

Please, just be a nightmare.

"Sweetheart…" A rough growl. "Are you ready to get the hell out of here?"

Her eyes flew open. She blinked twice. Midas stood in the open closet doorway. Light spilled behind him, and in that instant, he looked like an avenging angel come to save her.

She'd called him her angel before, and he'd denied the title.

Big, strong, and her absolute superhero. No one had ever looked as good as Midas did in that instant. A sob choked from her. The gag in her mouth muffled the cry, and his amber eyes narrowed with clear fury.

He crouched before her. His hands flew behind her head, and he yanked the knot free and tore the scarf-slash-gag from her mouth.

Her lips felt bone dry. Her jaw ached. From the gag? From the hit she'd taken?

She wet her lips. Didn't help. She licked them again.

His fingers slid under her jaw. "You already have a bruise." Low and filled with barely banked rage. "Be assured, the one I gave that SOB is a hell of a lot worse." He leaned toward her. His lips brushed over her jaw. "Pretty sure I broke the bastard's jaw. It will be lots of fun for him when he has to have it wired shut for weeks."

She shivered.

He pulled her against him. Lifted her up and got her out of the closet.

"M-my hands..." Now her teeth were chattering. She could still taste that stupid gag. Or maybe she was tasting her own fear. Her mouth was too dry. Her body too cold. All she wanted to do was hold tightly to Midas, but her hands were locked behind her back.

He put her down just outside of the closet. He eased her around and swore. "Fuck, baby, your wrists are raw and bloody."

"G-get them f-free—" She broke off because her gaze had just landed on the body a few feet away. The redhead. He sprawled on the floor, not moving at all.

Snick.

She flinched at that sound and turned to see that Midas had a wickedly sharp knife in his hand.

"Hold still," he ordered quietly.

She couldn't stay still. She would have very much liked to follow his order, but her body wouldn't stop shaking.

His fingers stroked lightly over her wrists. "Don't move. I don't want to cut you."

He sliced the zip ties. Immediately, pain seemed to shoot through her fingers. She let out a sharp cry.

He rubbed her hands and her wrists. "That's the feeling come back. Those sonsofbitches had the ties too tight." He kept rubbing. Stroking. "I know it hurts. It will get better. Trust me, okay? It will get better."

She trusted him completely. One hundred percent. He'd just saved her life. "How—" She winced at the pain. "How are you here?"

"You think I wasn't going to follow you?" More tender strokes of his fingers as he tried to ease her pain. "Sweetheart, I'd follow you to hell and back any day of the week."

Tears pricked her eyes again. She didn't want to cry. She wanted to be strong. Midas was strong.

Her gaze fell on the body. "Is he...dead?"

"Nope. Though I am tempted to make him that way."

A flinch jolted her body.

"Knocked him out. I'm going to cut the ties around your ankles. It's gonna hurt when the feeling comes back, but, actually, these ties aren't as tight so it might not be as bad."

He sliced through the ties. It was bad. But she bit her lower lip and tried hard not to cry out.

Be strong. Midas is strong. You can be strong, too. Her gaze remained on the fallen man. Curly red hair. Pale skin. Young. Maybe around twenty? Twenty-one? Much younger than she'd thought he would be.

"He has a pulse. He'll live." Midas moved in front of her and blocked her view of the sprawled man. "We need to haul ass. Someone else is coming. I don't know if it's one guy or a whole crew or what kind of weapons the others may have. I can't risk losing in a fight. If I lose, they'll have you."

She grabbed his shirt front. "Let's haul ass. Definitely."

He kissed her. Fast and hard and unexpected.

She wanted to keep clinging to him. But he'd already pulled back so quickly.

"Can you walk?" Midas asked her.

"I can run." She could do anything. She *wanted* to run. As fast as possible. Now, please.

He nodded. "Good. My ride is about two miles away from here. Had to hide it. Couldn't come straight in because I didn't want them to hear my vehicle and get tipped off. I was afraid of what they might do to you if they knew I was right outside."

Don't think about what they could have done. Don't.

"But we're going to have to trek through the snow to get back to my car."

He still hadn't said how he found her. Now wasn't the time to ask. As he'd said, it was the time to haul ass. Midas turned away and rushed for the door.

She rushed after him.

And fell to the floor. Her legs just seemed to give way, and she hit, almost landing on top of the redhead. She shoved away from him. Her palms pressed against the floor as she levered herself up.

"When you fall...you always get up."

Her head lifted at Midas's low words. "I'll get up. The, ah, the feeling just wasn't back in my feet." Was that even true? Her knees had given way on her in the closet. Fear had her shaking constantly now. But she could do this. She *would* do this. Two miles. They had to run two miles.

Her life depended on it. No, not just her life. Midas's. He was risking himself for her.

She pushed up to her feet.

Only to have Midas scoop her into his arms. "Screw walking. I'll carry you every step."

Her arm curled around his neck. Her lips pressed to his throat in a tender kiss. "Thank you." She wasn't just talking about him carrying her. She was thanking him for saving her. For giving her hope.

For risking himself, for her.

She'd never met anyone like Midas in her life. She never would meet anyone else like him. This man—a man she'd known for less than twenty-four hours—had risked everything for her.

He took her out of the cabin. Yanked the door closed behind them and leapt down the steps. A light dusting of snow began to fall, and the goose bumps on her body got even bigger.

"No clothes," he muttered. "Sorry, baby." He pulled her even closer against the heat of his body.

She did have on *some* clothes. They just offered practically zero protection. And she didn't have on shoes, so, yes, him carrying her—as long as she wasn't too heavy—was a great plan for her. And it wasn't his fault that she didn't have more clothing.

He took her to the tree line. Her gaze darted away from the black SUV. Her teeth locked as she remembered the terrible car ride. The absolute fear. Every moment, she'd been afraid of death. Been so sure they were just taking her away to hurt her. To kill her.

So sure she'd never see her home again.

Until Midas had opened that closet door.

Her hero. He'd said once that he was no guardian angel. He was so wrong.

He was her personal angel.

Snow crunched beneath his feet. How could he see where they were going? The farther they went from the cabin, the darker the woods grew. "Midas..." Alina whispered.

"Excellent night vision, sweetheart. Don't worry. And I came this way before. I know the path."

Okay, great. But how could she not worry given the situation?

Her teeth chattered. The snow fell a bit harder.

"Fuck this." He put her down. Her toes dipped into the snow, and she hissed out a breath.

He shouldered out of his coat. Put it on her shoulders. Shoved her arms into the sleeves. The coat practically swallowed her. It dipped way past her thighs. He zipped it up. Scooped her right back into his arms.

"Midas..." Her arm curled around his neck again. "You need to be warm."

"I'm fine." He maneuvered unerringly through the dark. "I told you, don't worry. I'm—"

The growl of an engine cut through his words. They were in the trees, but the drive to the cabin was close by. Headlights cut through the dark.

Midas immediately ducked behind a nearby tree. The growling engine came closer and closer.

She stopped breathing. The lights had almost hit them as the car turned on the drive. If they'd been seen...

They'll come after us. Take me back. Hurt— maybe kill—Midas. The drumbeat of her heart echoed in her ears as the vehicle slowly pulled past. She had the impression of another big SUV. Had to be with four-wheel drive in order to navigate out there.

Midas kept his grip on her but eased to the right so he could duck his head around the tree. "Can't see who is inside," he breathed. "Dark windows. Bright lights. Come on, come on...*dammit, can't see the tag.*"

But the vehicle was still moving. Going away from them. That was fabulous.

"Once they get to the cabin, they're gonna realize really fast that you aren't in there. Hold tight."

She already was holding pretty tightly to him and—

He took off. Far faster than before. Tree branches scratched at them as he seemed to torpedo through the woods. The sound of his footsteps pounded in the snow. The cold bit at her, but the coat he'd put on her provided Alina a welcome buffer. The coat was warm from his body and carried his scent.

Faster and faster, he ran.

And she tried not to think about who might have been in the car. Or what the occupants would do when they realized she wasn't in the cabin any longer.

***

He parked the vehicle in front of the cabin. Stared a moment at the snow as it fell down and covered his windshield. He'd always liked the cold. And when snow drifted down and spun in the air, it was really something beautiful to see.

He enjoyed beautiful things.

He enjoyed beautiful things even more when they were broken. After grabbing his bag, he climbed from the vehicle and headed up the steps. His eyes narrowed at the smoke drifting in the air. The scent from the fire had reached his nose the moment he exited his vehicle. The fools inside shouldn't be starting a fire, no matter how cold it was. Fire could attract attention to a cabin that wasn't supposed to be in use.

It was so hard to find good help.

He reached for the door. Unlocked. Seriously? The two idiots were far too complacent. Clearly, it was time they were replaced.

He pushed open the door and came to a dead stop. *Not fucking happening.* Shayne was on the floor. The man's hands were zip-tied in front of him, and his head sagged to the right. A few feet behind Shayne, the closet door hung open to show the completely empty interior.

Impossible.

He crouched next to Shayne. Drew back his hand. And hit the fool as hard as he could. Shayne barely stirred. So he hit him again.

A groan broke from Shayne. His eyes fluttered open. "Wh-what?"

"Where is the woman?"

Shayne's eyes closed.

"I will kill you here and now," he snarled. His knife already pressed over Shayne's heart. He'd put it there the minute Shayne's eyes began to flutter. "Where. Is. She?"

Shayne's eyes whipped open. "Big—big guy. He took her. Boyfriend?"

Was that a question? Or was he saying the boyfriend had taken her? And what boyfriend? Alina Bellamy had zero personal involvements. The lack of intimate connections had made her a perfect target. Not having close ties—other than the tie to her jackass of a father—should have made things easier. Friends or lovers wouldn't notice her absence. Mostly because Alina had no friends or lovers.

"He was here," Shayne gasped. "I-I think he did something to Fallon."

Like Fallon was even the guy's real name. That tattooed asshole just thought it sounded cool. But where the hell was Fallon? More importantly, *where is my prey?*

"Fallon...outside...thought he...heard something..."

He rose and sheathed his knife. How long had Shayne been out? Couldn't be that long, right? Maybe there was still time. He needed to get back in the car. Go back down the drive. If Alina had fled on foot—with her mystery rescuer—he could find her.

Maybe.

Woods were all around the cabin. Miles and miles of woods. Would he find Alina before she ran into some good Samaritan? Or, God forbid, the cops?

His gaze went back to Shayne. The man struggled to sit up.

"Get...these off..." Shayne held up his bound hands.

If Alina made it to the cops, she'd lead them back to the cabin. Shayne had been spread out in the cabin. No mask. She would have seen his face. She could identify him.

And Shayne can identify me.

Well, he had already been thinking it was time to replace his hunters.

He stepped closer to Shayne. Took out his knife once more. Brought it down as if he'd slice through the zip ties.

Shayne swallowed. Lifted his hands higher.

And he just shoved the knife right into Shayne's chest. "You shouldn't have let her get away."

CHAPTER SIX

Just through the twisting trees, his ride waited. Midas shot forward and held tightly to Alina. She kept shivering and shaking in his arms. He had to get her warmed up. Warmed up and then to a hospital because he wanted her thoroughly evaluated.

He opened the driver's side door and dropped her inside. She scrambled over to the passenger seat, clutching tightly to his coat. He slid in after her.

"You're bleeding," Alina said. Her hand reached for his forehead.

His hand flew out and locked around her wrist before she could touch him. "It's nothing." The light from the car's interior showed too many of his wounds. And it let him see the darkening bruise on her jaw. *I want to kill him.*

"Midas?" Her gaze searched his.

He let her go. Hauled his door shut and had the engine snarling. "Buckle up."

She did. His breath heaved in and out from the run, and he shifted the car into drive. When his foot hit the gas, the vehicle lurched forward. He'd hidden his ride. He'd followed the tag's tracking signal...until the fucking thing stopped. Until his phone had lost the signal because service in the middle of nowhere had been shit.

But he'd gotten close enough before he lost the signal. He'd actually had the black Benz within sight several times on the frantic drive. He hadn't gotten too close, though, for fear of spooking the driver. Midas had been afraid the guy might panic and do something stupid like, say...

Kill Alina.

So Midas had stayed out of sight.

But close.

Then he'd lost the signal, but, luckily, he'd already gotten a friend to help him figure out what potential hiding spots waited out in the woods. The friend in question? Memphis Camden. The Ice Breaker probably hadn't expected Midas to call back so quickly and ask for that promised backup. But there had been no choice.

I needed help. I had to get Alina back.

He'd hidden his car. Gone in on foot. Gotten her out. Now he just had to make sure that they made it safely to Colorado Springs. He whipped the vehicle around, and it slid a bit on the icy road.

Alina's hands flew out and grabbed the dashboard.

Hissing out a curse, he steadied the car. A quick check in his rearview mirror showed no one. For the moment. "We're fine. You're safe." Part of him wanted to go back to that cabin. A very, very big part. Find the man who'd been driving the car that had passed them while Midas and Alina had been in the woods. He wanted to find anyone and everyone who'd been involved. And rip them the hell apart.

But he knew she was the priority. Getting her to safety had to come first. Because if he went back, if he was outnumbered and outgunned, then who would protect Alina?

"We'll get a cell signal in about five minutes," he told her. Maybe a little less. "When we do, call the cops, got me? Tell them who you are. Tell them what's happening." He bit out the name of the road they were traveling on. "Tell them you were held in a cabin just off this road. The kidnappers are still there." For the moment, they were.

He glanced in the rearview mirror once more.

And lights flashed on in the distance.

Fucking hell. "That seatbelt is on, right?" He remembered her buckling it, but...

"It's on." A soft reply as she glanced back behind them. "That—that doesn't have to be the kidnappers."

No, it could be someone else...in the middle of the night, in the middle of absolute nowhere. He pushed down harder on the accelerator. His grip on the wheel was so tight he thought he might rip the thing off. "They aren't going to get you again."

"Midas?"

"They won't," he vowed. His gaze returned to the road ahead of him. He had the lead. He was getting down the mountain. The other car wouldn't catch him.

I just have to keep Alina safe.

"Call the cops as soon as you get the signal." His Bluetooth was connected. She could call through the car. "Get them to meet us." They could come in with lights flashing. The other driver would either get caught or he would flee from the authorities. All Midas had to do was make sure the guy didn't overtake him before the cavalry arrived.

Once more, he glanced in the rearview mirror. The lights were still there.

***

The sneaky sonofabitch had taken his prize.

He could make out the red taillights in the distance. The vehicle was driving fast, probably too fast for the icy roads, and there was only one person who could be behind the wheel.

Only one cabin out here. One inhabited cabin, anyway. Because he'd chosen this location specifically. Not like he wanted to be interrupted by nosey neighbors. He hated when his fun was ruined.

Like it had been tonight.

He lost sight of the taillights for a moment when the driver of the other vehicle took a turn. The curving roads were a bitch. Snaking and twisting. He accelerated as he gave chase.

He wanted his prize back. The prize didn't get to leave, not unless he'd been paid.

There had been no payment. No chance to even demand the ransom.

Because of the boyfriend. A boyfriend who shouldn't exist because Alina Bellamy was a loner. Introverted. Reserved. Shy. Focused on her skating and nothing else.

So where the hell had some Rambo wannabe come from? How had the prick chased them? How had he found—

He slammed on his brakes. Stopped his pursuit because...

You bastard...you're pulling me into a trap, aren't you? The man had followed Alina too easily. He'd gotten into the cabin...too easily. Defeated Shayne. As for Fallon, hell, he hadn't stopped to find that thug, but the jerk had to still be at the cabin.

You left Shayne alive. Did you leave Fallon alive, too? If Fallon was alive and the cops came swarming, then *Fallon will lead them to me.*

A snarl rumbled in his throat. The boyfriend wanted him to give chase. He'd bet his life that Shayne had confessed to him—told him that reinforcements were coming. If not Shayne, then Fallon. Fallon loved to dish out pain, but the prick could not take it.

If I keep chasing you, will you lead me straight to the cops?

Or, if he kept up the chase, would the cops swarm his cabin while he hunted? Would they find Fallon? Get him to talk?

He spun the vehicle around and headed back for the cabin. He knew where Alina would go. *Run home to daddy.* He could get her again.

He had to make sure the cops—and this prick of a boyfriend—didn't catch *him*.

He raced back to the cabin. Brought his car to a screeching halt. He took a quick moment to grab a new knife from the glove box, and he shoved it in the empty sheath on his waist. It paid to be prepared. And when he jumped out... "*Fallon!*" he bellowed. The cry seemed to echo around him. Snow fell harder. Not so beautiful now. Just a pain in his ass. He used the light on his phone to search the ground. The fresh snow would cover tracks soon but...

There. A boot print. Deep. Wide. Another. Another. Heading for the trees.

But...

There were different footprints, too. Another set. Even bigger. Also heading for the tree line.

"Fallon!" A roar this time.

And... "Help!" A faint cry.

He took off toward the cry. Cold fury seeped through his blood, turning his insides just as cold as the snow that fell on him. As he drew closer to his target, he heard the sound of thrashing.

His light fell on the figure who twisted and struggled on the ground. Fallon. With his hands zip-tied behind him and his ankles locked together.

Fallon's head tilted up as he glared at the light.

"How the hell did this happen?" he asked the bound man.

"Her...freak of a boyfriend! He f-followed us." The words, though...they came out all tangled together.

The man's jaw didn't look just right. Blood dripped from his lips. Was he missing a tooth? Looked to be the case.

"Need...hospital!" Fallon snapped. "J-jaw..."

Yes, the closer he got, the worse Fallon's jaw appeared. "How did he follow you?'

"Help—"

"I will help you," he soothed. "Just trying to figure out what went wrong. The other abductions were seamless. But not this time. This woman." A woman who should have been the easiest pickings of them all. "You got her from her bedroom? Just like I told you?"

"We...saw him outside."

"Outside her house?"

"Watching. Stalker."

His shoulders tensed. Blood had just flown from Fallon's mouth. It had almost touched him.

Fallon had managed to sit up, but not stand. He kept trying to stand, but he just fell back into the snow each time.

"You're telling me her boyfriend was outside, watching her house, while Alina slept?"

A jerky nod.

"And that didn't set off red flags for you? You didn't think you needed to *call me* and tell me what was happening?"

"We...saw them go out on a date. Thought at first, he was staying the night. But he l-left her place..." The teeth he still had chattered. The words thickened.

Talking had to be extremely hard—no doubt painful—with that jaw.

"He came b-back. Watched..."

"And you didn't abort."

Blood dripped on the snow near Fallon. "You would have been...mad."

He knelt in front of Fallon. "Alina is gone. Shayne is dead. How do you think I feel right now?" His hands lifted. Curled under Fallon's broken jaw.

Fallon hissed in pain. "Sh-Shayne is dead? That f-freak killed—"

He leaned close and whispered in Fallon's ear, "No, I did that." Then he eased back and stared into Fallon's eyes. "And I'm going to kill you, too."

Fallon opened his mouth to scream.

Can't have that...

***

The lights had vanished from the rearview mirror.

That didn't mean they weren't being followed. It could mean the tricky SOB had just turned off his headlights. *The better for me not to see him closing in.* But the roads were so twisting and sharp. It would practically be suicide to race down them in the dark.

Alina had called the cops. At first, the dispatcher had thought it was a prank call. Screw that bullshit. They'd set the record straight, fast.

The dispatcher had wanted them to pull over. To wait for the authorities.

Again, screw that bullshit.

Midas kept driving, never letting up on the gas pedal. The more distance he had between Alina and that cabin, the better.

"How can I ever repay you?" she asked quietly.

His teeth clenched so tightly that his jaw ached. "You don't."

"You saved my life! I definitely need to repay you." Her hand reached out. Her soft fingers traced over his upper arm.

He had one hell of a bruise there, but he didn't flinch because of the pain. He flinched because her touch unnerved him. No, unnerved wasn't the right word. Her touch just made him feel different. Edgy. Rough. *Wild.*

"How did you know I'd been taken?"

Because I was right outside your house. Because your dad hired me to guard you, and I didn't do a damn good job of it. "Alina, I need to tell you some things." Actually, hell, he needed to call her father. "Your dad," he began.

"He doesn't know!" Her hand flew away from him. "I have to call him. Tell him I'm okay, that you saved me—"

"He knows that you were taken." Ryker wouldn't know that she was okay, not yet. "But I need to inform him that I have you."

"He...knows?"

"I called him." Grim. *And he didn't want the cops involved. Only we've brought them in now, so your dad is gonna be pissed.*

Up ahead, he saw the flash of blue lights. The cops. Closing in. Finally.

"Safety," she whispered. Obviously, she'd caught sight of the cops, too. "Everything is going to be okay."

He wouldn't go that far. In fact, he thought quite the opposite. *The kidnappers aren't in custody.*

"They kept telling me that their 'boss' was coming," Alina suddenly revealed. "You got me out before he arrived." Her words shook. "What do you think he would have done to me?"

The flashing blue lights were brighter. Closer. "He's not ever going to do a damn thing to you." Midas pulled off the road. Turned on his hazard lights. That had been the plan. The dispatcher had said when he got close to the cops, he should turn on his hazards to signal them. "I won't let him get close."

But he needed to tell her the truth. About who he was. Why he was in her life.

He turned toward her. "Alina..." Shit, why did this feel like it was gonna hurt him? He'd just met the woman. A full twenty-four hours had not passed since he'd walked into that rink and seen her spinning on the ice. Spinning, then falling.

I don't want Alina falling.

The cop cars screeched to a halt. He saw two uniformed cops jump from the first vehicle and hurry toward them.

Alina caught his hand. "Don't leave me?"

His fingers twined with hers. "That shit just isn't happening." But he would have to tell her the truth, sooner or later.

Alina, I'm not your new boyfriend...

I'm your bodyguard.

One who'd done a clusterfuck of a job on day one.

CHAPTER SEVEN

He hadn't left her side.

Alina cast a quick glance at Midas. He'd stayed with her during the ambulance ride to the hospital. A ride she hadn't needed because she was *fine*. Just bruised. Meanwhile, he was the one with the lacerations. The one who'd been hit by a car. The one who—according to the EMT in the ambulance—had at least two bruised ribs.

But Midas had refused treatment for his injuries. He'd directed everyone to focus on *her*.

And he'd stayed by her side. Big, tough, protective.

Would she *ever* forget opening her eyes and seeing him fill that closet doorway? Never in a million years.

"Alina!" Her father burst into her hospital exam room. He ran to the bed. She'd been sitting on the edge, dressed in a paper gown, and swinging her sock-clad feet nervously. He threw his arms around her and held on tightly.

Over her father's shoulder, she saw Midas narrow his eyes.

"Thank God," her father muttered as his hold tightened even more. "*Thank God.*"

A nurse bustled in behind him. At the sound of footsteps, her father let Alina go and spun to face the nurse. "We need time alone!" An order.

Did her father get that he wasn't the one who was supposed to give orders in hospitals?

The nurse blinked at him. "I have a patient who needs my attention." Cool. "You can have your time *after* I've checked on her."

Her father immediately looked back at Alina. His hand rose and his fingers skimmed her jaw. "He could have broken it."

Could have. Hadn't. "It's just a little sore." So was the front of her head—where she'd been slammed into her front door. The doctor who'd examined her had said that she had a concussion. She was supposed to have someone watch her for the next twenty-four hours.

Midas had immediately volunteered for the job.

Like *he* probably didn't have a concussion? He'd been hit by a car. "Dad, you have to get Midas examined." Enough of his tough macho act. *Hit by a car.*

The nurse bustled closer. She raked a considering glance over Midas.

He remained standing near the exam table, with his arms crossed over his powerful chest.

The nurse began checking Alina's vitals. How many times were they going to do that process? This was the third time. Fourth? "I'm *fine*," she assured the nurse. "But Midas needs help. The cut over his eye might need stitches. His ribs could be broken." That was her fear. That they were broken, not bruised.

"Just bruised," Midas dismissed with a shrug. "And the cut stopped bleeding. I don't need treatment for a few scratches."

Like she did?

"I've had far worse," Midas assured her. "It's not a deal."

The nurse cleared her throat. "The police are waiting in the hallway. They have more questions for you."

She was sure they did. Only Alina didn't think she was going to have answers for them. She didn't know why she'd been taken. Didn't know who had taken her. She only knew that she was grateful to be alive.

Grateful to Midas.

"Please give me a moment with my daughter before the cops are escorted inside," Ryker said. His voice was less demanding. More charming.

The nurse nodded and slipped out.

Her father looked at Alina, then Midas. He turned from Alina and strode to Midas. Ryker reached out and clapped a hand around Midas's arm. "I knew you were the best."

She blinked.

"Did you eliminate them?" Low.

So low that maybe she'd misunderstood. Because surely her father hadn't just asked if Midas had *killed* the men who took her?

Midas broke from her father's grip and stalked toward Alina. He'd only been a few steps away, but he came touching-close. His amber eyes narrowed on her face. "We really need to talk."

The cops wanted to talk.

Her father wanted to talk.

Now Midas.

She nodded.

"I need to know what the situation is," her father trailed after Midas. "I have to get my lawyers on this, ASAP. Though, dammit, I told you I didn't want the cops involved. You should have listened to me. It would have made everything so much simpler. I could have made the problem vanish."

Her heart drummed hard in her chest. What was happening?

Midas stood right in front of her. "You need to take some deep breaths."

She released the breath she'd been holding. When had she even started holding her breath?

"You're safe, Alina. I am going to stay with you until the bastards are locked in cells."

"They're still alive?" Her father gasped. "But I told you—"

A knock sounded at the door. A woman with blond hair—twisted in a loose bun—popped her head inside. "Alina Bellamy?"

Alina nodded.

"I'm Detective Joyce Meriam." She pushed the door open fully. A tall, dark, broad-shouldered male stood behind her. His intense gaze took in the scene. "And this is my partner, Detective Calvin Booker."

Calvin dipped his head forward. His brown eyes swept over Alina and Midas.

"We've been assigned to your case," Joyce continued in her slightly friendly tone, "and we have quite a few questions."

Alina's lips parted.

"My daughter has been through a grueling ordeal," her father snapped as he moved into the path of the two detectives. "She is still being examined by doctors. This is *not* the time to question her. Shouldn't you be out there, hunting down the men who took her?"

"Oh, we think we have those men," Joyce said. Her lips pursed even as she sidestepped so that she could continue to study Alina and Midas. "Don't you worry about them. They aren't going to be hurting anyone else." Her bright blue gaze dipped to Midas. "Midas Monroe. I am very familiar with you."

Why would the detective be familiar with Midas? Alina's head ached, but then, it had been aching ever since she'd slammed into the door.

At the detective's words, Midas turned to partially face the detectives.

"You told the responding officers that you had secured two individuals who abducted Alina." Joyce strolled closer to him. "I believe you indicated that you had used zip ties you found in the rear of their vehicle in order to bind them."

"Yes." A flat response. "Though I wasn't sure if the men would still be at the cabin when the officers arrived."

"Oh, they were there," Calvin assured him. "Exactly where you told the uniforms. The redhead was inside the cabin. The other guy was in the woods, just past the tree line on the north side."

Alina exhaled in relief. "Then they can tell you about their boss."

All eyes locked on her.

She wet her lips. "They weren't supposed to hurt me." Her hand rose to skim over her jaw. "Not too much, anyway. Because of the boss. They were waiting for him. He was on his way there." Her gaze slid to Midas. "But Midas got to me first. He took me out of there. Carried me through the woods and got me to safety." Her hand reached out and curled over his. "He saved my life."

"Uh, huh. Saved you…" Joyce edged closer. "And he killed the two men who'd taken you?"

Alina's jaw dropped. It took her a moment to snap it closed and gasp, "What?" The detectives were wrong. Her head shook. "No, no, Midas didn't kill anyone!"

"Don't say another word until my lawyers are here," her father blasted. "Not you, Alina. Not you, Midas." He pointed at the cops. "My daughter is a victim. Her bodyguard is the hero. He saved her life. Your questions will wait. I will—"

Her father said more. He was in full command mode, but Alina didn't hear him. She'd gotten stuck on one word.

Bodyguard.

Her father was wrong. Or maybe she'd heard wrong. Midas wasn't her bodyguard. Maybe her father had meant to say boyfriend.

But…

We went on one date. My father wouldn't know about that date. She certainly hadn't told him about it.

The ache in her head grew worse.

Her hand began to pull away from Midas's.

His hand flipped over. Caught hers. Held tightly. "Alina."

Her gaze had fallen to their hands. Now it snapped back up to his face.

"Alina, I will explain everything to you," he swore. His amber eyes glittered. "I need you to trust me."

Joyce cleared her throat. "If she was taken under your watch, bodyguard, then you seemed to have been falling down on the job."

That word again. Bodyguard. "He's head of security at the rink," Alina blurted. Head of security didn't mean he was her personal bodyguard. "He didn't fall down on any job. I was at home. Sleeping." She'd told the other cops this information before—about what had happened when she was taken, but she'd tell it again. Clearly, there was some confusion. "I heard my bedroom door opening. I knew someone was in the house, and I woke up. They came at me, and I-I tried to fight." For a moment, the terror of that moment swamped her.

Her father darted back to her side. He pulled her hand from Midas's grasp. "Alina."

Her head turned toward him.

"Wait for the lawyer," he urged her.

But she wasn't saying anything wrong. "I grabbed the lamp. I fought. They were stronger." The words wanted to come out. She didn't try to stop them. *I am not saying anything wrong.* "I tried to run to the front door." They'd...they'd said something. Her brow furrowed. She glanced over at a still Midas. "They said someone was watching the house."

"I was," Midas told her. "I was on the street. I saw a light in your bedroom flash on, then turn off. Didn't seem right, so I went to your front door. When I knocked, you didn't answer."

Her father cursed.

Calvin raised one eyebrow. "Uniforms are at her place now. Seems her front door was broken open."

"Sure." An easy reply from Midas. "I kicked it in. I needed to get inside to her. When I got in, I realized they'd taken her out the back. I hunted for her. It was damn dark. I turned just as their car was coming right at me."

Her eyes squeezed closed. "They hit Midas." Thank goodness they hadn't killed him. Her heart seemed to jerk in her chest.

"A car hit you?" Joyce clarified with a slight clearing of her throat. "Like, it almost hit you or it actually *hit*—"

"I jumped on the hood," Midas informed her flatly. "Held on long enough to put a tracker on the vehicle. Hid it underneath the upper section of the hood, right near the windshield. The driver hit the brakes, I went flying, and they thought they left me behind." A pause. "They were wrong. I gave chase. Subdued the two men. Got her out of the cabin because their reinforcements were coming."

Alina saw the two detectives share a long look.

"And you didn't think to call the cops during this time?" A careful question from Joyce.

"*Enough,*" Ryker blasted. "I don't like the tone. I don't like the insinuations you seem to be making. The man was obviously busy *saving my daughter*."

Alina wasn't sure what the detective was insinuating. Maybe it was because of her concussion or the shock, but she felt like she was missing a whole lot.

Like...*bodyguard?* "Why were you outside my house?" Alina asked Midas. "Did you forget something?" Or maybe he'd been coming back to her. They'd shared that passionate kiss, and she'd wanted more. Perhaps he had, too.

Odd, though. The kiss seemed so long ago. But it had only been hours since that moment.

The night had distorted everything.

The faint lines near Midas's mouth deepened.

"If you'd been *in* the house," Calvin scratched his chin, "wouldn't that have been far more effective? She wouldn't have been taken if you'd been inside. I imagine it's exceedingly difficult to keep a close eye on your client when she's inside and you're camped out in your car."

"I'm not his client," Alina denied.

Calvin frowned. "Midas Monroe is well-known as a bodyguard for the wealthy and famous."

The paper gown suddenly seemed very rough against her skin. And the room had grown colder. Hospitals were always cold, but this chill felt different.

"I just assumed seeing as you are something of a celebrity, Alina—is it okay if I call you Alina?" Calvin asked.

She didn't care what he called her. Alina nodded.

"I assumed that you had hired Midas for protection. Why else would he be outside of your home in the middle of the night?"

"He...he supervises security at the rink." She'd told them that part already.

Calvin pursed his lips. "Is that what he does?" His stare shifted to her father. "That the story you are going to stick with? You feel good about that?"

Her father's face darkened. "I'm not telling you any story until my lawyers arrive."

Lawyers, as in plural, because her father always had an army of lawyers at the ready.

"My daughter has been through an ordeal," Ryker continued gruffly. "I am lucky she is safe. As for the men who took her—"

"The two dead men?" Joyce cut in. "The men who were found—still zip-tied, by the way, but *dead*—at the cabin? What about them?"

Very slowly, Midas turned his head so that he stared straight at the female detective. "I left them alive."

She grimaced. "Are you *sure* about that? Tense situation. Dangerous moments. They'd abducted your client. You were desperate to get her back. They got in your way. They made you look bad. Ruined that perfect bodyguard reputation you have. So you let loose with your fury."

"Midas isn't my bodyguard," Alina said. She jumped off the table. Grabbed tightly to the edge when her knees threatened to buckle. Her knees needed to get their act together. "And he didn't kill *anyone*. The redheaded man—he was alive when we left him."

Joyce tilted her head to the right. "Are you sure about that?"

"Yes, Midas said he'd checked his pulse. The man was sprawled on the floor, his hands were bound..." She looked down at her own hands. At the bandages around her raw wrists. Alina swallowed as she forced herself to focus on the detectives. "He was alive. Midas and I rushed out. Midas didn't kill anyone."

"So..." Once more, Calvin tapped his chin. "You weren't worried about the knife sticking out of the man's chest? That wasn't a concern for you? All the blood?"

Her mouth opened. Closed. "What knife?" No, no, he was wrong. Her head shook. "There was no blood. No knife in his chest."

The detectives glanced at each other.

They kept doing their silent communication bit, but that needed to stop. "Listen to me," Alina's voice rose. "There was no knife in his chest. I think I would have noticed that. Granted, I was *stressed* at the time." Try terrified. "But it's hard to miss a knife." She crept closer to Midas. He needed to know that she had his back. "Midas did not stab that man. Midas knocked him out, bound his hands, and then Midas carried me from the cabin."

Joyce's gaze dipped back to Midas. "That your story, too?"

"I didn't kill anyone tonight." He shrugged. "If the redhead was dead, that was probably due to him fucking up his job. He was supposed to keep Alina in that cabin. He failed. I imagine when his boss showed up that the guy wasn't too thrilled. It's hard to find good help, you know?"

Joyce's expression held plenty of suspicion. "That why the second man was dead, too? The one in the woods? A knife to the chest *and* a broken neck for him?"

Midas stiffened.

"You gonna tell us their boss did that, too? Or did you get a little overzealous in your attempts to subdue that individual?"

Alina reached out and curled her fingers around Midas's hand. She could feel eyes on her, but she didn't care. She wanted them all to know that she backed up Midas. He'd saved her. He didn't need to be treated like some kind of criminal.

"It's not easy to break someone's neck," Calvin mused. "Not at all like what you see in movies and TV shows. Takes a whole lot of power. Some specific know-how. You don't just wrench a neck to the side. If you're gonna break a neck, you need to know exactly what you're doing." His gaze sharpened on Midas. "But you'd know exactly what to do, wouldn't you? Tell me, did your father teach you those moves?"

Midas pulled from her. Both of his hands fisted, and she could feel the sudden surge of fury surrounding him.

"I am *nothing*," Midas gritted out, "like my father. Don't ever make that mistake about me."

His father? Lost, her gaze whipped around the room. It darted from person to person as Alina tried to figure out what was happening.

"Oh." From Joyce. She stared at Alina with a dawning realization. "You didn't know, did you? Like, you really, truly don't know who he is." Compassion flashed on her face. "They kept it from you, didn't they?" Her mouth tightened and she shot a look of disgust at Ryker. "Overprotective father bullshit. Didn't tell your daughter that you'd hired a bodyguard to watch over her, did you? And if you *hired* the bodyguard without telling her, it does make me wonder, did you know this abduction was coming? If so, how did you know?"

Ryker pulled out his phone, stared at the screen, and nodded. "Two of my best lawyers are in the parking lot. This discussion is over."

"Why are you stonewalling us?" Frustration seethed in Joyce's voice. "Don't you want to find out who arranged your daughter's abduction? Who the mysterious 'boss' is that she referenced?"

Ryker put his phone back in his pocket. Said nothing.

Midas had turned to stone.

And Alina stood there, in her paper hospital gown, with bandages around her wrists and ankles. She kept her chin up. Her spine straight.

"Fine. Don't talk to us, but I have something else to say because I happen to think Alina deserves some truth from *someone*." Joyce pointed at Midas. "This guy makes a living protecting the rich and famous. That was not bullshit. In plenty of elite circles, he's known as being the best bodyguard in the business. Alina, I suspect if we dig into your father's accounts, we'll see that he recently paid a very large sum of money to Mr. Midas Monroe. The man's services certainly aren't cheap." Her cheeks puffed out as she exhaled. "Though, considering the way the night went for you, I'd say you were lucky to have him."

"The two dead men weren't so lucky," Calvin noted.

She needed clothes. Real clothes. Or else maybe she'd just walk out in the hospital gown. Alina wanted to escape.

"But you should really dig a bit deeper into the lives of the people close to you. Midas has quite the backstory." Joyce grimaced. "One that just does not look so good considering the way one of your abductors died."

Midas stepped toward the detectives. The small hospital room felt even smaller with his movements. "I didn't kill anyone. Though the temptation was sure as hell there."

"Shit," Ryker muttered.

"They were alive when I left the men zip-tied. Look for their boss—he's the killer."

The door swung open. Two men in suits with crooked ties and askew hair spilled inside. "We're here, Mr. Bellamy!"

The lawyers.

Alina didn't pay them much attention. Midas had turned back toward her. His face seemed like such a hard, inscrutable mask. "I didn't kill them," he said, his voice low. Low and so deep.

She nodded.

"But..." His nostrils flared. "I *was* hired to be your bodyguard."

CHAPTER EIGHT

He didn't like staying at Ryker's mansion. Even if Midas and Alina were lodged in the guesthouse, he would have preferred to secure her in a place where he had total control.

Not like the guesthouse was small. Not by any means. Alina was actually up on the second floor. She'd gone to shower. To put on fresh clothes. Midas had already changed. New jeans. Old t-shirt. Same scuffed shoes.

The sun was about to rise, but he hoped like hell that Alina was going to get some sleep.

The cops hadn't been ready to let them go, even with the arrival of the lawyers. Or, more specifically, they hadn't wanted to let Midas go. *I didn't kill those goons.* But he truly had been tempted.

And the fact that one of them had been left with a broken neck? Like that shit didn't seem to be a message? One personally sent to Midas.

"I told you to leave the cops out of the situation." Ryker stood in front of the fireplace. His back was to Midas. "Why didn't you follow my orders?"

"Uh, because there was a *kidnapping?*" How did the guy not get this? "Because I had two men bound at the cabin who could point us in the direction of their boss? Because I was pretty sure I saw the boss driving to the cabin, but I couldn't go after him since I was the only one there to see to Alina's protection?"

Ryker kept staring into the twisting flames. "You think I fucked up."

"Absolutely." Midas didn't pull his punch. He never did. "They could have *killed* her while I was outside sitting in my car. You get that, don't you?"

Ryker's shoulders hunched. "Killing Alina wasn't the goal."

"How the hell do you know that?"

"Because torturing me was the goal." Ryker turned toward him. "Alina knows what you are now."

What. Not who. Screw that. He wasn't some *thing*.

"She could become...difficult."

A stair creaked. He didn't look toward the sound. "I can handle Alina. Difficult is my business."

Surprise—and what could have been relief—flashed in Ryker's eyes. Dark eyes just like Alina's. "You intend to continue the job? Even after what's happened?"

What had happened? Oh... "You mean the small matter of the cops suspecting I killed two men?"

Ryker stared back at him.

"I didn't kill them." *Despite the fact that you wanted me to.* The knowledge was there between them, unspoken. "They were the grunt workers. Killing them would make it harder for me to find the boss. I want the man who ordered her kidnapping."

Ryker's eyes widened. "You sound like you are going to hunt him."

Yes, that was precisely what Midas intended to do. "I'm a good multitasker. I can protect Alina and hunt down the piece of shit who ordered her abduction."

"He...he'll go away. He won't come after her again."

Keep telling yourself that. "Maybe. Maybe not. Either way, I don't intend to let the guy just scurry off into the dark. He's going to pay for what he did to her."

Ryker ran a hand through his hair. That hand shook a bit. "You protect. That's your thing. Protection. Bodyguard work. I've never heard anything about you *hunting* criminals."

"What can I say? I am a man of secrets." He was also a man with connections. "I've got some acquaintances who can help me out. One who specialized in hunting criminals for a very long time." Still did, in fact.

Memphis Camden was already flying down, with reinforcements. So maybe the guy wasn't such a sonofabitch.

"I don't want you hunting him."

Fear had trembled in those words. "What do you want, then? For him to come after your daughter again? For him to take her once more?"

Ryker surged toward him. Stopped less than a foot away. "I have others who can find him. All I need you to do is stay close to Alina. Be her shadow. She can't ditch you the way she's done other guards over the years. She's scared now. She'll let you stay at her side."

Scared wasn't quite the word for how he believed Alina felt.

"You protect her. I'll make certain the threat is eliminated. I just—I need you to stay with her until I give you the all clear to leave her."

The man was almost precious...the way he thought Midas would blindly follow his orders. Precious. Foolish. Delusional. "What aren't you telling me?"

"What?"

"You had a warning about the abduction, didn't you?"

Ryker swallowed. "It's late."

"Technically, it's early. Wait a little longer and the sun will rise."

Midas paused a beat. "Why didn't you want the cops involved?"

Silence.

Midas pushed, "What was it? An emailed threat? A letter that mysteriously appeared? Were you warned that if you called the cops, she'd die?"

Ryker flinched.

Paydirt. "She is not dying," Midas swore. "Count for fucking sure on that."

Ryker turned on his heel and marched for the front door. "You will stay in this house with her?"

Only until she rested. Then he'd find a better spot for them both. He already had a perfect place in mind. "I have no plans of leaving Alina."

Ryker paused at the door. He glanced at the darkened stairway. "I would never want my daughter in danger."

"Then maybe you need to put all your cards on the table." And if Ryker didn't, then Midas would just find the truth on his own.

"I think you're forgetting just who is cutting your check."

The stair creaked again.

Midas ground his back teeth together. "And I think you're assuming that I give a damn about that."

Ryker's head swung toward him.

"You need to understand this. I will find the man who ordered the kidnapping. No one will be screwing up my perfect record and walking away." But it wasn't about his protection record. Total BS.

It was about Alina.

Being taken.

Hurt.

Locked in a closet.

It was about the absolute terror that had covered her face when he opened that closet door—and the desperate hope that had flooded her eyes when she saw his face.

"You can be replaced," Ryker warned, voice gruff.

Midas laughed. "Nah. I can't. There's no one else like me. But good luck trying to find someone." He waited a beat. "I got her back. You think you can find someone else who would have gotten her back for you so quickly?"

No. The truth was right there in the heavy silence.

"Didn't think so." He rolled his shoulders. "Maybe my rates need to be higher." A taunt. One he regretted as soon as the words left his mouth because Ryker wasn't the only one listening to him.

Those words are totally going to bite me in the ass. But Ryker had gotten beneath his skin. The man was holding out on Midas. *When his own daughter is in jeopardy.* Midas wanted to rattle him.

And, sure enough, Ryker's hand shook even harder as he shoved his hair back once more. "You'd abandon my daughter?"

Midas turned toward the stairwell. "Not happening. Now, I get that you own the place, but how about you get the fuck out? I need to make sure she rests. She won't do that with you here."

"I'm her *father*—"

Oh, Midas knew exactly who he was.

"It's okay, dad." Alina's voice drifted down the stairs. "I'm safe, and, apparently, I have the best bodyguard that money can buy guarding my bedroom door." She climbed down the stairs. They creaked beneath her bare feet. She paused on the third step from the bottom. Her fingers trailed lightly over the wooden banister. "We'll talk after I've rested," Alina assured her father. "Who knows? Maybe by then, the cops will have caught the man who organized my kidnapping."

Midas snorted. She clearly had more faith in the cops than he did.

Alina bit her lower lip. "Dad, will you let Dimitri know that I won't be in for the practice? I don't want him thinking that I'm just standing him up."

Was she serious? The woman was actually worried about that Dimitri douche?

"I just need to rest for a little while, and then I can meet him at the rink," Alina continued.

No, she was *not* serious. "Fuck that," Midas announced flatly.

Alina's eyes widened. "Excuse me?"

"Fuck. That." He thought his words were pretty clear. He spared her gaping father a glance. "She won't be practicing today. Tell Dimitri she's resting. If he doesn't like that, he can deal with me." He motioned for the front door. Wait, on second thought, screw motioning for the door. He stalked forward and opened it for Ryker. *Time to hit the road.* "Good night. Good morning. Whatever the hell it is. My charge needs rest. Her safety comes first, so you'll excuse me if I drop the polite facade and just tell you to get the hell out."

Ryker blinked.

Hmmm. Perhaps Ryker had never been told to get the hell out before. Especially not when he technically owned the place. "There's a first time for everything," Midas assured him.

Yet still the older man lingered.

"You want me doing my job or not?" Midas snapped.

Ryker seemed to shake himself from his stupor. He lumbered forward and hesitated just a moment before the threshold. "You will protect her?"

"Got her back, didn't I?" But, so they were clear, he added, "I shouldn't have been outside. I should have been with Alina. You can damn well bet I won't be making the same mistake again. I *told* you I needed to be close. Consider me her freaking shadow from here on out. Wherever she goes, I go."

Ryker's fierce mask crumbled. "Thank you. Thank you for bringing her back to me. I-I *owe* you. I can pay—"

Midas pushed him out of the guesthouse. "Talk soon." He shut the door. Locked it. Then turned to face Alina.

She still stood on the third stair from the bottom. But her hand wasn't lightly tracing over the banister any longer. Instead, she clutched it in a death grip.

Okay, so... "Yell."

A cute little furrow appeared between her brows.

His gaze scanned down her body. She'd put on black yoga pants with a slight flare at the bottom. An oversized, gray sweatshirt dipped down to her thighs. No shoes. Dark blue polish on her toes.

His stare returned to her face. Her delicate jaw had hardened, and he really didn't like the dark smudges under her eyes. What he hated the most? The bruising along her jaw.

She didn't say a word. Definitely didn't do as he'd directed. No yells came from her.

Was she the type not to speak when she got pissed? He didn't do so well with silence. Midas motioned to himself. Then to her. "Want to get it out?"

"Get what out?" No emotion.

"We both know you want to scream at me."

Her tongue snaked over her lower lip. "As a rule, I try not to scream at anyone."

This was not going to end well for him. Taking his time, he closed in on her. And as he neared, she moved to the fourth step from the bottom.

"You don't need to retreat from me." He stared at her. "I would never hurt you."

"Liar."

It was his turn to blink. "Alina, I—"

"You lied to me from the moment we met, didn't you?"

Okay, well, at least she wasn't giving him the silent treatment. "Your father wanted me to work undercover."

"And that's what you usually do? Work undercover? Pretend to be someone you're not?"

They were both running on fumes. Maybe this talk should wait. "You're exhausted."

"Yes."

"Terrified."

"Terror does keep clawing through me, absolutely." She stopped gripping the banister and instead wrapped her arms around her stomach. "But I also think I deserve some answers."

"Fair enough." He kept his hands loose at his sides. "I don't usually work this way, no. My clients typically know exactly who I am and what my job is—makes things easier that way." *So you're not say, sitting in a car outside when your charge gets abducted on day freaking one.*

She swallowed. "Typically?"

"You're the first who didn't know what I was doing. Got to tell you, it was a real pain in my ass."

Alina flinched.

Yep, that had not been the right thing to say. "You aren't a pain in my ass. The job is," Midas clarified.

She sucked in a breath. And turned to rush up the stairs.

Hell. "Alina!" He gave chase. Caught her at the top. He didn't spin her around. He just scooped her into his arms.

"Stop it! Put me down!"

Yes, again, not the right thing. Holding her was not right. So he put her down in front of the bedroom that she'd chosen for the night—or day. Or… "Dammit." He blew out a hard breath. "I wanted to tell you, okay? I warned your old man that this was a terrible idea. I can't work with my hands tied."

"Your hands are currently on me."

Yes, they were. Stroking her shoulders. Whoops. "My bad."

"They are *still* on me."

Once again, yes. He pulled them away. "Your dad wanted you focused on your skating. He thought if you knew you had a bodyguard watching your every move, it would make you nervous." Like she didn't have cause to be nervous…

Her chin lifted. "Who had the idea that you should pretend to be interested in me?"

Oh, yeah. He could see the landmine in front of him just waiting to explode. "You need rest."

"I need some answers. My body won't stop shaking. I'm afraid someone is going to come rushing in the door and attack me any moment, and I just found out that you lied to me from the moment we met." Her lips pressed together. Then, "Rest is not exactly going to come easily."

"You probably have too much adrenaline coursing through your blood." Midas tried to make his voice sound soothing. A hard feat because he typically sounded like a growling bear and growling bears were not soothing. "You'll feel a crash soon, and you'll be out like a light."

She stepped closer. "Did you have the idea to fake being interested in me?"

Her scent teased him. She'd showered, and her hair was still wet, and she smelled like that sweet, sweet vanilla cream again. Good enough to eat.

And he wanted a bite.

So not the time. But his dick never listened to reason. And his dick couldn't tell time for shit.

"Was it your idea or did my father tell you what cover to use?"

He whipped his gaze off her delectable lips. "He mentioned that you were sheltered. That you didn't have a lot of experience with men and—"

Her face flamed.

His back teeth ground together. "I'm shit with words sometimes."

"No, you seem to be explaining just fine. My father told you that I'd trip over myself with eagerness if you showed interest in me. And I did, didn't I? Asked you out after we'd barely had a conversation." Her cheeks darkened even more. "How convenient for you."

"No, nothing about this case has been convenient. It's been a cluster from the first moment."

Her lower lip trembled. *Trembled!* He'd just done that. "Do *not* cry."

"Do *not* be an asshole!" Alina threw right back.

"Impossible. I'm always an asshole." His hand lifted because a tear had slid down her left cheek and the sight of that lone tear was like a punch right to his gut. "I have rules with charges."

"Charges?"

"I'm in charge of taking care of you. Your dad is the client. You're the charge."

Her brow furrowed. Her head turned into his hand.

Then away.

His hand fell back to his side. "I have never worked undercover with a client before. Normally, I would have told your old man to piss off. Being undercover meant that from the first moment, I'd be at a disadvantage."

"Then why did you do it? No, wait. Let me guess. He offered you a great deal of money, didn't he?"

"Yes, but—"

"I think I'm projecting," she suddenly said, and her spine stopped being so straight. It slumped, as did her shoulders. "I used to do that a lot. A counselor told me—after my mother's death, I saw this lady for a while—and she told me..." But Alina's words trailed off. "I'm scared and I'm angry because I was so helpless. All those feelings are getting pushed onto you. You saved me." A nod. "I should be grateful. I *am* grateful. But I'm also hurt because..." A low exhale. "It was a lie. I thought it was something special, but it wasn't. It was just you pretending."

It seemed as if another punch pounded into his gut. "Maybe we should start over."

Starting over was a whole lot better than ending. He couldn't let her end things between them.

She was still in danger. And he just—*we can't end.*

"How do you normally start with your, ah, charges?"

"I give them a set of rules."

"Rules," Alina repeated. With a weary hand, she pushed back a heavy lock of hair that had fallen forward. "What is rule one?"

Yeah, okay. This probably wasn't the best thing to say. "Uh..."

"What's the first rule?"

"Don't go falling for me. Don't go getting emotionally involved." *I'm not here to be your lover or your best friend. I'm just here to watch your ass.*

Her eyes widened. Her hand froze in mid push with her hair.

"I don't cross lines," he heard himself say. "So I let my charges know that nothing personal is gonna happen between us. I'm there to do a job. Nothing more." Personal involvements would screw a case to hell and back.

Her long lashes swept down to hide her eyes even as her hand slid down to her side. "You kissed me."

He wanted to kiss her again. And again. And again.

"But that was part of the undercover mission, huh? Nothing personal. Just getting close." Her lashes swept up. "You're close now."

He wanted to be even closer and that was the problem. "I'm your bodyguard."

"So I've discovered." A dip of her head. "Thanks for saving my life, by the way." Stiff. Cold.

He didn't like her that way. He wanted her warm. Smiling. The light shining in her dark eyes. But that light was gone. She was too pale. The bruise along her jaw was too dark, and her body seemed far, far too fragile. "No one is going to hurt you."

"Because you're going to stand between me and every threat?" Mocking. Or at least, she probably meant for the words to be mocking.

"Damn straight. Until the danger is over, where you go, I go."

She looked over her shoulder. "I'm going to bed."

Take me with you. Nope. No way. Not gonna say that. "I'll be downstairs. No one will get past me."

"There is a bed in the next room." She returned her attention to him. "You haven't slept tonight, either. You need rest. I'm sure you can protect me just as well from that room as you can from downstairs."

"I can protect you best if I'm in the same room with you."

Her body stiffened.

He shouldn't have said that. Oh, well. "But I can see where you might not want that to happen. I'll bunk on the couch. That way, in order to get to the stairs, in order to get to you, any perp would truly have to get past me first." He wanted to keep an eye on the ground level. "I'm sure the cops will be knocking at your door with more questions in a few hours. I'll keep them away until you've had enough rest."

"You're the best bodyguard in the business. The female detective said that."

He shrugged one shoulder and lifted his head. "That's why your dad hired me."

"Who was your last client? Uh, charge?"

"An action star." He told her the name. "He has a place close by, so I was in the area when your dad needed someone to step in with you."

"Then I'm grateful. Without you, I don't know what would have happened to me."

Not like Midas wanted to think about that shit. "You won't be hurt again."

She eased away. Opened the bedroom door. And left him there. Her scent lingered in the air. Surrounded him.

The door closed.

He wanted to open it. To go inside and tell her—

What was he supposed to tell her?

That she wasn't just a case? That none of his normal rules applied to her? That he had been ready to kill and destroy in order to get her back?

She'd been through enough. That was hardly the crap she wanted to hear.

That was hardly—

Her door flew open. "You didn't have to pretend that you wanted me."

What?

"Unnecessary," she bit out. "You didn't have to kiss me. You didn't have to act like you needed me, you didn't have to—"

His hands curled around her waist. He lifted her up so they were eye to eye. "I had to kiss you."

Alina shook her head.

"But I didn't have to pretend. I *didn't* pretend. I wanted you from the first moment." His eyes were on her lips. "And you know what? I still do." So...*I'm gonna take what I want.*

His mouth locked on hers.

CHAPTER NINE

Angry. Scared. Hurt.

Alina's emotions battered at her even as she wrapped her arms around Midas and kissed him back with every bit of passion that burned through her. This was wrong. They were wrong. He was wrong. A man who'd lied to her. Misled her.

Saved her.

A man she wanted too badly to bother caring about anything else. Especially not all of the reasons why she should not be kissing him.

She'd *never* felt this way. Never wanted someone so much that the need twisted and consumed her.

He kissed her with a wild, feverish passion. His wicked tongue took and tormented, and the hands on her waist seemed to brand her. He'd lifted her up, held her so easily with that casual strength he possessed. Her legs wrapped around his hips. The better to hold on tight. There was no missing the long, thick length of his cock pressing against her.

He might have lied. But he wasn't pretending at that moment. There were some things that couldn't be faked. That massive erection of his? That would be one of those things.

His mouth tore from hers. "I shouldn't do this," he rasped.

Her lips went to his throat. She kissed him. Licked. Felt the racing of his pulse beneath her mouth. One hundred percent, they shouldn't be doing this.

He hissed when her teeth bit lightly against him. His hold on her tightened and then he was moving. Striding into her bedroom. She'd left all the lights on in that room. She'd been afraid of the dark. How ridiculous was that? But she'd been afraid to be alone in the dark. The instant she'd closed the door and looked around...

Fear.

Anger.

I need Midas. She'd gone right back to him. And now he was taking her to the bed. Lowering her down but not leaving her. Coming on top of her. Kissing her once again. Putting her on the mattress, but not crushing her with his much bigger body. He levered himself up. Pushed his hand on the mattress so that his weight was off her.

His mouth took hers once more. Her legs were still locked around his hips, and she realized with a little shock that she was arching against his dick. Rubbing and rocking against him.

"Alina!" Again, he'd pulled his mouth from hers. His breath sawed out. "You do not want this."

She rolled her eyes. "Really? Do tell me more about what I want."

His jaw clenched. His amber gaze seemed to blaze as he stared down at her. "You had one hell of a night."

Like she needed that reminder.

"Your emotions are running crazy. You're scared and angry and right now, I bet you're pissed as hell at me, even though you want me."

Her nostrils flared. "Maybe you should get off me." The man certainly knew how to kill a mood.

"I don't want to get off you. I want to strip you. Fuck you. Make you scream my name. And I want to give you so much pleasure that you forget every moment of fear you've ever felt in your life."

Her breath whispered out.

"But I also don't want you to hate me when the adrenaline crashes and the terror leaves and your world returns to normal." A muscle flexed along his jaw. "You hating me? It matters. I've already had enough missteps. I can't afford more."

Missteps? Was that what she was?

"Said that wrong, didn't I? Dammit. *You're important.* I'm trying not to screw up more."

"You're the one on top of me." Still. "And you want me." Just so they were clear. She wasn't lost in this madness alone.

The amber of his eyes deepened. "I never faked wanting you. My dick gets hard whenever you're near."

She jerked.

"Sorry. No, not sorry. That was too crass for you? Sweetheart, I am crass. I'm crass and dangerous, and some would say I'm one of the most evil sonsofbitches to ever walk the earth."

She did not know what was happening. Her heart kept pounding. She could taste him. Need wracked her. And her legs were still wrapped around his hips. She should let him go. Instead, she asked, "Why would someone say you were evil?"

His eyes squeezed closed. "I cannot have this conversation while I'm in bed with you. Not while your yoga pants are too thin, and I can feel your heat against me, and I just want *inside*." His right hand moved between their bodies. "Tell me to stop."

His hand slid down. Down. He shifted his hips away enough so that his hand could wedge between them. That big hand went to her core and began to stroke her through what was, indeed, thin fabric.

She bit her lip to hold back a hungry cry. And that was *not* her telling him to stop.

"You're so beautiful. I could have you screaming..."

She'd never screamed. Her sexual experience to date had been, well, it had been practically zero. Not that she intended to tell Midas.

She wanted him to keep stroking her. To stroke *harder*. To push her to the edge and then over it.

Instead, he pulled his hand away. Caught her legs and lowered them to the bed. Then the man jumped away from her and the bed like he'd just been scalded. "You don't want me touching you."

Alina sat up. Glaring, she said, "You seem to know an awful lot about what *I* want." What she wanted was for him to finish what he'd just started.

"You're class. You're substance. You're good." His hands fisted. "If you knew the real me, you would never let me put my hands on you."

"I don't know the real you." He was right on that score. "Due to the fact that you lied to me." That hindered the whole real-me process.

"You're gonna know. The cops will tell you. They think I killed those two men."

Moments before, she'd been kissing Midas. They'd been hot. Passionate. Now—this? "You didn't. I was there. The redhead was alive. There was certainly no knife sticking out of his chest. I would have noticed that." Hard to miss something like that.

"The other man was stabbed and had his neck broken."

"Yes, I heard that." Scary. But what did that have to do with Midas?

"Your father told me that you wouldn't know about my past. It was a long time ago. Hell, I was barely nineteen when they locked me up."

Her shoulders stiffened. "When who locked you up?"

"A lot of people have forgotten. You would have been so young then. The memory would have passed for you by now, and hell, only true crime buffs are familiar with the dirty details these days."

Her hands clenched in the covers. "You are losing me, Midas. I don't understand what you are talking about."

A jerky nod. "Right. And this isn't the time to tell you. You're already terrorized enough." He took a step back. "Go to sleep, Alina."

"You're bossy, you know that?"

"I'm a straight A bastard, that's what I am. Don't ever think otherwise." A shadow seemed to darken his face. He sawed a hand over the beard along his hard jaw. "But I can keep you safe. I can protect you better than anyone else. So when you do learn all the dirty details, remember that, would you?"

Enough of the mystery. "Just spit it out, Midas. Tell me what you're hiding. I am sick of secrets."

"You won't sleep. You have enough fear as it is. Adding more to it now..."

This was crazy. He couldn't just leave her in the dark.

He turned for the door. "If you need me, I'll be a shout away."

No. Absolutely not. "You don't drop bombshells and walk away."

He didn't look back.

"Fine. Should I do an internet search on you? I'm sure I'll get some hits. Whatever dirty secrets you're keeping, I'm certain I can uncover them. But don't you think it would just be better for you to tell me the truth?"

Slowly, he faced her.

"Why were you locked up, Midas?"

"Alina..."

"You lied to me before. Let's agree that you won't lie to me ever again. You don't lie to me. I don't lie to you." She wet her lips. Tasted him. Ached for him. "Fair?"

His head jerked.

She guessed that was a yes. "Why were you locked up? And, clearly, you were innocent. So someone was framing you."

A furrow appeared between his brows. "Clearly?"

Yes, clearly. "My father wouldn't have hired a criminal to guard me."

"Why not? Criminals know all the best tricks."

She shivered. Tiredness had begun to pull at her, and she feared the adrenaline coursing through her body might be preparing for the promised crash. Not that she'd confess that info to Midas. "Don't joke."

"I wasn't."

"Midas..."

"I was suspected of killing three women."

Her heart stopped.

"Breaking their necks and thrusting knives into their hearts. A very specific signature, I can assure you."

The room seemed to spin. It was a lucky thing that she was already on the bed. "Wh-what?"

With deliberate steps, he came back to the bed. Leaned forward. Put his hands on either side of her. "That's fear."

Her mouth had gone dry.

"The way your voice trembled? You're afraid. The way you are *looking* at me right now? You're afraid. And that's why I need to keep my hands off you. I warned you that when you knew the truth, you wouldn't want me touching you."

She couldn't look away from his eyes. "You didn't kill those women."

"For a while, no one believed me when I said that very thing."

He'd been locked away? For multiple murders?

"There was a very, very good frame job in place, you see. DNA evidence left behind. Witnesses who saw a man fitting my description. In case you didn't notice, I do tend to stick out in a crowd."

Her hand rose and pressed to his chest. Right over his heart. "Who framed you?"

"The real killer, of course. Isn't that how these stories go? He needed a fall guy. He picked me. A dumb kid who trusted the wrong person. Lucky for me, though, a young FBI agent came along. Someone who believed me. Who helped me to prove my innocence. The real killer was caught. Convicted. Sent to live the rest of his life in a cage. End of story."

If that was the end, then why was he pulling away? And he was. He'd already retreated from her. "I didn't hear dirty details. I heard…" She wet her lips again. "I heard a terrible story about you being put through hell. But you were innocent. You were cleared. And now you protect people." She wouldn't touch on him lying to her. Or how it hurt. Or how she didn't know what to feel or think any longer.

"The real killer was a true monster. He got off on the pain he gave to his victims. And he had a whole lot more than just three vics." Midas had made it to the bedroom door. It was partially open. When they'd rushed inside, kissing, feverish, they hadn't shut it. He opened it fully. His hand curled around the wood along the edge of the door. "The detectives were right about one thing at the hospital. It isn't easy to break someone's neck. Not at all like you see in TV shows. It takes considerable force." He stared at his hand as it gripped the door's edge. "But when you're someone like me—with my size and strength—and the vic...the victim is someone like..." He trailed off. Swallowed. "When the victim is someone so much smaller and delicate, it gets easier. You just have to know how to snap the bones in the right way."

Nausea rolled within her.

"He was big like me. And he found out—dammit, I don't need to tell you this. You already have enough nightmares." A ragged exhale. "Why am I giving you more? You don't need more."

She climbed from the bed and found herself creeping toward him. Her hand reached out to him. "Midas."

"He was my own fucking father. He'd killed women—so many of them—during my whole life. Sometimes, I was even in the same house with him, and I didn't know what he was doing." His fingers tightened even more around the edge of the door. His knuckles turned white. "He was going to have me pay for his crimes while he got off scot-free. My dear old bastard of a dad."

Alina sucked in a sharp breath.

His head turned so that his gaze collided with hers. "And those are the dirty details. I'm the son of the devil, sweetheart. And you don't want to fuck me. You don't want my hands on you. You don't want anything *personal* happening between us. That's why I have my rules. Because no one wants the evil that is buried in me. But I swear, I *swear* I can keep you safe. I will keep you safe. Because I know how to fight monsters. I've been doing it my whole life."

She didn't know what to say.

Before she could find words, he'd walked out. Closed the door.

And left her alone.

***

He'd just screwed that to hell and back. Midas stood in the hallway, his hands clenching and releasing, clenching and releasing. Part of him—a very, very big part—wished that she'd wrench open the bedroom door again. That she'd come out for him, just as she had before.

And tell him that it didn't matter.

Sometimes, Midas worried he was as delusional as his dear old dick of a dad.

I shouldn't have told her. Not now. Not when she'd been coming off her own nightmare. But, no, he'd opened his big mouth and just sent her spiraling from one nightmare straight into another one.

I had to tell her. If I hadn't done it, she would have found the truth online. Not like it was overly hard to discover. His dad was an infamous serial killer. And if she hadn't looked online, the cops would have told her. They'd almost spilled the truth at the hospital.

He'd thought it would be better to tell her himself.

He…he hadn't wanted to lie to her.

Let's agree that you won't lie to me ever again. You don't lie to me. I don't lie to you. Her soft voice whispered through his mind. He'd like to only give her the truth. He hated lies. His father was a master when it came to manipulation and lies, and Midas's entire life had been nothing but one horrific lie after the other.

And the worst lie of all? My mother didn't walk out on us. That bastard, he—

The door opened.

Midas whipped back in surprise.

"Your father did that to you?" Alina asked him softly.

"Yes." Jeez. Could his voice sound more like sandpaper?

She stepped forward and wrapped her arms around him.

His own arms hovered awkwardly in the air. He wanted to hug her tightly, but if he did, Midas wasn't too sure he'd be able to let her go. *I told her the truth. I warned her.*

And she'd opened the door for him again.

"I'm sorry," Alina told him. "I can't imagine the pain you must have felt." Her head tilted back, but she didn't let him go. "You aren't your father."

She didn't know him. They'd just met.

So why does it seem like I've known Alina forever?

"You saved me. You fought for me. You were hit by a *car,* and you didn't stop." Her eyes widened and she hurriedly stepped back. "Your bruised ribs! I'm sorry! I forgot about them."

"You didn't hurt me." He hadn't noticed any pain. It had just felt good to have her body against his. "You're supposed to be pissed at me."

"I am."

The immediate reply caught him by surprise. "Then why are you out here trying to comfort me?" He should comfort her. Instead, he'd just dropped the big bombshell of his backstory on her.

"Because you need me to be here."

His mouth dropped open. "You..." He shut his mouth and struggled to figure out what to say. Finally, Midas settled on, "You were the one taken today. You were the one hurt."

Her hand carefully trailed down his body to press softly over his ribs. Then that same hand rose to his face. She feathered her fingers over the bruises and scrapes on his cheeks and forehead. "If I was the one hurt, then why are you the one with all the injuries?"

"They don't matter."

"I happen to think things that hurt you do matter."

She was going to wreck him. He knew it. Accepted it with one hundred percent certainty in that moment and understood—

I can't ever let her go.

"I'm sorry he hurt you," she said as her gaze never broke from Midas's. "I'm sorry you went through that nightmare."

He couldn't be hearing her right.

Her hand pressed to his cheek, then dipped to press over the beard that covered his jaw. The beard he always kept because it hid his scars.

Scars his father had given to him.

When he'd turned his knife on me.

Her long lashes flickered. "I think that promised adrenaline crash is hitting me. My knees are weak. I'm trembling."

She was. He could feel the faint tremble in her fingers as she touched him.

"But I'm scared to close my eyes."

Her confession broke something in him.

"I closed my eyes before, and I woke up to fear." She wet her lips. "I know I'm safe here. I know you'll just be downstairs. You won't let anyone get to me."

"I won't." A vow. He'd keep that promise no matter what it took.

"But I'm still scared. Scared to turn out the lights and scared to sleep alone." Her hand pulled away. "Could you—will you just stay with me until I go to sleep? The bed is big. You saw it. You can stay on one side. I'll stay on the other."

When you were Midas's size, a bed was never big enough. And there were a thousand reasons why it would be a bad idea to go back into that bedroom with Alina.

"Please, Midas. I'm scared."

And there was one reason to go in. She needed him.

He scooped her into his arms.

"Why are you doing this? I can walk."

Sure. "Your knees were weak. Why risk it?" Besides, he liked carrying her. Liked touching her. Being close to her. Liked her.

He carried her to the bed. Put her down and then carefully pulled the covers over her.

"Midas, are you tucking me into bed?"

"Yeah, got to say it's the first time I ever tucked a woman *in* bed." Usually, he did a whole lot of other things. And not that he wasn't tempted to do all of those things with Alina. *More than tempted.*

He reached for the lamp, but her hand flew out and caught his hand. "Leave that one on," she whispered.

Nodding, he did. But he turned out the overhead light. He shut the door. Locked them inside. Then he walked around the bed. Midas emptied his pockets. Ditched his shoes but kept on his clothes. And he climbed on top of the covers. Midas stretched out his body and tried really, really hard not to touch her.

Impossible. He was too big.

"Uh, Midas?" A sleepy yawn.

"Yeah, sweetheart?"

"Shouldn't you be *under* the covers?"

"Nope."

Another yawn. "Why not?"

He turned on the pillow and found her sleepy gaze on him. His hand reached over, and he tucked a lock of hair behind her ear. "Because I'm trying to avoid temptation."

"Temptation?"

"That would be you. We need something between us." Though the covers weren't much in the way of a barrier. "Don't worry. I'm not gonna pounce."

Her eyes closed. "Didn't think you were. I tried to get you to do that earlier..." Her voice slurred. "You have...good control."

"It's my middle name." No, it wasn't. His full name was Midas Henry Monroe. Henry...his father's name.

Because his father had wanted his son to be just like him.

A chip off the old block.

A chip off the murdering, sadistic block.

His hand lingered on Alina.

Like father, like son.

CHAPTER TEN

His phone buzzed. Midas jerked, and the buzzing continued. His eyes opened. For a moment, disorientation filled him. *Where the hell am I?* He didn't recognize the ceiling. Or the darkly painted walls or—

His head turned. His gaze landed on the profile of the woman who slept peacefully beside him. Alina. Her hand had stretched out, and her fingers pressed lightly over his stomach.

She touched him while she slept.

The woman looked like sweet sin. Perfect temptation. His waking fantasy.

The phone buzzed again. A low ring followed, one that—thankfully—hadn't stirred Alina. She needed all the sleep she could get.

I fell asleep with her. He hadn't meant to do that. He'd just intended to stay in bed long enough for Alina to drift off before he slipped back downstairs. But he hadn't left her. He'd slept deeper and harder than he could remember sleeping in months.

And his phone would not stop buzzing.

Midas reached for the nightstand. He'd put his phone down before climbing into bed. He grabbed the phone and brought the device up to his face. When he saw the number on the screen—saw the caller ID displayed—

He shoved the phone to his ear. "Has something happened to him?" Because it was the penitentiary calling. The warden had Midas's direct line and instructions to call only in the case of an emergency. As in...

Death.

His father had been convicted in North Dakota. The death penalty had never been a possibility for him there. Instead, he'd gotten multiple life sentences.

"Midas."

Wait, that wasn't the warden's slightly nasal voice. It was the uptight, too much money, upper West Side accent that belonged to Henry Monroe's lawyer, Xander Palmer.

"Midas, don't hang up!"

Someone had just read his mind because he'd sure as hell been about to disconnect the call. Midas's grip tightened on the phone. "Why are you calling from the warden's number?" Low. He didn't want to wake Alina. Midas slid from beneath her touch and eased from the bed.

"The warden is right beside me. So is DA Terrance Peters."

Well, weren't they quite the group? Not like Midas was pleased to hear about the DA. At one point, Terrance had been dead set on locking Midas away.

"I called from Warden Walker's number because I knew you'd actually *take* the call. You've been dodging me and the DA for weeks."

Yep, due to the fact that he had nothing to say to them. "I've been on assignment." He looked down at a sleeping Alina. "I'm still on assignment."

"It's important." Tension boiled in Xander's voice. "Listen to me, please. I need you to—"

"Give me the damn phone," someone burst out in the background. Then... "Midas, it's Terrance."

His jaw hardened. Midas flipped the lock on the bedroom door then grasped the doorknob.

"Henry is willing to tell us about the other victims, but *only* if you come and talk with him. He's given us twenty-four hours. Did you hear me? Twenty-four hours." Urgency vibrated in each word.

Midas felt his blood turn to ice. This news was the last thing he'd expected.

"He's said there are at least seven more. *Seven.* And some of the vics that we suspected were linked to him? The ones that the families keep coming to me about, over and over? Henry is hinting that he'll take us to those bodies. But you only have twenty-four hours to get your ass up here."

"He's playing games with you." Angrily, Midas wrenched open the door. Then caught himself. Midas glanced over his shoulder.

Alina's eyes had flown open. Fear filled her stare.

It's okay, he mouthed.

She sat up and tugged the covers with her. One hand brushed back a tousled lock of her hair.

"This is no game." Terrance was adamant. "He gave us one vic location already."

Midas's feet had become rooted to the spot.

"It was his show of good faith," Terrance continued. "Look, I'm putting you on speaker. Xander wants to say—"

"I want to say that there will be *no* additional information provided from my client until he sees his son." Xander's voice filled Midas's ear. "That was the arrangement. And the deadline is tomorrow at noon. The clock is ticking. So either Midas arrives at the penitentiary by noon tomorrow and sees his father, or Henry Monroe has vowed to completely stop cooperating with the authorities."

Alina climbed from the bed. Her feet made no sound as she crept toward him. Worry was etched onto her face. *What is happening?* Her lips moved to shape those words though no sound emerged from her mouth.

"Get on a plane," Terrance urged him. "We need you. The vics out there need you."

Ah, the old guilt angle. Like he didn't feel enough of that already. "I'm working on a case right now," Midas returned. "I can't just up and leave." Not an option. Alina needed him.

"Have someone else cover your case!" Terrance exploded. "This is important! This is—"

"My charge is important," Midas cut through Terrance's words. "She was abducted once already, and I'm not leaving her side."

"Fine, then bring her with you." Terrance threw that out like it was the obvious choice.

Uh, bring Alina around Henry? Over my dead body. "Not happening."

Terrance ignored those words. "I'll fly you both into town. Put you up in a secure location. *I need this. The families need this.* Your father will only cooperate if you are here. This is our chance, don't you see?"

What Midas saw was that his prick of a father was still playing games, even after all these years. And since Terrance had always been an ambitious man, the DA saw this as his chance to make headlines again. Just as he'd tried to make headlines when he first tossed Midas into a cell. "I'm working a case," he said again. "Tell my father to screw himself." He hung up.

But...

Seven more victims. He'd always known there were more out there. Would his father really reveal their locations if Midas went to see him?

"What is happening right now?" Alina wrapped her arms around her stomach. "Because I hate to use the old cliché, but you look like you've just seen a ghost."

"Not seen one. Just had the bastard call me." Midas shook his head. "Forget about it. I didn't mean to wake you." He'd wrenched open the door too hard. His mistake. "I'll go downstairs and get us some breakfast." Though was it closer to lunch time? Yeah, it was.

Her hand reached out and her fingers fluttered over his arm. "I'm not forgetting it. Whoever was on the line upset you. *Talk* to me." Her lips thinned. Her hair was a beautiful, sexy tangle around her face, and her eyes seemed so dark and deep. "I don't want secrets between us. No secrets. No lies. Remember?"

He remembered everything that involved her. "You don't have to worry, it's not about you. The call had nothing to do with you." And he wanted to keep it that way. He never wanted any part of his father's darkness to touch Alina.

"But it had everything to do with you." Her head tilted, and her hair trailed over her shoulder. "You're upset."

Hell, yes, he was. "My father," he gritted out.

She waited. Watched. No judgment showed on her face.

"That was the DA and my dad's current attorney—my dad says that he will reveal more vics and their locations."

Her lips parted. "That's good, isn't it? For the families?"

A grim nod. "If he's not lying. My dad is very, very good at lying." He raised his chin. "And there's a catch. There is always a catch with him. He never does anything out of the goodness of his heart because there is no goodness in him." His father only existed to destroy the good things in the world. "My father said he'll only reveal the info if I come and talk to him."

"Go."

He blinked. "Excuse me?"

"Go," she repeated. "If there are people out there who have missing loved ones—wives or daughters or friends—and this can end their cases, then go."

"Not that simple. Nothing is ever simple with my father." No, everything was always a game. A chessboard set up so that his father planned every single move in advance. "And I'm not leaving you."

Her fingers pressed harder to his arm. "Midas..."

He looked at her hand, then at her face. "I'm not leaving you," he said again. And it was probably callous and brutal, but he still told her, "Those vics are dead, Alina. Cold in the ground. No one ever escaped from my father. I can't bring them back, no matter what I do." But what he could do? "I can protect you." She was living. Breathing. Beautiful. Alive, right in front of him. "The man who orchestrated your kidnapping is still out there. I will not leave you alone."

His father could rot in hell.

Midas would not be seeing him again.

***

"We are prepared to offer a deal, of sorts." Terrance Peters stared across the table at Henry Monroe. Terrance made an effort not to let any emotion show on his face or in his voice. He was good at keeping his mask in place.

But, deep inside...

Henry Monroe freaks me the hell out. It wasn't the man's massive size. Though, if anything, he'd gotten even bigger in the years that he'd been incarcerated. Probably because the man had plenty of time to work out. Over and over again.

Henry Monroe was still in the prime of his life. He'd had his son Midas when Henry had just been eighteen years old. He easily could have passed for Midas's older brother. The two men looked so very similar.

And that is one of the reasons it was easy for Henry to set up his own son.

Henry Monroe could be charming. So many people had said that during the countless interviews before the trial—correction, *trials*. Charming. Seemingly kind. A big guy with a big heart.

Such bullshit descriptions. When they were away from the public eye, when it was just Terrance staring across the table at Henry, Terrance saw the other man for exactly what he was.

A stone-cold, sadistic predator.

"Better accommodations," Terrance said. He hated offering anything to Henry, but there was no choice. More vics? He'd been after this intel for years, and Henry had steadfastly refused to cooperate.

Until recently.

Until the out-of-the-blue phone call from Henry's lawyer.

Xander Palmer sat near Henry at the little table. Terrance noted that Xander made sure not to get touching-close to Henry. A smart move, though Xander was hardly the man's type.

No, Henry preferred female victims. Small. Delicate. Breakable.

"Better accommodations," Terrance repeated, "and that would mean a bigger cell. Maybe one with a bigger window? A little more time outside. Bet you'd like that, wouldn't you?"

"I'd like to see my son."

Right. *But your son doesn't want to see you.* Not that Terrance could blame the man. In all the years that Henry had been locked away, Midas hadn't visited him even one time.

Henry focused on his lawyer. "Did you give Midas the twenty-four hour timeline?"

Sweat trickled down Xander's left temple. It wasn't even particularly warm in that room. "He's...working with a client."

"So?"

"So he can't make the trip here right now," Terrance informed Henry.

Henry's head turned—snake-like—toward him. "He can let someone else watch the client."

"No." A quick rush of breath from Xander. "Midas said the client had been abducted once. He wanted to stay close."

Because Terrance was watching Henry so closely, he caught the faintest of smiles that tipped up the other man's lips. A smile that came and vanished in a blink.

But that momentary smile was enough to have every one of Terrance's alarm bells ringing.

"Forty-eight hours," Henry murmured. "In the interest of cooperating. I'll let my son get his client settled...or perhaps..." A roll of his broad shoulders. "Midas should just bring her with him."

Terrance did not let his mask falter. But Henry had just made a mistake. *No one mentioned that the client was a woman.* So how had Henry known that fact?

"Forty-eight hours." Henry inclined his head. "And then my memory might just become cloudy. I'd hate for that to happen." He made a tsk-tsk sound. "So unfortunate for those looking for their lost loved ones." His gaze pinned Terrance. "So unfortunate for you. How will you get your face on cameras again if you don't have big news from the monster you locked away?"

Anger hummed through Terrance. "I don't do this job for the cameras." He wasn't some smart-ass kid looking to make a name for himself. Years had passed. The job *was* his life. The victims mattered. Every person mattered.

Henry folded his hands together. "Tell my son that I will reveal the location of my first victim. My very first." A soft sigh escaped him. "But the offer will not last forever. Forty-eight hours is all he'll get."

He hated the bastard sitting across from him. "Why the hell should Midas care whether it's the first vic or the last?" Terrance snarled. "The man doesn't want to see you. You can't yank on his strings like some puppeteer. I am offering you better accommodations. I will allow more privileges." He didn't want to give this psycho shit. But that wasn't the way the system worked.

"He'll care." Henry was smug. "He's always cared about her."

Terrance's stomach twisted.

***

Midas had locked down. Alina slanted him a quick glance from the corner of her eye. They'd both showered. Dressed. She'd winced when she'd seen her own reflection in the mirror. The bruise along her jaw was much darker, and she'd done her best to disguise it with makeup.

Not a perfect job.

But, better.

She'd put fresh bandages around the marks on her wrists and ankles. She wasn't bleeding any longer so she could probably ditch the bandages soon. The marks were so red and dark. Each time she looked at them, she seemed to jump right back into the closet.

So don't look at them.

She'd deliberately picked a top with long sleeves that dipped past her wrists.

They'd had a quick breakfast—well, lunch. Midas had barely spoken during the meal. He'd barely even glanced her way. Meanwhile, she hadn't been able to take her eyes off him.

A cloud of menace and darkness seemed to cling to him. Ever since that phone call, his face had been set in heavy lines. She could feel the anger pouring from him.

His father is a serial killer? Not like that was an easy burden to carry. "Midas, I—"

Someone knocked at the front door.

He rose immediately and stalked toward the front of the guesthouse. He peeked through the curtain near the door. "Cops," he muttered.

She'd crept up behind him. "We figured they'd show up, sooner or later." Though Alina had been praying for much later.

He grunted. "Was hoping for a phone call first."

Her hands twisted. "Maybe they found the 'boss' guy?"

Midas glanced back at her. His expression told her that he didn't think that had been the case. At all.

"Maybe," she repeated stubbornly. She was trying to be positive and not give in to the nerves that wanted to shake her body apart.

The knock came again. More demanding this time.

He flipped the lock. Opened the door.

Detective Joyce Meriam stood on the threshold. Her partner was right behind her. Alina's father hovered on the edge of the small porch. But her dad wasn't alone. Alina recognized the well-dressed, fit man with the salt-and-pepper hair who stood at his side. Bradford Wells, chief counsel and lead partner at Wells, Mayo, and Abernathy. The two lawyers who'd come to the hospital last night? They worked at the law firm. But Bradford was one of the three founders.

Her father had clearly brought in the big guns.

"Midas." Joyce inclined her head toward him. "I see you are still on bodyguard duty."

Alina didn't stiffen but she felt that dig. *Bodyguard.* A reminder that Midas had lied. Her chin angled up a notch. "He's the best in the business," Alina returned as she stepped up to Midas's side. "I want the best."

Joyce pursed her lips. "Quite the change from last night."

"We cleared the air," Midas returned flatly.

"Uh, huh. I'm sure you did." Her right hand went to her hip, and the movement pushed back her jacket to reveal the holster beneath her arm. "Alina, we'd like for you to come with us."

Her father announced immediately, "You don't have to go anywhere with them, Alina! You are under no obligation to see the bodies."

Bodies? Her gaze darted from her father to Joyce.

"We'd like for you to officially ID the men in the morgue. Confirm that they were the individuals who abducted you last night."

Alina's arm brushed against Midas. "I only saw the redhead. I never saw the other man's face."

"I gave you pictures of them both, detective," Midas groused. "ID'ing them should be a snap."

Joyce sent him a grim smile. "That you did. But having the actual victim ID the men would be very helpful." She jerked her thumb over her shoulder. "Your lawyer can come along, of course."

Bradford sniffed. "As if I would leave my client alone without representation."

"And your bodyguard. You can bring him, too." It was Calvin who'd added that part. "Certainly wouldn't want you going anywhere without him at your side."

"Where she goes, I go." A flat response from Midas.

They wanted her to see the bodies? "I..."

"Your help is vital to the investigation." Joyce shifted her weight. "A firm ID is the first step for us. Then we can backtrack through the lives of these men and find out who they were working for. The ID won't take long, I assure you."

Was there a choice? She wanted to find their boss. She wanted to cooperate. Alina released a long breath. "Okay." If this would help find the man behind the attack, yes, she'd do it.

"I want this kept out of the news." Her father's voice was as grim as his expression. "I don't want Alina's abduction being tabloid fodder. There is no need to release her name to the press. She's a victim and should remain anonymous."

Calvin scratched his chin. "That's not exactly the way these sorts of investigations tend to go."

"It's how I told the mayor it *would* be going when we had breakfast together this morning." Her dad arched one eyebrow. "And when I spoke to your supervisor at the police station, I told him the same thing. I want the press learning as little about my daughter's involvement as possible. We're cooperating, but you *will* do your part, too."

Bradford ran his hand over his bright blue tie. "Don't worry, Ryker. I'll be on hand to make certain everyone is on the same page."

In other words, Bradford would make certain that everyone followed her father's orders. That was the way he'd always worked. When her father said jump, Bradford made sure that everyone leapt into the sky.

Midas's phone rang.

Automatically, her gaze jerked down. The ringing came from the front pocket of his jeans.

Midas made no move to pull out his phone.

Joyce frowned. "You need to get that?"

"Nope," Midas replied, voice smooth. "It's just a wrong number."

"How do you know that?" Calvin demanded. "You didn't even look at the phone!"

The phone rang again.

Sighing, Midas pulled it out of his pocket. He briefly glanced at the screen. "Yep, like I said, wrong number."

But his grip seemed too tight around the phone.

"Same number called earlier," he murmured. "Calling me was a mistake then, and it's a mistake now."

Her gaze whipped to his face. The call earlier had been about his father. About the victims he claimed were out there.

Midas turned his head and met her gaze. "Wrong number," he said once more.

CHAPTER ELEVEN

"We both know it wasn't a wrong number." The first words that Alina had spoken since the limo had left her father's estate.

Her father had insisted that they use the car and his driver. A privacy screen separated Midas and Alina from the man up front. Tinted windows prevented anyone from peering in the back and watching them.

As for the lawyer in what had probably been a three-thousand-dollar suit? He'd left on his own but vowed to meet them for the actual viewing of the bodies. He'd high-tailed it away before Midas and Alina had left her father's estate.

The remainder of their group? The detectives were driving in front of the limo. Yep, they had a whole caravan routine going.

And Alina was staring at him with worry in her eyes.

Midas's legs sprawled in front of him. Alina perched next to him. He knew she was not going to let this matter go. Meanwhile, it was the last thing he wanted to talk about.

"It was your father, wasn't it? On the phone?"

"They don't just let convicted killers call whoever they want, so, no, that wasn't Henry." A roll of one shoulder. "But it was the warden's number again, yes."

"And you ignored the call."

Indeed, he had. "Kinda busy with you right now."

Her eyes narrowed.

How was she not getting this? *"You* are the priority for me." He didn't like that the cops wanted her to ID the bodies. He'd seen the suspicion in the detectives' eyes. They thought Midas was guilty. That he'd stepped over the line and killed the two men who'd taken Alina.

But these murders weren't his.

"After we finish at the lab, you and I will be moving to a new location." He'd finalized arrangements while she'd been finishing in the shower earlier.

"Why?"

Okay, this was where she was probably going to get pissed. No help for it. She'd asked for honesty from him, so he'd give it to her. "Because I don't trust your father."

Her jaw dropped.

His phone vibrated. His nostrils flared as he pulled the phone from his pocket. Then he read the text from Terrance.

Henry says he will reveal the location of the first victim. His very first. He is giving you forty-eight hours to appear and meet with him, then the offer vanishes.

The first victim. Midas's heartbeat raced too fast and hard.

My mother?
What a sonofabitch.

"I don't trust yours," he rasped. "And I fucking hate mine." The thundering of his heartbeat seemed extra loud in his ears. Midas tossed the phone onto the nearby seat.

"But—but why—"

His head turned, and he watched the other cars glide past through the window. "Told you before, but I'll revisit and tell you again. My father is a murdering psychopath who likes torturing his prey. He's dangerous, conniving, and most of the words that come out of his mouth are lies." *He won't tell me where my mother is buried. It's just another lie.*

"Um, I actually completely get why you hate your father." Her hand touched his cheek.

Midas flinched. His stare whipped back to her.

She sent him a weak smile. Not the high wattage one that he adored. The smile trembled on her lips. Then faded. "What I don't get is why you don't trust mine."

His hands fisted. The better to not reach out and touch her. Her scent had already wrapped around him. Tempted him. "With my past, trust never comes easy."

"Again, I can get that."

"When he originally hired me, your father acted like some obsessed fan or stalker had you in his sights."

Her tongue swiped over her lower lip.

His gaze became fixated on her mouth. Still, he made himself continue talking. "Then you were abducted. He didn't want me going to the cops. He barely let you talk to them at all last night. My instincts tell me that your father knows one hell of a lot more than he's saying. Now he's pulled in some top dog lawyer because he wants to make sure that neither one of us says anything we shouldn't to the detectives."

She sucked in a sharp breath. "Ransom."

Midas nodded. "Yeah, that's what I suspect. You were going to be held for ransom. Maybe they even reached out to your father after you were taken, but he won't tell me jack. I need to know everything so I can find the bastard in charge and make him pay." A bastard who Midas suspected—with every fiber of his being—was a killer. "But your father is stonewalling me."

"No, no, when I was taken, one of the men—it was the redhead you took out inside of the cabin—he said..." Another nervous lick of her tongue. "He said the last one who was taken didn't get home. I didn't tell the cops that part."

She'd barely had time to tell the cops anything, thanks to her father.

"I-I actually haven't told anyone but you. He said the last one didn't follow the rules. That she wasn't good." Her body had tensed. "He kept telling me that I needed to be good."

"You *are* good, sweetheart."

"The last one didn't get home." Husky. "He said that. Told me she hadn't followed the rules, so she didn't get home."

Midas began to see dots in his mind. Leading down a trail he did not like. "Anything else you remember?" The night had to be a swirl of fear for her.

But she nodded. "He told me that there had been others. That it didn't always have to end the way it had...for the last one." A lone tear streaked down her cheek. "If you hadn't been there, I might never have survived."

He hated her tears. They made him want to rip the world apart. Or to find the bastards who'd taken her—and make them pay. *Too late. Someone else killed them for me.* "I will always protect you."

"Because it's your job. I'm your charge."

"Yeah. That's what you are." He brushed away the tear. His hand was too damn big. He was too big. Big and rough and he'd known from the first time that he saw her that he shouldn't be touching Alina.

There was no undercover assignment any longer. He didn't have to pretend to be her boyfriend. He'd never wanted to pretend.

I want to be the real thing with her. No, no. He shut the thought down. But—

He could see the darkness along her jaw. She'd tried to hide the mark with makeup. His fingers slid under her chin. Tilted up her jaw.

"Midas?"

"You're not mad at me." His fingers trailed carefully over the bruise. Dipped softly down her neck.

"M-Midas?"

"Why aren't you mad? I lied to you. You should be mad." *You should hate me, but, please, God, don't. I don't want you to hate me.*

"You said this last night." She swallowed, and he felt the movement beneath his fingers. "Hard to be properly mad with someone when he saves your life."

"You're grateful." He didn't want her gratitude. What he did want? *Her.*

"Yes, I'm grateful." A whisper. "But it's a whole lot more complicated than that."

They were complicated. His head lowered, and he pressed a soft kiss along her bruised jaw. "You won't be hurt again."

"Because..." Her voice had gone husky. "I'm your charge."

"Because you're mine." The words just rumbled from him. They shouldn't have. He'd never claimed anyone as his, and this wasn't the time. It wasn't the place.

But she is mine. He felt it all the way to his bones. Hell, hadn't he felt it from the very first moment when he'd seen her on the ice? He'd looked at her and just frozen. He never froze. But he'd been held spellbound as he watched her on the ice. From that first instant, he'd wanted her.

And that wanting just grew stronger, more dangerous, with every moment that passed. "I shouldn't think of you that way, but I do. You're mine."

A soft gasp escaped her, only to be swallowed by his mouth. Because he needed to kiss her. Had to do it. Her plump lips parted eagerly beneath his. His tongue slid into her mouth. He tasted her. Reveled in her. Got lost and didn't care about anything else in that moment. Only Alina.

His charge.

His.

His hands grabbed her waist, and he lifted her so that she sat astride him. Her hands grabbed for his shoulders as she held tightly to him. Her fingers dug into his coat.

He could kiss her forever. Taste her endlessly.

Fuck her until they were too limp to move.

That was what he wanted. Alina, naked, calling his name. He didn't want to be taking her to view dead bodies. He wanted her shielded from everything dark and dangerous in the entire world. He would be her shield.

He'd be everything, for her.

But she pulled away. Her breath heaved in and out, and her mouth was red from his kiss. "What are you doing?" She still sat astride him. His hard dick shoved against the spread V of her legs.

"If you don't know, then I can't be doing it right."

Her cheeks flamed. "Midas."

"I want you." There. Didn't get any more stark than those gravelly words. "You want me." A dare.

"Yes."

"What are we going to do about that?" The limo was still driving. His hard-on was still raging.

Her gaze searched his. "I have no idea."

"Yeah, me, too, sweetheart. That's why the situation is an absolute clusterfuck." He kissed her again. Softer. She deserved some softness.

"No," she breathed against his lips.

His head rose.

"I mean...I haven't done this before. So I'm not sure what we do about it. You'll have to lead the way."

Thud. That sound was his heart slamming into his chest. And he remembered that her father had described her as shy. Reserved.

Fuck, fuck, fuck. And Midas was just enough of a territorial asshole that the knowledge Alina had been with no one else just turned him on all the more. He hadn't thought it was possible for his dick to get any bigger. He'd thought wrong. The damn thing jerked eagerly against her, but his hands were already tight around her waist and he lifted her up. Off him. And he put her on the seat to his right.

Then he scooted aside. A good foot.

"Midas?" Her brows rose.

He held up his hand. He was gonna need a minute or two in order to be able to actually talk. If he tried right then, he'd just growl. Not his usual growl-like words. But potentially full-on animal sounds. He felt like an animal. Hungry. Primitive. Territorial.

He would be her first. Her only.

He could take her right there. In the back of the limo. Take what he wanted so much.

But I am not an animal, and she deserves better than me.

"It's not like you can catch virginity," her cool voice informed him. "You don't need to suddenly act like I've got the plague or something."

His head whipped up. He'd been staring at his clenched fists—clenched so he wouldn't grab her again—and trying to count to ten. Then to twenty. Midas shook his head.

Her eyebrows snapped together. Her cheeks also flushed. Dark. "I get that many men don't like being with a woman who is inexperienced. And I do have *some* experience, FYI. I just haven't gone all the way."

Some experience. "Bastards." Yep, a growl.

"I couldn't make out what you said." She bit her lower lip. "I haven't had time for relationships. No, I don't think that's the real truth. How about this? I haven't ever met anyone that I wanted from the first touch. But when you first touched me, I felt it all the way to my bones. You heated up parts of me that I didn't even realize were cold." Her nose scrunched in the cutest way. "That doesn't sound right, does it? Not like I'm trying to say I'm frigid or anything. I just—" A hard exhale. "I just hadn't wanted anyone that strongly until I met you. I didn't even think that kind of instant physical attraction was real until you came along."

She thought he was hot. Great. He thought she was freaking fire. "Definitely *not* frigid." Okay, that was better. Actual words. "Love it."

"What do you love?" A little line appeared between her brows.

"That I'll be your first." *Only. Be her only.* Nope. Not gonna say those words. He had enough sense to hold them back.

"Oh." The blush deepened. "Then why did you move me away from you?"

"Trying not to have your first time be in the back of a limo while we're on our way to view dead bodies."

Her hand pressed to the seat between them. "Here? You want to have sex *here?*"

Anywhere. He pulled in a breath. Let it out. Pulled it in. "First times are supposed to be special." Even he knew that. His head shook. "Why in the world would you want to waste yours on someone like me?" Then a terrible thought slapped him in the face. "No."

She inched closer. "No—what?"

"It had sure as shit better not be because you are grateful to me. I was just doing a job."

She flinched.

Sonofa— "That's not what I meant."

Her head tilted. The limo was slowing. There wasn't much time left.

"Don't fuck me because you're grateful," he rasped. "Fuck me because you can't take another breath without wanting me."

The limo stopped.

He slid forward because he wanted to get out first and assess the scene. If he didn't think the area was secure, Alina would not be exiting. But her hand curled over his arm. His gaze darted from her fingers to her face.

"I've been grateful to coaches who helped me win national titles."

Did she mean that prick Dmitri?

"I've been grateful to corporate presidents because they helped provide me with sponsorships."

What corporate presidents?

"I didn't ever want to fuck them." Her lips twisted. "I may be inexperienced when it comes to sex, but I don't trade my body for anything."

He was such a dumbass. "That's not what I meant to say."

She waited.

He should be checking the scene. But first he had to fix her heart. "There's a lot happening between us. A lot going down fast. I just want you to be sure. Once I have you, everything will be different." A warning, but he wasn't sure she clearly understood just how serious he was.

"I've never been more sure of anyone." And her high-voltage smile flashed.

His breath froze.

The driver opened the door. "We're here, Mr. Monroe."

Midas's head whipped around so he could glare at the guy. Mood killer. They'd been having a moment.

One that was now over, courtesy of the driver. But Midas had a job to do. And it wasn't to fuck Alina in the back of the limo. Though he'd been more than tempted to do that very thing.

"You'll need to come this way," Calvin Booker announced. The detective's voice drifted into the vehicle.

Midas slowly exited. He took his time surveying the surrounding area. They'd parked behind the big, square building in a twisting alley. The two detectives waited with impatient expressions on their faces. No sign of anyone else. Definitely no reporters. Despite Ryker's wishes, Midas knew the story wasn't going to stay under wraps for long. And when the news broke, a swarm would descend on them.

"Joyce will take Alina to view the bodies," Calvin told him smoothly. "You can stay in the hallway with me. We'll be just outside of the lab area."

Uh, huh. Like that wasn't some deliberate divide and conquer BS. Midas knew Calvin planned to grill him. "Where is the lawyer?" He reached his hand back into the limo. Alina's soft fingers took his.

"Meeting us inside," Joyce assured him. "Now how about we get moving? This alley reeks."

Yeah, it did. The whole scene reeked, as far as Midas was concerned.

Alina climbed out of the vehicle. She stared up at Midas. "I've never seen a dead body before. You'll stay with me?"

"Nope," Calvin denied as he wrenched open the door at the back of the building. A uniformed guard waited on the other side of the door. "He isn't allowed to actually go in with you. You know, seeing as how we still have questions about Midas and the two deaths. Questions that we do hope will be answered soon."

Alina stiffened. "I told you, Midas had nothing to do with their deaths. They were *alive* when we left them."

"How about you ID the bodies?" Joyce urged. "Then we'll get to the Q&A portion of the day."

Footsteps tapped from inside the building. The guard at the rear door stepped aside as Bradford came to greet them. "Did someone say Q&A?" A shake of Bradford's head. "Not without me." A tiger's smile flashed. "But nice try, detectives."

***

It was cold in the lab or exam room or—or whatever it was. Alina wrapped her arms around her stomach and followed Joyce inside. Bradford was right on their trail.

She'd known Bradford for most of her life. Her father always invited him over for big events. Every party? Every gathering at the Bellamy estate? Bradford would be there. Her father had been his friend through Bradford's three divorces. The men belonged to the same clubs, the same charity groups.

She also suspected that Bradford knew every secret her father possessed. And he was paid well to make sure those secrets never saw the light of day.

"It's all right," Bradford murmured to Alina. "Just take some deep breaths. The last thing I want is for you to feel lightheaded. Lot of people don't react so well to the sight of a dead body."

Consider her one of those people. She already felt lightheaded. There was an odd scent in the air. One that burned her nose.

"This is Dr. Edward Hatch." Joyce motioned to the man who stood beside an exam table. "He's a forensic pathologist who will be completing the autopsies." She touched his shoulder. "I need her to see their faces."

The light gleamed off Edward's balding head. Round glasses perched on his nose. He wore a white lab coat and gloves. His gloved hands reached for the first subject.

"I only saw the face of one man," Alina rushed to say. "I already told you that it was—"

The redhead's face was revealed.

Alina stepped back. Her elbow bumped into Bradford.

His hands closed over her shoulders. "It's all right."

The redhead's skin had a waxy look. His eyes were closed, and he—he appeared so young. "That's one of them. He..." She swallowed. "He said if I was good, then I might be able to go home. The other man—he threatened me." Her hand rose to her cheek. "Said he was going to slice my face. This one was...nicer." That sounded so strange to say. But it was true. *He was nicer than the man who wanted to cut my face open.* Alina pulled her gaze from the dead man.

She found Joyce staring straight at her.

"Seeing him reminded you of a few things?" Joyce inquired.

Alina knew Joyce had planned this scene. Her chin lifted. "Yes." Not that she'd forgotten. How could she? But last night, everything had been *on fire*. Or at least, that was how Alina had felt. Too much fear. Too much horror.

"Your statements last night were very brief. You told us you were held in a closet. You didn't mention that someone threatened to cut you." Joyce never took her stare off Alina. "Was Midas aware of the fact that one of these men wanted to use a knife on you?"

Her breath stuttered out as she looked at the dead man. "Can you cover him up now?"

"You didn't answer—"

"Alina Bellamy is cooperating with you," Bradford cut in. His tone was smooth and easy but brooked no argument. "She identified the first man. Shall we move to the second?"

Joyce's lips thinned, but she motioned to Edward.

The forensic pathologist covered up the redheaded man. Alina sucked in a breath, but the breath didn't help. The room was too cold. And the smell? Too antiseptic. Too harsh. "I never saw the second man. He was tall." She remembered him standing in the closet doorway. "About six one. Lean but muscled."

Edward had moved toward a second exam table.

"He was...he was the one who hit me." She didn't touch her bruised jaw. Mostly because her hands had twisted in front of her.

"That does make sense," Joyce allowed.

How did that make sense?

The second body was revealed.

Young, just like the other man. Early twenties? Dark, shaggy hair. That waxy-looking skin tone that came from death. And—

She flinched.

"He's got a broken jaw. That's why it looks that way. Bruised and distorted. I guess Midas didn't like that the man had hit you? So he hit him back."

Alina couldn't look away from the body. She recalled what Midas had told her as he got her out of that terrible closet. *You already have a bruise.* He'd looked at her jaw. His face had been angry. So hard. *Be assured, the one I gave that SOB is a hell of a lot worse. Pretty sure I broke the bastard's jaw.*

"Midas packs quite a punch, doesn't he?" Joyce mused.

CHAPTER TWELVE

"What's it like?" Calvin asked him.

Midas kept his attention on the closed door that led to the exam room. Alina had been inside for several minutes. Just how long would this scene take? He didn't like not having her within sight. "Being awesome? Utterly exhausting." A flippant reply.

Calvin laughed.

Ah, so we're playing the friend game, huh? Not like it was his first time to face an interrogation from a police detective. Hardly. And he knew every trick in the book when it came to cops.

Clearly, this whole scene was just a divide-and-conquer setup. Alina was viewing the bodies—something meant to unsettle her, perhaps push her into revealing more than she'd shared with the cops before—while Midas got to cool his heels with the male detective. And, of course, Calvin had pounced with his questions.

"No, I meant…" The fake laughter ended. "What's it like having a killer for a father?"

Midas turned his head from the closed door and focused on the detective. "Is this your first big case?"

"No. In fact, Joy—ah, Joyce and I have quite the closure rate. Best in the city."

"Wonderful. Fabulous for you both. Hopefully, that fantastic closure rate means you'll do your job and find the man who organized Alina's abduction and likely killed the two men in that exam room."

"Ah, still sticking to that story, are you? That they were killed by their mysterious boss?"

"Sticking to the truth, you mean? Yeah, I am." His gaze swept back to the door.

"You broke the jaw of one of her abductors."

Midas shrugged. "The dark-haired one? I took a swing at him. The man was coming at me with a knife. What else was I supposed to do? Shake his hand?" All of this was in the statement he'd given to the responding officers the previous night. But cops liked to go over details again and again, always hoping that a suspect would slip up.

Midas wasn't in the mood to slip. "I have a powerful punch. It took him down. I used that time to restrain him with the zip ties I'd taken from the rear of the vehicle on scene."

"And once you'd restrained him, it was easy to break his neck and plunge a knife into his heart?"

Midas didn't blink.

"That *is* the order of operations, correct? Broken neck first, then the knife plunge. At least, that's what your father always did."

"I am not my father." He kept his hands loose at his sides. His voice remained cool and unemotional.

"Were you angry that Alina had been taken?"

"Wasn't thrilled."

"And were you angry that these men tried to kill you? They did hit you with their vehicle. Our techs found dents on the hood. Scratches. Plus, the locator tag was exactly where you told us it would be."

"So my story checked out. How wonderful."

"They took Alina. They tried to kill you. And, hey, I believe a lot of what you've said. Maybe when you got to the cabin, Fallon White did attack you with his knife."

Ah. And this is why I'm talking to the cop instead of staying silent. Because I can get more information from him than he will get from me. "That the guy's name?"

"Yes, the man with the broken jaw is Fallon White. Well, that's one of his aliases. Real name is Fred White. Guess he thought Fallon had more of an edge than Fred."

Midas grunted. "He was not wrong."

"The redhead was Shayne Preston. Both men had records. Lots of petty crimes for Shayne. A few assault charges for Fallon."

All of this fit with what Midas suspected about the two men. "They were the goons. There for the grunt work. Someone else was pulling their strings."

"And you saw that someone driving to the cabin. Then driving *after* you when you fled with

Alina? I believe that's what you said to the cops on scene."

Yes, he had said that. "You believe correctly."

"Odd. If the leader was right there, I would have thought a guy like you would have gone after him."

He'd wanted to go after the SOB. "Getting Alina to safety was the priority."

"And now that she's safe? Now that she's home, what is your priority? Is it protecting her?"

Of course.

"Or is it going after the man who took her? The ringleader? Are you planning to hunt him on your own?"

Absolutely. "I like to multitask," Midas said, trying to sound modest. His gaze didn't leave the door. "And, for the record, it was absolute hell."

Calvin edged closer. "Excuse me?"

"Growing up with a serial killer as a father? Hell. What else could it be? But when you walk through hell, it teaches you how to handle fire."

The door flew open before Calvin could respond. Alina rushed out with her eyes too wide and her face far too pale. Midas immediately stepped forward and caught her in his arms. "Alina."

Her breath shuddered out. "I think I'm gonna be sick."

Swearing, he scooped her into his arms and rushed toward the nearest restroom. He shoved open the door and hurried toward the sink.

"Midas, this is the *women's* restroom!"

"Yeah, sweetheart, and you're a woman." He sat her down on the countertop and grabbed for some paper towels. He wet them. And lifted them toward her forehead. "I want you to breathe. Or, hell, maybe you should put your head between your knees? Is the room spinning? Are you dizzy? Faint?"

She caught his wrist and stopped him before he could put the damp towel on her forehead. "I'm fine."

"What?"

"I wanted to get away from the cops."

Water dripped from the paper towels.

"Didn't think you'd spirit me away quite so fast—or that you'd rush into the *women's restroom* with me, but...it works."

He wasn't following.

"Can you look beneath the stalls to make sure we're alone?"

Midas tossed the dripping paper towels and scanned beneath the stalls. "Clear." He closed back in on her. Midas flattened his hands on the counter on either side of her body. "Explain." Critically, he eyed her. Alina's face was far too pale. She hadn't been acting, not completely. The woman was obviously shaken.

"You broke his jaw."

Ah. Yes. He had. He'd even told her that very thing back at the godforsaken cabin. But maybe seeing the damage hit different than just hearing about it. "The detective ID'd the guy as Fallon White." *Fred*. "And, yeah, I did."

"He punched me."

Midas clenched his own jaw. "Heard him talking about that outside. I was waiting in the tree line, trying to figure out the best way to get you out of that cabin. Fallon had a loud voice. Heard him talking to the other one—Shayne Preston."

"You knew what Fallon had done to me."

A nod. "Knew about the punch and the knife." That bastard had thought to slice open her silken cheek? Hell, no.

"You...you broke his jaw because he hit me."

Again, they had covered this when he got her out of the closet. But she'd probably been in shock then.

Midas studied her for a moment in silence. Was that why they were in the bathroom? Alina was having second thoughts about him? "I broke his jaw because he came at me with a knife." *And, of course, because of what he did to you. He deserved some pain.* "But what do you really want to know? Are you trying to ask if I killed him?" He leaned in closer to her.

"I'm asking if you broke his jaw because of what he'd done to me."

"I broke his jaw because the prick was running at me with a knife." Each word sawed from between his gritted teeth. "But, dammit, *yes*. I punched hard because no man should ever hit a woman. No one should ever hurt you. I wanted him to see what it was like to be on the receiving end of a punch. I hit him. Knocked him out. Zip-tied him. I did *not* kill him." There. Done.

Her hands rose to cup his jaw. "I know you didn't kill either of them. Despite what Joyce suggests, I truly would have noticed a knife sticking out of the redhead's chest. Sort of hard to miss something like that, even when I was shaking apart with fear." A careful exhale. "Their boss killed them. He would probably have killed me, but you saved me. Thank you, Midas." Her lips pressed to his.

He was violent. Savage. Barely in control.

And she kissed him with gentle tenderness.

The bathroom door flew open. "Everything okay in—" Joyce's words stopped.

Midas finished the kiss. Lifted his head and saw the detective's shocked expression in the mirror that ran above the sinks. "Great news," he replied without any hesitation. "Alina is feeling better."

And your divide-and-conquer BS did not work.

***

"You need to go home, Alina," Bradford urged her as their little group left through the back door. There had been more questions from the cops. Some, they had answered. Others, they hadn't. Bradford had stepped in when he felt like the questions were out of line.

Alina wasn't even sure where the line was. "I need to practice." The words were automatic. She *wanted* to go to the rink. To lose herself on the ice.

"Not happening," Midas retorted as his gaze swept the area. The limo waited about ten feet away. "And she's not going home, either, Bradford. Tell your boss I have her. We'll be contacting him later."

"What?" Shock rolled in Bradford's voice. "Of course, she's returning home. Alina's safety is of the utmost importance!"

"Tell me something I don't know." Midas seemed to be searching for someone. Only no one else was in that little alley.

"Then you *know* she needs to return to her father's property. You are working for him."

Midas grunted.

"You follow his orders," Bradford fumed. "So put her in the damn car!"

Right then, a man in khakis and a blue blazer rushed around the building. He barreled straight toward Alina, and as he did, he yanked something out of his pocket.

Fear rushed through her, but Midas was there. And by there—he jumped into the man's path. The guy had been so focused on Alina that he hadn't even noticed Midas. Something that should have been impossible because Midas was a very hard man to miss. The guy in the khakis barreled into Midas then stumbled back as if he'd hit a brick wall. He pretty much had, after all.

The item he'd been clutching—a phone, she could see that now—went flying.

When it landed, Midas stepped on top of it. The crack seemed extra loud.

"What are you doing?" the man howled. "That's my phone!"

"Whoops." Midas shrugged. She was also sure that he stepped down harder on the device.

The guy gaped, then strained to peer around Midas. "Alina! Alina Bellamy, is it true that you were kidnapped last night? Were you taken from your home? Were your abductors killed during the course of your rescue?"

Midas sighed. "Where there is one, there will be more."

Was that man hurling the questions a reporter? Shouldn't he have a crew with him?

As if on cue, two more people hurried around the building. A woman. A man. The man carried an expensive-looking camera.

"Limo," Bradford ordered, voice curt. *"Now."*

Alina took a step toward the limo, but the sudden roar of a motorcycle had her jerking and whipping around. A black beast of a motorcycle roared down the alley. The rider wore a black leather coat and a black helmet. The visor covered his face.

Everyone scrambled out of his path. Everyone but Midas.

The driver braked near him. Kicked down the stand. Rose. He pulled off the helmet.

Dangerous. The one word blasted through her mind. She had no idea who this guy was, but he sure didn't look like a reporter. An air of menace clung to him, and Alina started to inch toward the safety of the limo once more.

"Got your text," the man said to Midas. "Looks like I arrived just in time. More reporters are out front. Someone definitely leaked the story." His gaze swung toward her. "Just hold on to Midas, and you'll be fine."

Hold on to him?

Midas climbed onto the motorcycle. He extended one hand toward her.

Alina crept toward him.

Bradford locked his hands around her shoulders. "Do not go anywhere with him. Your father wants you back home. You'll be safe there."

"You're safe with me, Alina," Midas assured her. "You know that. I'll protect you from any and every threat."

Bradford's grip tightened. "You work for her father. You can't—"

Were the reporters filming? She feared they were. Alina wanted out of that alley. And, for her, safety meant Midas. She broke free of Bradford and rushed to take Midas's hand.

But even as his fingers closed over hers, the stranger plunked the helmet on her head. "Hold tight to Midas," the man directed as he made a few adjustments to the helmet. "I'll be seeing you both soon."

Midas swung her onto the back of the motorcycle. The engine revved again.

"Ever been on one of these before?" Midas asked.

"No." She wasn't exactly thrilled about being on one right then, either.

The intense stranger had already walked away.

Bradford shouted something at her, but she couldn't make out his words.

"Hold on," Midas commanded. "Tight."

She *could* clearly understand Midas's words. She grabbed for him.

"Tighter."

She held tighter. Her body smashed against his.

The motorcycle flew forward.

***

Bradford Wells gaped after the motorcycle. He was trying to wrap his head around what the hell had just happened. The limo driver stumbled forward. Bradford knew the man because Milo Shaw had been Ryker's driver for years.

Scratching his jaw, Milo asked, "Am I supposed to be following them?"

The motorcycle was long gone. Following them wouldn't be an option. Something that Bradford suspected was deliberate. He whipped out his phone and had Ryker on the line in seconds.

The reporters kept milling around. He heard one guy muttering about his broken phone. *Cry me a freaking river.*

"What's happening?" Ryker demanded. "Is everything under control?"

Bradford almost laughed. His friend valued control over all things, and this was most definitely not a controlled situation. "The bodyguard just swept your daughter away." He should have been informed *before* Ryker hired Midas. He would have told his friend that Midas Monroe was too much of a loose cannon. Too dangerous. Too impulsive.

"What?" Shock cracked in the word.

"I'm strongly suspecting they are not returning to your estate." Just seemed appropriate to give the man a heads-up. "He does answer to you, yes?"

"Yes," Ryker gritted out.

"Then you might want to reach out to him." He watched as the two detectives—Joyce Meriam and Calvin Booker—opened the building's rear door and stared around. Zero surprise showed on their faces when they noticed the reporters. Like it was hard to figure out who'd tipped them off. "The story will also be airing on the news. Thought you might want to be aware of the situation. I'll handle as much as I can on this end, but you'll want to pull in your PR team, too." STAT.

"The abduction made it to the news? How?"

"I suspect it's due to the two smug-looking detectives I'm watching. Now, unfortunately, the reporters are coming my way, so I have to go. Damage control, you know."

"*Where is my daughter?*"

Ryker would hate this but... "The last time I saw her, she was on the back of a motorcycle and holding tight to her bodyguard."

"*What?*"

"Maybe consider firing him and bringing in someone new? Someone who will actually follow your orders so that Alina can stay alive? That's some helpful advice from your attorney." He hung up. The reporters had closed in on him.

"Bradford Wells," a woman with stylishly cut, dark hair lasered in on him. He was hardly surprised to be recognized by the press. The surprise would have been them *not* recognizing him. "Is it true that Alina Bellamy was abducted last night? Is someone trying to stop her from competing in the Olympics?"

Competition had nothing to do with this case. The detectives thought ransom was the motive. That it was about cold, hard cash. Wasn't it usually?

He opened his mouth to reply, but then felt a sudden awareness pulse at the back of his neck. His head turned. A stranger stood a few feet away. The man who'd gotten off the motorcycle. His arms were crossed over his chest as he leaned against the back of the building. His eyes were on Bradford. A direct, intense gaze.

Then that stare moved to the reporters.

Then to the whispering detectives.

Bradford had encountered all sorts of people during his days practicing law. When he'd first started, he'd gone into criminal law. Had even handled several homicide cases before deciding that he was much better suited for corporate law. If you lost a case in corporate law, your client would lose a ton of money.

But not his life.

Yes, he'd handled all sorts of cases over the years. Met all kinds of people. Some of those people had been very, very dangerous. So he knew a hunter when he saw one.

The stranger who'd come to help Midas Monroe was definitely a hunter.

But that only seemed fitting, considering that Bradford knew Midas was exactly the same. A modern-day hunter. A predator straight to his core.

And that predator had just vanished with Alina.

CHAPTER THIRTEEN

The motorcycle braked to a halt. For a moment, Alina didn't move. During the drive, she'd closed her eyes because there had been more than a few turns that threatened to give her a heart attack. She'd closed her eyes and gripped him as tightly as she could. The result was that her body was plastered to his.

This had been her first time on a motorcycle. No doubt Midas probably enjoyed those adrenaline-inducing rides all the time. Meanwhile, Alina was pretty sure that when she got off the bike, her body would collapse in a quivering pile. She could still feel the vibrations rolling through her.

"We're here, sweetheart," Midas told her. "All safe and sound."

She pushed away from him and looked around. With shaking hands, she pulled off the helmet. He hadn't worn a helmet. That seemed crazy dangerous to her. She'd scooted back as she tried to take in the scene around her. Midas kicked down the stand and climbed from the bike. He turned back to her. Offered his hand.

He'd done that before. Behind the building, when the reporters had been surging toward them, he'd extended his hand to her. Even though she'd been afraid of the bike, she'd taken his hand because she wasn't afraid of Midas.

There were plenty of things she did fear in this world, but he wasn't one of them.

So, once more, she took his hand. He helped her off the bike. He'd parked it inside of a garage, and as they walked forward, he hit a button on the wall and the garage door lowered behind them.

Then they were heading through a well-lit hallway. Midas unlocked a door. Typed in a code on a security panel. Took them inside what turned out to be an enormous house.

One with a view of the mountains that was even better than the one her father had. "Where are we?" Alina asked as she looked around in confusion.

"Your new safe house."

Her head whipped back toward him. "Say again?"

He sent her a quick smile. "Your new safe house," he repeated. "Top-of-the-line security. Way better than what your father *thinks* he has. Cameras are installed all along the outside perimeter. Sensors. If someone tries to get close without us knowing, well, let's just say they will be in for a fun surprise." He let go of her hand. "I made arrangements earlier. Had your clothes and personal items brought over from your house. It's not safe for you to go back there, and I think you know that. Again, your dad's idea of security and mine are two different things. The kidnappers got past the system at your house far too easily. The same will not be said of this place." His hands went to his hips. "No intruders will get inside here."

Her gaze darted around the immaculately decorated house. "Who owns this place?"

"An acquaintance. I made arrangements for us to stay here for a while."

Her head craned toward him. "You really can't protect me at my father's estate?"

"I told you—"

"You don't trust him," she finished as her stomach knotted.

"He can't hold back with me. Not when your safety is at stake. And the security *is* better here. It has to be. I oversaw the installation myself." He headed toward the window that overlooked the mountains. "The action star I told you about? This was his place. He's off filming, and when I realized you needed a good safe house, I sent some texts and arranged to use this place. A...friend brought my things—and yours—over for us."

A friend? Had that been the guy who oozed danger? "Who was the man on the motorcycle?"

"Memphis Camden."

The name meant nothing to her.

"He's a former bounty hunter and current cold case solver."

She could feel the furrow between her brow deepening. "My case isn't exactly cold."

"No, it's not. In fact, it's red-hot. We need to keep it that way. I'm not gonna let the case fade away. After a week, maybe two, your dad and you will think you're safe. If the guy doesn't come for you again and more time passes, you'll start to let down your guard. Hell, I've rarely ever heard of a kidnapper going after a specific target twice."

"That's good news for me, isn't it?" It would mean that she *would* be safe.

"Not if you get complacent. Not if your father sends me away and you're on your own and the bastard is just waiting. I can't let that happen. I can't let you become prey again. That's why I'm planning to hunt him. I will not leave you on your own with him just hiding in the shadows and waiting for the perfect moment to come after you again."

She blinked. "You're hunting him." Alina crept closer to Midas.

"Memphis will help me. You've confirmed something I already suspected—there were other victims. One went home, that's what you told me. We find her, and we might find answers."

Her heart raced. "Answers would be great. Getting the guy who planned all of this tossed into a cell for the rest of his life? That would be even better." But, just so they were clear. "When you find the woman who got away, I'm coming with you. I want to be there with you to talk to her."

"Like I was planning to leave you behind."

She was right beside him now. Only he turned away from the mountain view and focused completely on her. "Told you, Alina, where you go, I go. The same is true for me. I am not going to leave you behind. This case is about you. I think you deserve to be with me every step of the way for the investigation."

Before she could respond, his phone rang. A loud peal of sound. He didn't move at all. Alina wet her lips. "You going to try telling me that's a wrong number?"

The phone pealed again. "Nah," he said. "That's the ring tone I assigned to your dad."

She released a low breath. "We should answer him."

"Fair enough." He pulled the phone from his pocket. Swiped his finger over the screen and put the call on speaker. "Midas."

"Where the hell did you take my daughter?"

"To a safe location," Midas responded easily. "Don't worry, I have my eyes on her."

Her father thundered, "Fuck that!"

Her brows climbed. Alina started to speak, but Midas shook his head. "She's okay," he said.

"No, she's not. She's being hunted. You need to get her back here, now. You were supposed to return her in the limo, but Bradford called and said you'd taken her away."

"Yep." Again, an easy reply. Completely at odds with her father's furious voice. "I wanted her someplace safe. If the kidnapper is planning to target her again, he'll figure out real fast that you have her at your estate. And despite what you think, the security there is trash. I brought her to a better location. She's safe here. I used the motorcycle to make sure no one followed us. This location buys me time. I can work with my team to track down the kidnapper before he finds Alina."

Silence. Then... "What team? I thought you worked alone."

"Not this time." His gaze remained on Alina. "And you need to tell me the truth."

"What the hell are you talking about? Listen, I am paying you. You will do what I say!"

"I'll do what's best for Alina."

Her heart raced.

"*You're on my payroll!* If you can't follow orders, then I will find someone else. I don't care what Agent Foxx said. I'll hire another bodyguard."

"You gonna trust someone else with her? Really? Think other bodyguards will protect her the way I will? Because I can assure you, I will kill before I let anyone hurt Alina."

Her head shook. She didn't want Midas killing for her.

More silence. Then… "That's why I hired you."

Her eyes widened. Had her father just said—

"Tell me what you're holding back," Midas ordered him. "This abduction isn't just about money, is it?"

Her whole body tensed.

"No," her father rasped. "It's about the sins of the past. Even though I tried to atone."

What in the world did that mean?

"He will come after her again." Her father seemed certain. "Stop him."

"I intend to do just that."

"Tell me where you are—"

"Can't do that," Midas said and for the first time during the conversation, his tone wasn't quite so easy. "You see, I don't trust you."

"*What?*"

"I also don't trust the people around you. I'm betting some of your staff had the security code to her house. Or at least access to get the code. I believe they also had a key to the rink. If we'd stayed at the guesthouse longer, it would have only been a matter of time until something happened there. Anyone can be bought, you should know that. I'll have my associates take a hard look at the people around you. Be careful, Ryker. Sometimes, you just can't trust anyone."

"Fuck," her father snarled. Then... "Only Alina matters. You do whatever has to be done...*Only Alina matters*." He hung up.

Midas tossed aside the phone. "Finally, we agree on something."

Her muscles had turned to stone. "Don't kill for me."

He shrugged. *Shrugged*.

"Midas, don't! That's not what I want."

He stepped toward her. Put his hands on her. And it was just like it *always* was when he touched her. Heat—fire seemed to whip through her blood. "I will do whatever is necessary to keep you safe."

Her head tilted back as she stared up at him. The whole world seemed to suddenly narrow in focus so that only he remained. "You aren't a killer."

He brought his mouth down toward her. "Yes." A breath. "I am."

Then he let her go. Walked away.

Oh, hell, no.

Anger pumped through her body. Anger, fear, adrenaline. Lust. That dangerous combination that pushed her and emboldened her. "Stop!"

He did.

"You think you're going to scare me, don't you?"

Midas didn't glance back at her.

"Think that if you say the right things—or the wrong ones—you'll make me afraid of you."

His hands fisted. "I don't want you afraid."

"No? Then stop dropping ridiculous lines saying that you're a killer."

He spun toward her. "I have told you before—"

"You're a bodyguard. You protect people. That's your whole gig. You *saved* me. I don't care who your father is." She marched toward him. Determined. "I don't care why you came into my life. I just care that you are here now. You're not some killer. You might just be the craziest, bravest man I've ever met, but you *aren't* a killer."

He smiled at her. That slightly cruel smile should have chilled her. It didn't. "If you think I would hesitate to kill if it meant keeping you safe…"

Her heart pounded even faster.

"I wouldn't. Not even for a second. I would destroy anyone who tried to hurt you."

"Because…you're protective of me."

"That I am."

"Because…I'm your charge."

His hands curled around her waist. "Thought we covered this before…you're just mine." His mouth pressed to hers. Her lips were open. His tongue dipped inside.

Her blood ignited.

That was just the way it was with him. Her body had a mind of its own. When he touched her, she yearned. When he kissed her, she melted.

Did he have the same reaction? His body didn't seem to be melting, but Midas sure did seem plenty hard. In the limo, she'd told him her secret. No past lovers. No way to compare the riot of feelings that thundered through her when they touched. Everything was fresh. New. Consuming with him.

He tasted her and she moaned and her hands clutched desperately for him. He lifted her, and it was natural to wrap her legs around his hips and to just kiss him deeper. To savor his taste. He was carrying her somewhere. She didn't break from him to see where. She kept kissing him. Her nipples had turned into tight peaks that ached, and her hips rocked against him with every step that he took.

Alina knew she should stop. This wasn't the time. They were still little more than strangers. Except...

She trusted Midas completely. How could she not? He'd walked through hell to save her.

He lowered her down. Lifted his mouth from hers. Alina blinked and realized she was on a bed. The mattress was soft and big beneath her. Midas towered over her. His hands were still around her waist.

"Want me to stop?" A rumble from him.

"Don't you dare." A demand from her.

She saw his pupils flare at her words. "Remember you said that," he told her, voice so deep and dark.

She'd remember everything about this moment.

His hands slid under the edge of her blouse. Such warm hands. His fingers were callused, a little rough, but Alina found she liked that roughness. Up, up, his fingers went, and then he was cupping her breasts through the bra she wore.

It wasn't enough.

She was on the side of the bed. Her legs splayed over the edge. Midas stood between her legs. Leaned over her. He touched her through the bra, and it just wasn't good enough. Her hips kept surging up against him. She ached. She needed.

He eased back. Stared at her with amber eyes that glittered. Then Midas nodded. "Your first time has to be with me."

Not like she was planning to go out and jump anyone else so... "The clothes have to go."

"Oh, baby, they will." He yanked her shirt over her head. Tossed it on the bed. Alina arched her back, and his hands slid under her so he could undo her bra. It fell away, and his mouth closed over one tight nipple.

Desire knifed through her, and she gasped. Her hands scraped over the bedding.

He licked her. Sucked her nipple. Gave her a sensual bite.

"Midas!"

His mouth moved to her other breast. He licked and sucked and her hands clenched that bedding even as his fingers trailed down her body.

Over her stomach. Down to the top of her jeans. He unhooked the snap. Eased down the zipper. His mouth left her breast, and she watched as he stepped back.

He pulled the jeans down her legs. Her jeans and her panties. Her shoes hit the floor. He yanked away her socks and the jeans and panties and left her totally naked.

Unease slithered through her. Nerves. When they were kissing, passion dominated. She didn't have to think. She could only feel. Alina wanted to keep feeling. No thinking. Thinking brought doubt and fear and a thousand other things.

He stared at her. Didn't touch her again. His eyes trailed over her breasts. Down her body. Locked on her spread thighs.

More of that unease came again. No, not unease. Vulnerability. She was naked. He was completely dressed. He was so much bigger than she was. More experienced. Alina didn't know what to do or say and the silence stretched as he stared at her and—

"You are the most beautiful thing I've ever seen in my life." His hands moved to cover hers as she fisted the bedding. "Trust me?"

Her head moved in a nod against the covers. His hands were so big they swallowed hers. His gaze slid to the right. To their hands. His jaw hardened. "You are so small. Every part of you." His stare—with the amber burning so brightly—returned to hers. "I have to make sure you're ready. The last thing I want is to hurt you."

"First times..." Alina licked her lips. "There's always a little pain."

"Screw that. I want you to have pleasure." He let go of her hands. His fingers curled around her waist. He pushed her farther back on the bed. Then his head lowered and his mouth pressed to her stomach. "Let's see how you taste. I'm betting you'll be sweet cream. You'll taste just like you smell."

Her eyes widened. "Midas, I—"

He was already kissing a path down her body. Her stomach quivered. Her legs shifted restlessly. This was like dipping a toe in the shallow end of the pool one moment and then diving into the deep end in the next instant. Him putting his mouth on her core seemed incredibly intimate. Too personal.

Oh, right, like sex isn't personal? But she wanted to have sex with him. When she'd been in that damn closet, Alina had been convinced she'd never escape. That she'd die in there.

Die and miss so many experiences that others had every single day.

Dying a virgin? *No, thank you.* She wanted more. She wanted passion. She wanted Midas.

She was also just scared as hell.

"Trust me," he urged again. And he pushed her legs wider apart. His mouth lowered between her thighs. She felt the stir of his breath against her. Then he kissed her core.

She would have bolted off the bed, but his hands were wrapped around her waist, and he chained her against the mattress. His lips parted. His tongue stroked her. Light, teasing licks that had her squirming to try and get a little closer because the touch of his tongue felt so good, but she wanted even more.

His tongue dipped into her.

She jerked.

One hand left her waist. It slid between her thighs. That big, strong hand. His callused fingertips teased her even as he kept licking. Then it wasn't his tongue dipping into her, it was one finger.

He sucked on her clit. Licked. "So tight," he rasped against her. The rasp had her shivering. No, his tongue had her doing that. Because he was licking her harder. Stroking her deeper. She was arching around that probing finger, trying to take more of him. And he put another finger inside of her and stretched her even as his mouth turned more demanding and feverish. Her whole body had gone bow tight. Release teased her. Alina could feel it. She was almost there.

Her wild gaze flew down her body. Locked on him as he took her with his mouth and fingers and he was relentless and greedy and she was—coming. Hard. A fast explosion that just swept through her body and had her crying out for him as her inner muscles clamped greedily around his fingers. The quakes shook her and tossed her headlong into a storm, and she loved it. Her heels dug into the mattress as her body arched up against him. But Midas didn't stop. Not even for a second. If anything, his mouth became ever harder. More demanding. Possessive and consuming and the climax didn't stop. She could do nothing but take the pleasure as it soared through her body.

When it ended, his head lifted, and Alina found that she couldn't breathe when she met his stare. The amber didn't just blaze. It had gone absolutely molten. A primitive, untamed desire stared back at her from the depths of his eyes. More need than she'd ever seen in her life. Alina hadn't even thought someone could look that way.

Savage.

Primal.

"I could eat you up," he growled.

I thought you just did.

"You are so tight." His fingers were still in her, and he stretched them.

A half moan, half whimper escaped her because that movement sent off a little aftershock of pleasure within her.

"You will feel insane around my dick."

A quiver went through her. This was happening. *He's taking me. I'm taking him.* The vulnerability stirred, but she pushed it back. She wanted this man.

His fingers slid from her body, and a moan of protest broke from her lips. He left her briefly, and she hated his absence. Alina vaguely heard the rustle of clothing. Then he was back. The head of his cock pushed against her.

"Are you ready for me?" Midas asked.

"Yes." Breathless.

Then he began to push against her sex. The broad, round head of his cock dipped just inside of her. His eyes glittered as he stared at her. His face was a rough mask of control, but need blazed so clearly from his eyes. Her hips started to arch up because she wanted to take all of him inside of her.

But at the slight tilt, his hands clamped tightly around her waist and held her in place.

"Slow, sweetheart," he gritted. "I am not hurting you. *Slow.*"

She wanted more. All of him. Alina squirmed in his hold even as she became aware of a distant beeping.

Steady. Pulsing. Getting...louder?

Midas stared into her eyes. His jaw had locked tightly. Sweat beaded his brow, testament to his self-control. And then—

"Fuck!"

He withdrew from her.

"Midas!" she cried in dismay.

He'd spun from the bed. Yanked his jeans back up and zipped them. Buttoned them. She didn't remember him *unbuttoning* the jeans. Maybe she'd been in climax bliss. But he fixed his clothes in a flash and, with his jaw still tightly clenched, he snarled, "Company is here."

"Company?" Alina parroted.

His hand jerked through his hair. "What the hell was I thinking?"

She hoped he'd been thinking about making love to her. Her body still ached. Still craved him. But she grabbed the covers and yanked them partially over her body because the feelings of vulnerability and awkwardness had returned.

"I knew he was coming to meet us. What the fuck?" Midas shook his head. "Wanted you so much. *This isn't fucking me.*"

It looked like Midas to her.

The beeping continued.

"Get dressed," he groused.

"But I was having so much fun being naked," she muttered. That was actually true.

His eyes narrowed.

They stared at each other. His expression seemed so stark...and hungry.

"I didn't have on a rubber."

Her brows climbed.

"That's how fucking far gone I was. I was in you bare, Alina."

"You...you didn't come in." Not all the way. Just the broad head of his dick had teased her. She was still technically a virgin. Wasn't she? Was there even a technical component to the situation? "And I'm on birth control. There's no risk that way."

"I want in." Hungry. Rough. "I will be..." He swallowed. "Just so you know, I'm clean. Get checked regularly, and despite what I did just then with you..." His gaze slid over her body. "I've been careful with other lovers. I hold my control." He spun away. "The alarm is sounding because Memphis is here. Probably brought a partner with him."

So his...friends were rushing to the safe house, and she was naked. She'd been coming a few moments ago. Far and away the best orgasm of her life. Far better than the ones she gave herself.

He paused in the doorway and glanced back at her. "We will finish." A vow.

"Good to know," she whispered.

"By the way..." The amber in his eyes gleamed. "You taste incredible."

Then he was gone.

She was naked. He was gone. And her body kept quivering.

Alina exhaled.

***

What the fuck am I doing? What the fuck was I thinking? Why the hell am I still not fucking her?

Midas disabled the alarm that had been beeping—a sensor that told him company had arrived on the property. He'd known that Memphis would be showing up. And Midas sure as hell hadn't planned to spread Alina out and make a feast of her in the middle of the day but—

But I did. And I want more. He could still feel her around the tip of his dick. Hot and wet. Sweet cream. He'd wanted to drive balls deep into her and claim her completely, but he'd been trying to take care with her.

Really? 'Cause you were bareback in her. You've never gone bare in a woman before. Where the hell is your sense?

He checked the monitors. Saw Memphis and his companion on the screen. Midas's eyebrows rose as he recognized the guy with Memphis.

Fantastic. Like I need more drama.

But he hurried to the front door. Opened it and waited for Memphis to finish climbing up the steps. And, of course, he should have known that Memphis would—

"You look like shit," Memphis told him cheerfully. "But I guess you had one hell of a night, huh?"

Midas swiped a hand over his hair. Tension still hummed in his body. Sexual frustration poured through his veins. *I was so close to taking Alina.* "Memphis. Still a pain in the ass, I see. Good to know some things just don't change."

Memphis grunted. He entered the house, and his gaze immediately went to assess every inch of the place.

Midas stood by the doorway while he waited for the second man to enter. Silent, intense, with green eyes that raked over Midas. A man he'd met on a previous case.

Lane Lawson.

Suspected serial killer.

Jail escapee.

And a man who'd been…proven innocent. With some serious effort. It had actually been Midas's buddy FBI Special Agent Oliver Foxx who had first put Lane behind bars. And it had been Oliver—and Lane's twin sister, Lark—who had eventually succeeded in clearing his name.

Now Lane was free, and he'd taken up a side hobby. Being a cold case solver. Not that Midas could blame the man. Midas had thought about joining the Ice Breaker crew a time or twenty, too. Once you'd been accused of committing heinous crimes, you had a tendency to want to make certain that real justice was carried out.

So, yeah, he felt a kinship with Lane. Though he hadn't expected to see the man on his doorstep. Midas shut the door. Reset all of his alarms. "So what—you two are fulltime best friends now?" Midas asked.

Memphis turned back toward him. "You seem off."

Hell.

"Where's the skater?" Memphis asked in the next breath.

"Getting dressed." *Wrong* response. Because Memphis's eyes had narrowed. "She's freshening up," he clarified with a vague wave of his hand. "Just got back from viewing bodies. Her first time to get a trip to the lab. So you'll understand if she's shaken."

Memphis strode close to Midas. Memphis was tall, but Midas still had him by a few inches. "Something you want to tell me about this case? Got something to share with the group?"

"Yeah, it's a cluster." He crossed his arms. "The two men who took Alina are dead, the cops keep eyeing me because they're jerks—"

"They're having an affair," Memphis cut in to say. "Bad idea, if you ask me. Personal involvements always cloud things." The words seemed to be a warning.

Midas did a double-take. "Who's having an affair?"

"The two detectives. Joyce and Calvin. Saw the way he touched her when they went back in the building after you raced from the alley. You were right about them tipping off the reporters, by the way. I chatted briefly with one guy on the scene. You broke his phone. Remember him? *That guy.* He was pretty salty. And very chatty.

Found out that Joyce was the one to call him. The detectives definitely want attention put on you."

Footsteps padded toward them.

Midas glanced over Memphis's shoulder. Alina was dressed, thankfully. Blouse back in place. *Hopefully, her bra, too.* Jeans on. Tennis shoes on her feet. But her hair was a bit disheveled. Sexy, but it definitely looked like she'd just taken a side trip to bed.

I did that.

And her cheeks were flushed. Her lips were also red and swollen from his mouth, and, hell, had he left a small mark on her neck?

Memphis sent him a knowing, sideways glance.

Midas fired right back with a *don't-say-anything* glare.

"Thought you knew better," Memphis muttered. "What happened to your rules?"

Seriously? Memphis had freaking *married* the woman he'd gone to protect years ago. Like Midas needed judgment from him. Thanks, but no thanks.

Alina stopped a few feet away and surveyed the men. The faint flush in her cheeks deepened. She shoved her hands into the back pockets of her jeans and rocked forward. Her gaze drifted over the group and lingered for a moment on Memphis. "You're the man who brought the motorcycle to us."

"Guilty as charged." Memphis ambled toward her. He extended his hand. "Memphis Camden."

Her hand came up to shake his. "Midas mentioned you. Thank you for helping me."

"Haven't done much yet. Just gave you a getaway vehicle and arranged for some gear to be brought over here earlier for you. No big deal. Besides, I'm hoping you can help me. I think your case might just coincide with another I've been working." He released her hand and motioned toward Lane. "That's Lane Lawson. He's here in a...training capacity."

"Training capacity, my ass." Lane headed for Alina. He extended his hand. "Sorry for what happened to you."

Alina shook his hand. "I—thank you." She let go of him. "You're both here to help? And just what other case is it that, uh, coincides?"

"Maureen O'Sullivan. The woman who was found dead recently. Broken neck. Knife through her heart. You know, the same MO that Midas's father used on his vics," Memphis responded in an oh-so-helpful asshole way.

Midas hurried to Alina's side. As usual, Memphis wasn't pulling any punches.

"Got those pics you sent of the two men who abducted Alina," Memphis continued with a nod of his head. "Smart of you to snag them. We've got a new tech whiz who ran them through some facial recognition software BS stuff. Got to say, though, Midas, you are *not* gonna like the results."

Alina rubbed her temple and peered at Midas. "When did you send pictures to them?"

Right after he'd met up with the cops on that mountain road. He'd known that he needed a team to help, and Memphis had skills and reach that Midas wanted on her case.

"And when did you call them to come help us?" Alina continued as she motioned to the two other men.

"We were already working on Maureen's case. Or, trying to work on it," Memphis clarified. "Feds and local cops are stonewalling us. Such dick moves. Hate it when they do that."

Lane watched silently.

"Maureen's the second vic. And you're the third. At least, that's what we suspect." Memphis pursed his lips. "Probably more. Aren't there always more?"

Alina rubbed her temple again. "How can we figure out the first vic?"

"Oh, we already know who she is." He flashed a shark's smile. "Who she is and where she is. Are you impressed?"

Actually, dammit, Midas was. Memphis had just saved him a shit-ton of legwork.

"Kiera Thatch. Also from a wealthy family, close to your age, and, from what we can tell, Kiera vanished for three days before she finally turned up again. Of course, her family never reported the abduction, but we received a tip from a concerned friend."

That concerned tip was sure helping them out. "When did you get the tip?" Midas asked, unable to keep the suspicion from his voice.

"Before you let me know that you'd just rescued your charge from a cabin in the middle of nowhere." Flat. "Didn't exactly take me long to put the pieces together. That's one of the reasons I hauled ass so fast to get to your side." Memphis's gaze dipped to Alina's wrists. "Kiera was treated at a hospital for abrasions around her wrists and ankles."

She tugged down the sleeve of her blouse. The long sleeves had covered her bandages, so the tug wasn't necessary. But at the movement, guilt spiked in Midas. *Was I careful with her hands?* No, fuck, he hadn't been. He'd just been a greedy, horny bastard.

A low sigh escaped Memphis. "The police tried to follow up with the family after her hospital visit, but they were shut down. The...friend is the one who was concerned. You see, Kiera has since refused to leave her home. She has guards with her all the time. And she's been seeing a shrink. She fits the victim pattern that the Ice Breakers are establishing. She made it home. Maureen didn't. And then, of course, there's you."

Alina reached out to touch Midas. "You're telling me that these men are just—they are serial kidnappers?" She turned her head toward Midas. "That fits with what they told me," she said. "Remember, the redhead revealed that someone had gone home? It fits. Kiera could have been the one he meant."

"Yeah..." Memphis sawed a hand over his jaw. "It fits with what we've found, too. The Ice Breakers have been able to place Shayne Preston and Fallon White in the areas where both Maureen and Kiera lived. Normally, I don't buy that proximity equals guilt—"

Lane grunted. "Yeah, because that shit *can* be wrong."

It had certainly been wrong in Lane's case.

"But with the new intel we uncovered about Fallon, we have to assume the worst."

Lane's nostrils flared, but he'd gone back to being silent.

Midas waited.

Memphis just looked all intense and somber, a look the guy did all the freaking time.

"Well?" Midas pushed when the silence stretched too long. "You gonna tell me or just stare at us all day?" Because he already had plans spinning in his head. First step, get the surviving vic to talk. They had to make sure that she actually had been abducted, and the only way to do that? A one-on-one chat with her. And while she might have shut down anyone else who tried to get close to her, he had a feeling she'd talk with Alina.

Because Alina had been through the same hell.

"So..." Memphis rolled back his shoulders. "I happen to have a question or two of my own. Let's start with this one. How did you come to be on this case, Midas?"

"Oliver recommended me to her father."

Memphis and Lane shared a long glance.

Wonderful. Now those two were doing the silent communication bit? He'd thought they were pretty much enemies. Now they acted like besties. "Look, I already tried to reach out to Oliver—twice—but he's off on some tropical isle with your sister." Midas pointed at Lane. "Oliver is great at profiling, and I want his input, STAT." So, yeah, he was gonna interrupt his friend's honeymoon.

"I talked to my sister this morning," Lane revealed. "Told her about the case. Oliver heard me. He...didn't know anything about Alina. Or about you protecting her."

"What?" That made zero sense. No, Lane was misinformed. "Oliver told Alina's father to hire me. He's the whole reason I'm here with her now."

Memphis's expression turned extra grim.

Shit. What now? "Memphis?" he barked.

"That new tech whiz I told you about who is working with the Ice Breakers? The woman is all about finding patterns and links. She found a link with Fallon White."

"Don't keep me in fucking suspense, spit it out. A link to what?"

"You're not gonna like it," Memphis muttered.

"Who the hell cares? Just say it—"

"Fallon's older brother is in the same penitentiary that houses your father. In fact, they were briefly in the same cell."

Midas felt every muscle in his body stiffen. Not possible. What he was saying...the idea that Midas was getting in his mind... "My dad isn't involved in this."

Memphis just stared at him.

"My father is locked away! Maximum security!"

"Just like Fallon's older brother," Memphis agreed.

"My father isn't—" But he stopped.

"I believe Fallon was found with a broken neck," Memphis murmured. "And with a knife plunged into his heart. Pretty sure we are all familiar with that particular MO."

***

Henry Monroe smiled as he stared through his window. It had been so long since he'd seen his son. Granted, the last time they had been touching-close…

I used my knife on him.

But that was only because he'd been so angry with Midas. The man could be such a disappointment sometimes.

Enough was enough, though. Henry had come to that decision weeks ago.

His smile spread. He was sure that, by this time tomorrow, he'd be sitting down with his son for a wonderful face-to-face chat. Quality time was so important for a family.

They really had quite a bit of catching up to do.

CHAPTER FOURTEEN

"You gave Ryker Bellany my name," Midas said as he gripped his phone tightly and paced in the bedroom. He'd left the others. He knew Memphis wouldn't let Alina leave the house.

This can't be happening.

"Uh, hello, to you, too, Midas," Oliver Foxx returned. "I'm enjoying my honeymoon, thanks so much for asking. I'm good and you are—"

"Lane said you didn't know a damn thing about the case. Ryker Bellany *told me* that you referred him to me for bodyguard services." He didn't have time for BS small talk. "What is happening?"

"I don't know." All humor vanished from Oliver's voice. "But I do wish I wasn't five thousand miles away because I don't like where this is going." A pause. Midas could have sworn he heard the roar of waves in the background. Probably because Oliver was on a sunny beach. "Look, I don't know how long I'll have service out here but understand this...I have never talked to Ryker Bellamy. I don't even know who the hell he is."

The twisting knots in Midas's stomach grew worse. "I'm protecting his daughter."

"The one who was abducted last night? Lane told me about that, and I'm glad you were there—"

"I was there because someone wanted me to be." *And it couldn't be...no way could it be...*

He shut down the thought.

"Go talk to Ryker," Oliver suggested. "Find out why the hell he told you I was the one to recommend you."

Oh, he planned to talk to Ryker. Immediately.

"And watch your back, man." The ocean roared. "Because I'm feeling like you are a piece on a chessboard, and someone is moving you around in a game you didn't know you were playing."

***

"I have eyes on Kiera Thatch," the man who'd identified himself as Memphis Camden told Alina. "Her parents are keeping close tabs on her, too. She's not even talking to her best friends, but I think I can get you close to her."

Alina tugged at her sleeves again. For some reason, she wanted to keep hiding the bandages that still encircled her wrists. She hadn't thought about the bandages at all when she'd been with Midas in the bedroom.

Her gaze darted to the bedroom door. Midas had rushed in there moments before, saying that he needed to make calls.

"He's talking to my brother-in-law."

Her stare whipped to the other man, Lane. He...unnerved her. A handsome man, yes, but there was something unsettling about the intensity of his eyes and the grimness that seemed to cling to him.

Midas was always controlled. *Too controlled?*

But this man felt like a volcano that was getting ready to explode.

Lane's lashes flickered. "You look like you're afraid of me." His lips thinned. "I take it that you're familiar with my story?"

Alina shook her head. "Should I be?"

He backed up a step. Surprise flashed, momentarily lightening the grimness of his features.

"She's on the ice twenty-four, seven," Memphis noted with a wave of his hand. "Guess she missed your news coverage."

She seemed to be missing a lot of news.

"Did you know about Midas's past?" Lane asked.

"I—" Her attention shifted back to the closed bedroom door. "When I first met Midas, I didn't even know he'd been hired as my bodyguard."

"Sonofabitch," Lane exclaimed.

***

"Listen, you sonofabitch," Midas snarled into the phone. "I want answers. I am trying to keep your daughter safe, and you are *lying* to me."

"I want my daughter home! I need her—"

"I just spoke to Oliver Foxx. He has no idea who you are. He swears he didn't tell you to hire me."

"But, but—" The words fell into a stark silence. Then... "I-I was sent an email from him. I *called* the number listed and talked to him personally."

No, he hadn't. "When did you talk to him?"

"The day before you came to my office."

Midas closed his eyes. "Oliver Foxx has been on his honeymoon for the last two weeks. He's been island hopping, and he only got phone service today." One of the reasons for the trip—Oliver had wanted to be completely alone with Lark. But Lane had reached him earlier, and Midas had just made contact with him and—

And whoever actually talked to Ryker knew that Oliver would be unreachable for an extended period of time. Someone has been planning this. Working so carefully.

"What's happening?" Ryker demanded, and a note of fear had entered his voice.

***

"Liars really piss me the hell off." A muscle flexed along Lane's jaw. "People should be exactly who they say they are."

Memphis slanted him a glance. "This about your sister and Oliver? Dude, the man apologized. If I can get past you locking me in a freezer, then you can get past—"

"Being locked away for murders I didn't commit? No, I can't. And you're not over that freezer shit, either. Don't act like you are."

Memphis pursed his lips. "You're right. I hold grudges, too. Guilty."

Alina gaped at them, then she backed up. *Lane had locked Memphis in a freezer?*

"Fabulous." Memphis threw his hands into the air. "Now you've scared her. Saying scary things is not the way to reassure victims. Write that down in a notebook somewhere, would you?"

"Considering the mess going on in her life, she should probably be scared," Lane retorted. He did not pull out a notebook.

The bedroom door flew open. "Oliver Foxx never spoke with Ryker Bellamy. He never told her father to hire me." Midas stormed forward to join them.

"Told him this already," Lane noted with a roll of one shoulder. "But what's new? People don't believe me. Always got to find extra proof."

"Someone is playing with us. I don't like being anyone's toy."

She was trying to follow along. Truly. But... "Who told my dad to hire you?"

His nostrils flared.

"I think," Lane announced, voice considering, "that might be the million-dollar question."

Midas stopped at Alina's side. "We need to talk with Kiera Thatch, now."

"Yep, figured that would be on your to-do list." Memphis rocked back on his heels. "I'm also figuring that as soon as she sees the news stories about Alina, Kiera will be in the mood to chat with you two. So, I'll give you her address and you guys can hit the road." He smiled. "Am I a man with a plan or what?"

"Or what," Midas threw back.

Memphis's smile dimmed. "While you're chatting with Kiera, I'll be talking to Maureen O'Sullivan's brother. The man is grieving his heart out, and I know he wants justice. Maybe he can give me more intel."

Lane frowned at Memphis.

And Midas nodded. "Done. Let's get this investigation moving, now." Anger roughed his words. "Someone is dicking around with us. And *no one* plays with me."

***

"Texted you the address," Memphis said as he exited the house. Lane stood near the waiting SUV. Memphis lingered with Midas on the wraparound porch. "Like I told you before, I have eyes on Kiera. I'm worried she might get spooked when she first sees the news stories. If she runs, I'll have her tailed."

"I appreciate the help," Midas replied.

Memphis slapped him on the shoulder. "Did that hurt to say? Sounded a little bit choked coming out. Maybe you want to try it again? Louder and with more feeling?"

He didn't say another word.

"Well, then how about *I* say something?" The slap on the shoulder changed. Memphis curled his fingers around Midas's shoulder and hauled him closer. "Keep your dick in your pants, man."

Midas glared at him. "Don't be concerned about my dick."

"Yeah, you wish. I'm warning you as someone who has been in your shoes—you are about to fuck up."

"You have never been in my shoes." Not even close.

"You want her."

Midas didn't blink. But, *want* seemed far too tame a word. Maybe crave would work better?

"I read body language. A little hobby I picked up over the years. I can also tell when a woman was just in the middle of a serious make-out session. You left a hickey on Alina's neck, and her mouth was still swollen from yours."

"*Watch it.*" Dammit, he *had* left a mark on her neck. He'd have to be more careful.

"No, you watch it. Take my advice. Keep your hands to yourself and your dick in your jeans."

Midas shook his head. "There you go again, worrying about my dick."

"I'm worried about the woman." Solemn. "And about you. You're both pawns, and pawns have a way of getting tossed from the game. Be careful." He let Midas go. Turned and waved to Lane. "On my way, asshole! Stop glaring at me!" He hurried toward Lane.

Midas watched the two men climb into the SUV and drive away.

"Not a pawn," he rasped. "I'm the fucking king." But, of course, the king wasn't really the most powerful piece in the chess game. Midas glanced over his shoulder.

Alina stared back at him with her dark and mysterious eyes.

Everyone knew that the queen really controlled the board.

***

"So...they're fucking," Lane said with a sigh. "He could barely keep his eyes off her for a second, and did you see the way he kept moving to stand beside her? The man is obsessed."

"He's her bodyguard," Memphis replied as he gripped the steering wheel a little too tightly. "He's supposed to keep his eyes on her and stay close to his charge."

"Yeah, but there's close and then there's—whoa! Why the hell are you stopping?" Lane's hands hit the dashboard before he turned to glare at Memphis.

He was stopping because he had a plan. "There's a car rental company across the street. I want you to get a ride, and I want you going to the address I have for Kiera Thatch." He whipped out his phone and sent a text with the address to Lane's phone right then. "You've been riding me for more work with the Ice Breakers, so this is your chance. Go. Hurry." Before Midas got too big of a lead on them.

But Lane lingered. "You want me to go and interview Kiera? I-I'm not sure if I'm the best with vics."

Memphis rolled his eyes. Lord save him from amateurs. *No, buddy, you suck with vic interaction.* "I want you watching Midas's ass.

The man is being set up. He needs help. And you're going to be there in case things go to hell."

"All right, all right. Got it." Lane climbed from the vehicle. He started to slam the door—

"Do *not* lock anyone in a freezer."

Lane's gaze hardened. "I will if some asshole deserves it."

Such a bastard. "Just stay back and watch, got me? Don't go in with guns blazing and don't take any unnecessary risks. Understand?"

"Oh, absolutely. You want me to go in with my guns blazing and take every risk in the world." Lane saluted him. "Mission understood, boss." He slammed the door and headed for the rental company.

The guy was such a prick.

But...with the right training, he would also be one fine Ice Breaker. After all, it did take considerable talent in order to break out of a maximum-security facility. Not everyone had that skill set.

Lane Lawson showed definite promise. Provided he could stop being such a major pain in Memphis's ass.

***

An hour and a half later, Midas pulled onto a long, winding drive. Alina leaned forward to get a better view of the house up ahead. Perched on a hill, the windows in the two-story structure gleamed in the waning light. When they'd turned on the drive, she'd noticed the security cameras perched discretely.

As they neared the house, she caught sight of more cameras. Small, white, positioned on both the lower and upper levels of the house.

The ride had been tense. Uneasy. She and Midas hadn't talked about what happened in the bedroom. What had *almost* happened? He'd been too intent on getting her to Kiera.

As for Alina, she'd been trying to figure out just what she should say to the woman who might be a victim of the same kidnappers.

Midas drew the vehicle—a jeep they'd taken from the safe house's big garage—to a stop. But as soon as he did, a man with a shaved head and a big, leather jacket immediately approached the vehicle. His hand went to the side of his coat where a bulge pushed out the leather.

Midas lowered the driver's side window. "Easy," Midas told him. "We are just here to talk with Kiera."

"Ms. Kiera doesn't want to talk with anyone," the guy threw back. His voice was low, grating. "You're on private property, and you need to get the hell out of here, now." His gaze slid to Alina. Then went right back to Midas.

"She wants to see us," Midas assured the other man. He sounded so confident that Alina almost believed him. "If you send us away, she'll be very upset with you."

"Ms. Kiera doesn't want to see *anyone*. That's why I guard the door."

Alina thought the man made an excellent point. "Uh, Midas..."

He remained focused on the guard. "Tell her that Alina Bellamy is out front. Take out your phone. Call inside. Tell Kiera. Tell her that Alina Bellamy was abducted last night and that her two abductors are dead."

The man hesitated. His blue gaze swung back to Alina.

"Tell her," Midas repeated. "And if she says for you to kick us off the property, then I will turn right around without you needing to pull out that gun that you have strapped beneath your coat."

She'd feared the man might have a weapon.

But he was pulling out his phone. Making a phone call and... "Bowie? Got two people out here who say that Ms. Kiera wants to see them." The black spiderweb tattoo on the back of his hand flexed. "Woman says she was abducted last night. Her name is—" He squinted at Alina. "Who the hell are you again?"

"Alina Bellamy," Midas said softly.

"Alina B—" He stopped. "Yeah, yeah, okay. I'll send them in." He shoved the phone back into his pocket. "You can go in. Bowie said Ms. Kiera will see you."

"Is Bowie another bodyguard?" Alina asked.

The man's head jerked in agreement.

Midas killed the engine, and they exited the ride, but before they could approach the house, the man with the spiderweb tats—tats that Alina had noticed covered the backs of both his hands—had moved into their path. "Got to pat you down first. No one gets near her without being cleared by me."

Midas lifted his hands. "You certainly take security very seriously here."

The man started patting him down. And he pulled out a knife—two knives—that Midas had been carrying. One had been under Midas's shirt, hooked onto his belt. Another had been in a sheath around his ankle.

The man also took Midas's phone. Then he turned to Alina.

"Keep the hands only where they need to be," Midas warned him. "And we won't have a problem."

Grunting, the guy patted her down. Quickly. Impersonally. Then he took her phone. "Can't have phones inside. Ms. Kiera doesn't want anyone recording her."

Alina peered at the double doors that led into the house.

"Nice tats," she heard Midas say.

"Thanks."

"Where'd you get them?"

The man didn't answer. One of the double doors had opened. A dark-haired male in a black t-shirt and jeans stood in the doorway. Muscled, but not close to Midas's scale. Sharp eyes. Hard jaw. His assessing stare swept over them both. "You checked them for weapons, Ray?"

"Yeah, they're clear. Now."

He nodded and waved them inside. "You have ten minutes."

CHAPTER FIFTEEN

Alina went in first, with Midas at her heels.

"I'm Bowie, one of Kiera's bodyguards." He shut the door behind them. Locked it. Then briefly looked at his watch. "She can't be stressed. Do *not* stress her, understand? Answer her questions, then get the hell out."

"The friendly welcome is overwhelming. You're a ray of sunshine," Midas returned.

"No, Midas, I'm not." the man said, surprising her because Midas had not given his name to anyone. But, clearly, this guy recognized him. "I'm just a bodyguard, same as you, trying to protect my client."

Midas raised his brows. "You know me? Should I be flattered?"

Bowie hurried into the den. "You should be faster. Time is ticking." Then he looked over his shoulder. "And after the news story I saw this morning—with you featured prominently as both hero and potential killer—I think everyone is going to know your face soon."

"Good to know."

Alina ignored the men and focused on the woman she'd just seen in the den. Thin, fragile, with hair that hung limply around her shoulders. She sat on the edge of the couch with her feet firmly planted on the floor, but her hands moved nervously on her lap.

The bodyguard—Bowie—moved to stand near the fireplace. His body remained alert. Watchful.

Kiera looked up at Alina. "I saw you on TV." Her voice was...hoarse. Careful.

Alina moved closer to her.

Kiera tensed. "I don't...please, just sit in the chair." She pointed to the chair across from her. "I don't like being close to people."

Alina glanced around the den. She noticed that every light was on and all the curtains were drawn back to let in a maximum amount of illumination. *You don't like the dark either, do you?*

Alina took the indicated seat. Midas stood beside her. Stood, even though there were plenty of other seats. She could feel the tension rolling off him.

Kiera licked her lips. "You were...abducted."

"Yes." Alina's spine was straight. "Two men broke into my bedroom." She lifted her hands. Pushed back the sleeves of her blouse and revealed the bandages still around her wrists. "They zip-tied my hands behind my back. Zip-tied my ankles, too. They put me in an SUV and took me to a cabin in the middle of nowhere."

Kiera swallowed.

"They locked me in a closet. One of the men threatened me with a knife. He put it to my cheek and said if I wasn't good, he'd slice me."

A growl rumbled from Midas.

Alina stretched out her hand. Caught his fingers. Squeezed. Then let go.

Bowie watched them all with a hard gaze.

And Alina...her stare tracked to the thin scar on Kiera's right cheek.

"I screamed too loudly," Kiera murmured. "But I learned from my mistake. After the first cut, I didn't make another sound."

Oh, God. "I'm sorry," Alina told her, and she meant those words. Pain seemed to pour off the woman before her. "So very sorry for everything that happened to you."

Kiera tilted her head to the right. "How did you get away?"

"Midas." Her attention darted to him, then back to Kiera. "He followed me. Got me out."

"And killed the men who took you," Kiera finished.

Alina shook her head.

"No," Midas responded, but his voice was low. Careful. "I left them subdued. Someone came to the cabin after we left. Their boss."

Kiera flinched.

That flinch had been very, very telling. "You know about the boss, don't you?" Alina asked her.

Once more, Kiera wet her lips. Her trembling hands tugged on the sleeves of her blouse. But the edge of the right sleeve had ridden up a bit.

Red lines. Scars?

Deeper than the marks on Alina's wrists. *Because she had the zip ties on longer? Because she fought longer?* There had been no Midas to rush to Kiera's rescue. Alina wanted to get up and go hug the other woman.

But Kiera didn't want to be touched. Not that Alina blamed her.

"They said he was coming," Alina added. She shuddered.

"Did you see the boss?" Midas continued to use his careful voice. One that wasn't exactly soft. Alina didn't think his voice could ever be called soft. But it was oddly gentle.

A tear slid down Kiera's cheek. "The men who took you—what did they look like? The news didn't show photos."

"One had red hair."

Another flinch from Kiera. "I could...see his hair. Poking out from beneath the black cap he wore." Her right hand rose to touch her head. "Ski cap. Ski mask, too. He seemed...kinder than the other one. He tried to stop his partner from cutting me."

"I've learned that you were missing for three days." Midas shifted his position slightly.

Bowie stiffened. "Who the hell told you that?"

Midas didn't glance his way. "Where were you during that time?"

"In the closet. It was so dark." She looked around. "Bowie keeps the lights on for me."

Bowie's lips thinned. "Yeah, I do."

Kiera exhaled slowly. "I'm glad they are dead." She focused back on Alina. "Is that wrong?" She shook her head. "Don't answer."

Alina leaned forward. Right or wrong, this nightmare wasn't over yet. "The boss is still out there."

A shudder shook Kiera's slender form.

"He was coming that very night to see me," Alina told the other woman. "Is that what he did with you, too? Came the first night that you were taken?"

Kiera's body rocked forward, then back.

A low whistle escaped Midas. "You saw him, didn't you?"

"Mask," Kiera bit out. Her eyes squeezed shut. "Always wore a mask." Her hands went to her throat. "So easy to snap."

Horror roared through Alina. She knew the boss had threatened to break Kiera's neck. Maybe he'd put his hands on her throat. Had teased her with the pain he could give.

Kiera's hand trailed down her chest. Rested over her heart. "Just a nick."

Oh, God. "Do you have more scars, Kiera?"

Her eyes opened. "I think he liked hurting me. But my father paid the money. Sent it to the offshore account just like he was ordered to do. The boss said it wasn't enough vengeance, but it was a start. He said—"

"Time's up," Bowie announced.

"Screw that," Midas fired right back. "Kiera is talking to us. She wants to help us." He took a step forward. "Don't you, Kiera?"

Kiera jumped to her feet.

"Tell us everything you remember about the boss," Midas told her. "We'll find him. We'll stop him. Then you won't need to be afraid any longer. You won't have to keep every light on because he will never come for you again."

So Midas had noticed the lights, too.

Kiera's head moved in a fast nod. "I-I want him stopped. I want—"

"There are two of them, Midas," Bowie said suddenly as his voice cracked like a whip. "You can't protect them both. Alina or Kiera. You have to choose. Bet I know who you'll pick."

Alina's stunned stare flew to him. Bowie had pulled a gun from behind his body. He had it aimed at Alina. He smiled at her.

"What the hell are you doing?" Midas thundered.

"My job." Bowie swung his hand a bit, and the gun pointed at a frozen Kiera. "You should have just stayed silent. But you got brave when you heard her story, didn't you?" Then he swung the gun back to Alina. "Two women. Honestly, I think I can take them both out before you can get to me, Midas. I am that fast. Good thing I made sure you didn't have any weapons before coming inside, huh, hero?"

He was going to shoot her. Alina knew it. The man who should have been protecting Kiera was about to pull the trigger. He'd shoot her, then Kiera. Then...*Midas?* He was going to kill them all. "Why?" Alina asked.

"Because the dead don't talk. Don't worry, the cops will think it was Midas. That's what I'll tell them." The gun swung between Alina and Kiera. And—

Came back to Kiera. Then Alina.

The gun swung back and forth like a twisted game of *eeny-meeny-miny—*

She opened her mouth to scream but the gun blasted. Even as it blasted, Midas had slammed her to the floor. But the bullet hadn't come tearing toward her. Alina's head turned.

Kiera had also hit the floor. Blood covered her chest. Her eyes were wide open. Shocked. Her lips parted. "Help..."

The front door flew open. "Ms. Kiera!" The other bodyguard—Ray—ran forward. He came to a dead stop as he gaped at the sight of a bleeding Kiera. "Ms. Kiera...?"

Midas leapt off Alina. He threw his body at Bowie. Alina scrambled up as she watched them. Bowie turned at the last moment, and he brought up his gun. She knew he intended to fire it at Midas. "No!" Alina screamed.

Midas caught the man's hand—the hand that gripped the gun. Midas yanked Bowie closer.

Boom.

Who'd been hit? "Midas!" she screamed.

Midas rammed his head into Bowie's. A brutal headbutt that had the other man stumbling back. And when Bowie stumbled back, she saw the blood on his shirt.

He'd been hit. Not Midas. And Midas had just wrenched the gun out of Bowie's hand. Her breath shuddered out.

"Shoot him!" Bowie roared as he clutched his bleeding stomach. "He hurt Kiera! Shoot him, Ray! Now!"

Ray had yanked a gun from the holster at his side. The webs on his hands twisted and quaked as he lifted the weapon and aimed it at Midas.

"No!" Alina yelled. She rushed at Ray. "It's not him! Midas doesn't even have a gun—you searched him yourself! *It's not him!*" She plowed into Ray.

He shook her off, or tried to, but Alina hung on tenaciously. She could not let him hurt Midas. Midas hadn't done anything to Kiera.

Ray brought the gun up and pointed it straight at Alina.

She stopped breathing.

"I don't want to hurt you," he mumbled. The weapon shook in his grasp. "So you get back, lady. Right now."

A fist slammed into the side of Ray's face. The blow had Ray staggering back as Alina leapt away.

"Damn straight you don't want to hurt her," Midas snarled. "Because then I'd hurt you extra bad."

Ray tried to bring up his gun, but Midas delivered another punch, then a kick to the guy's midsection. Ray stumbled. The next kick from Midas sent the gun flying from Ray's hand.

"I am *not* the bad guy here," Midas blasted. "Jesus! Stop trying to shoot at me!"

Her gaze whipped behind him. Bowie had slumped on the floor. Blood soaked the middle of his shirt. But as she watched, he heaved himself up and began to reach toward his ankle.

Midas had kept a knife stored in the sheath attached to his ankle. Bowie must have a backup weapon hidden near his ankle, too. "Midas!" Alina yelled her warning. There wasn't time to get to Bowie. Midas was between her and the attacker.

Midas whipped around. But he didn't turn toward Bowie. He'd turned toward Alina.

She saw Bowie straighten and bring up a gun. Point it at her. No, no, at Midas because Midas had just stepped to the side and now blocked her completely with his body. A shield between her and everyone else. And—

The window to the right of the couch shattered. "Freeze!" A woman's yell as her body came hurtling into the den. Glass flew everywhere. Smashed into the floor. Ricocheted up and one piece sliced Alina across the back of her hand.

The woman landed in a crouch with her dark hair a curtain around her head.

Bowie had turned instinctively at her arrival, and because he was closer to the window, more chunks of glass hit him. He swung his gun around and pointed it at her. "Who the fuck are you?"

Her head lifted. "The place is surrounded. Cops have you locked in from every direction. Drop the weapon, right now, and you might get to live and see another day." She rose. One hand went behind her back. Shards of broken glass rained down her body and over the all-black outfit that she wore.

Midas crept toward Bowie.

Ray let out a long groan and slowly sat up. He seemed to realize that all was not as he'd originally thought. "Ms. Kiera..." He crawled toward her.

Kiera choked and blood slid from the corner of her mouth.

Bowie swung around, and his weapon slid over everyone as he seemed to realize that he'd screwed up. If the cops were outside, he couldn't escape.

"No one is gonna believe the story that *I* hurt Kiera," Midas said. "Not now. There is no escape for you. The cops will take you into custody. They'll make you tell them about your boss."

Ray crouched over Kiera. His hands pressed to her chest. Blood covered his fingers. His head tilted back, and he gazed at Bowie in horror. "What did you do?"

"What I was paid to do."

"You shouldn't have," Ray cried back. "Not her. *Not her.*"

Bowie's left hand clutched his blood-drenched stomach. His breath heaved in and out, and he weaved on his feet. He swallowed. "Fuck me. At least...going out with a bang." And his shaking weapon landed on Midas. "Your father says hi—"

Lane Lawson ran through the open front door. "What in the hell is happening?"

Boom.

A bullet tore into Bowie, and he jerked backward. His shoulders hit the wall behind him. His eyes widened.

And he fell to the floor.

CHAPTER SIXTEEN

Darkness waited outside the window of the private plane. They were cruising, the pilot had things completely under control, and Midas wanted to rip the world apart.

Your father says hi.

The last words spoken by Bowie Dodge.

Because after those words, Ray had fired a shot that hit Bowie in the head. Lane's sudden appearance had caught Bowie off guard. In that instant of confusion, Ray had pulled out his backup weapon—didn't everyone have a freaking backup?—and blasted at Bowie even as Ray's other hand had pressed to Kiera's chest in an effort to stop the blood flow.

He'd fired four times. The first bullet had connected with Bowie. The other three had thudded into the wall. Midas had grabbed Alina and covered her until the bullets stopped firing.

"Are you going to say anything?" Alina sat across from him. Deep, dark eyes. Nervous hands that gripped the armrests.

"You shouldn't be here." That was saying plenty.

"Yes, I got that you wanted to leave me behind with Memphis and Lane. And their mysterious partner."

Their partner—that would have been the woman who came hurtling through the window. She'd said that she needed to cause a distraction. That she'd realized what was happening inside because she'd been watching them. She'd been the pair of "eyes" that Memphis had mentioned before.

Ophelia. Ophelia Raine. She'd gone to the hospital with Kiera. For the moment, Kiera was still alive. Midas hoped like hell that she would stay that way.

In the meantime, he had an appointment to keep.

"I thought you'd said that where I go, you'd go," Alina continued in her careful, subdued voice. "But you were trying to ditch me at the first opportunity. That's hardly the way to keep a close watch on your charge."

He swallowed. "I don't want you anywhere around my father." And that was where he was headed. Like there was a choice. His father was involved in this mess, no doubt about it, and the bastard was only going to talk if Midas sat down in the same room with him.

"I don't want you facing him alone."

His gaze locked on her.

She sent him a weak, half-smile. "You keep saving me. I'd like the chance to help you."

He shouldn't have let her get on the plane. But he hadn't been able to just walk away from her, either. Local cops and Feds had swarmed the scene at Kiera Thatch's home. Everything was in serious screwed-to-hell-and-back mode, and Midas had needed to pull in every favor he had in order to smooth things over with the authorities.

Terrance had helped him out. The DA had spoken to the right people and convinced them that Midas had to get on a flight to North Dakota, STAT.

So here he was. And Alina sat right across from him.

He wanted to reach out and touch her, but it felt like the closer and closer he got to his father, the darker and more dangerous he became. "Memphis would have protected you while I was gone."

Her lips pressed together. She nodded. "But he isn't you." She unhooked her seatbelt. Eased from the seat.

Midas shook his head. "Don't come closer." A stark warning. She did not get what was happening to him.

Bowie could have shot her. Could have killed her right in front of me.

Completely ignoring his order, she slid into the seat beside Midas. Her hand reached out and curled around his. For a moment, he just looked at their hands. The drumming of his heartbeat seemed extra loud in his ears. "I didn't think I could save you." He'd been too afraid that Bowie would fire right at her.

Midas had launched at her, just wanting to get between Alina and the bullet. Then the bullet had flown at Kiera instead of hitting Alina.

"I was worried about saving you, too."

Her words had his gaze lifting.

"When he came into the house, Ray didn't understand who'd hurt Kiera. He had his weapon aimed at you."

Another moment burned into his memory. Midas's hand slid from beneath hers, and he gripped her chin. "You could have been killed." She never needed to risk herself for him. "I'm the bodyguard, not you."

"Someone has to protect the bodyguard."

Not you.

"Besides, I think I'm safer with you than I could ever be with anyone else."

"Don't be too sure about that." Low. The way he felt, she wasn't safe at all.

Her lashes fluttered. "But I am sure. All you do is protect me."

Adrenaline rode him. So did fury. His freak of a father was pulling him back into his dark web, and there was nothing that Midas could do about it. *I have to see him.* The Feds wanted him to meet with his father. The DA wanted him talking to the bastard. The victims' families—they all wanted Midas in a room with his father.

And his dear old sadistic dad wanted it, too.

As for what Midas wanted? He was looking at her. "I'm not good for you."

"I think I can make my own decisions about that."

She'd insisted on staying with him, even when Memphis and Lane had offered protection. They'd vowed to secure her in the safe house. She'd ignored them, packed a small overnight bag, and gone with Midas.

They'd be staying in a hotel room together when they touched down.

Not too long until their descent.

The darkness seemed to pull harder at him. "I'm not…I'm trying to warn you."

"I got that. You don't need to warn me, though. I understand that your father has done terrible things."

A rough bark of laughter escaped him. "Sweetheart, my father is the devil incarnate." His father would *not* see her. On this point, Midas was adamant. "He loves giving pain. He's as sadistic as they come, but the man is also a freaking genius when it comes to manipulation. He plays long games when other people don't even realize they are on his board. Every word he says is a deception. All he wants to do is hurt and leave hell in his wake."

Sympathy showed on her face. "And you grew up with him."

He didn't want her sympathy or her pity or even her understanding. Not then. He was too raw and wild. *Closer and closer to hell. That's where we are flying. Closer and closer…* "I grew up with him," he said, jerking his head in a nod. "He wanted me to be just like him."

"But you're not."

Don't be too sure.

"You protect people. He hurts them. You're the exact opposite of what he is."

"I planned to kill Bowie Dodge. The instant he pulled that gun and threatened you, I wanted him dead. But I wanted to get answers from him first. He could have told us more." He released her chin. "Ray just beat me to the shot. I would have killed Bowie. Other people would balk at the idea of ending someone's life. I don't feel that hesitation." Truth be told, he wasn't always sure that he *felt* things the way normal people did.

He was good at pretending. At making jokes. Smiling like the world was some grand theme park ride. But the truth was that so much of what he did was only on the surface. When you peeled back the surface...

Show them what you want the world to see, boy. We're big and strong, and people will be afraid because of our size. If they think we're too dangerous, we'll never get close. So you have to smile. You have to charm. You have to get beneath their guards. That way, they can forget you're a threat. They'll think you're just like them.

But we aren't. We will never be like everyone else.

Her cream scent teased him. Greedily, he drank it in even as he said, "You should get back in your seat."

"You were only doing what was necessary to protect me. You are *not* your father."

"Why do you think I'm in the bodyguard business?"

"Because you're good at protecting people."

A negative shake of his head. "No, sweetheart. It's because I'm good at violence. Good at figuring out the threats because I know how to think like a predator. And when the threats do come, I enjoy fighting back." *I like it too much.*

A determined shake of her head. "You're not going to scare me into thinking you're some kind of monster, Midas."

"You need to get back in your seat."

"Why? What is so wrong with me being close—"

"My control is shredding with every second that passes. Violence leaves a mark on me. Adrenaline. Fury. I told you before that I knew all about the rush that comes in the aftermath. My blood is practically burning, and I want you."

She swallowed.

"I want to fuck you right here in this plane seat, and I don't really give a shit that the pilot will be able to hear every sound you make."

Another swallow. Her eyes had seemed to get bigger with every word he spoke.

"I want to sink into you again and again and I don't give a shit," he said again, deliberately crass, "that it will be your first time. I want to be rough and hard. I just want to take and take until nothing else exists but you." Because...

Because she pulled him from the darkness.

Only he didn't say that part.

"You're a virgin, and you are not ready for what I want from you. *So get back in your seat.* When we land, it would be...wise not to touch me." Talk about an understatement. "I'll sleep on the floor at the hotel room." Because getting a second room wasn't an option. He had to stay close to her. Bad enough that he'd brought her on the plane, but...

I want her where I can see her. Yes, I trust Memphis but... He doesn't understand how important she is. Doesn't get that nothing matters but her safety. Yes, Memphis would watch her but...

Midas would take a bullet to protect her. He'd rip the world apart to shield her.

He'd kill his own father to keep her safe.

No, he did *not* have his customary control. In fact, he was as out of control as he'd ever been.

Alina turned her head and looked at the seat across from him. Then, without a word, she got up and returned to that seat. Put her seatbelt back into place.

He sucked in a deep breath. Her scent lingered around him and maybe he drank it up like the thirsty bastard he was.

"I don't want the pilot overhearing." Her cheeks pinkened. "And I'm not too sure how we could work out the logistics in the plane seat, anyway. You're pretty much too big for the seat as it is."

It was Midas's turn to clasp the handrests in a death grip.

Her dark gaze held him captive. "But when the plane lands and we are alone, I will most definitely touch you. I certainly hope that you will touch me, too. Everywhere. Because I feel that adrenaline rush again. My emotions feel out of control. My body is aching. And I just want you." Her shoulders squared. "You need to finish what you started before, Midas."

"Alina..." She could not be saying this to him. *Pushing me closer to the edge.*

"I want you to be my first. I told you that. You're not going to scare me away by saying how big, bad, and dangerous you are."

That wasn't what he'd been doing. Was it?

"I want your mouth on me."

His grip tightened even more on the handrests. He was about to shatter them.

"I want your hands on me. I want your fingers stroking my breasts, and I want them dipping into my body."

Yeah, he'd rip the handrests apart in about five seconds.

"I want you naked. I want you thrusting into me until I can't feel anything else but pleasure. Until *you* can't feel anything else but the pleasure we give each other."

His dick shoved hard against the front of his jeans. *In her. I want in her.*

One time fucking her wouldn't be enough. He'd want her over and over again. *She can't handle what I need. It's her first time. She can't handle me.*

"I want your dick in my mouth."

He lunged out of his seat. Caught himself right before he pounced. He towered over her, and Alina tilted back her head to stare up at him.

His hands flew down and curled around the top of her seat. "Be...careful." Guttural.

"Why? I've been careful my whole life. Know what it's gotten me? A lonely bed. An aching body. Practice after practice session on the ice and so much loneliness."

"So I'm a cure for your loneliness?" Was that all he was?

"No." Her hair slid over her shoulder. "You're pretty much everything I've ever wanted, and I didn't know it until I met you."

Fuck. Fuck. Fuck.

"I want you to touch me, Midas. I want you to fuck me. And when we land, be assured that I *will* be touching you. That is, unless you say that you just don't want me." Her gaze swept over his body. Dropped to the dick that saluted her. Alina's tongue snaked over her lips. "I don't think that's the case." Her stare rose. "Do you?"

"Baby, I love it when you talk dirty." His head lowered over hers. "I'll want you as long as I have breath in my body."

"So that's a yes?"

His mouth crashed onto hers. His tongue dipped past her lips so that he could take all the sweetness that he craved. It wasn't just a yes. It was a *hell yes*.

Her hands pressed to his chest. Singed him through the clothes. He wanted to haul her out of the seat and introduce her to the mile high club right then and there. He could hold her against him and thrust all the way into her and she could come around him and they could both ignore the rest of the world.

Nothing else would matter.

Nothing...

The pilot made an announcement. The words didn't even register at first because Midas was too lost in Alina.

Then the pilot spoke again, and Midas heard him say they were preparing for landing.

He needed to get his ass back in his seat.

He needed to get his mouth off Alina. For now.

Slowly, he did. He pulled away. Retreated back to his seat. Buckled the belt. But his gaze stayed on her. Every second. And he said, "You're mine."

Because he'd given her a chance. He'd tried to do one final, good thing.

But the plane was landing.

The darkness was calling.

It was almost time for her to see who he really was.

***

It was the nicest hotel in town. The one with the best security. Which, unfortunately, wasn't saying much. But the DA had made sure that uniform cops were stationed downstairs. One of Midas's conditions for coming to the meeting. Once he'd realized that Alina wasn't going to be dissuaded from accompanying him, he'd taken steps to ensure her safety.

But who will protect her from me?

He shut the door to their room. Made sure to secure all the locks. He dropped their bags near his feet. Alina had already walked toward the bed. Bed as in singular. One big, king bed. He wondered if this might be the point where she'd lose her nerve. Maybe the adrenaline had worn off for her, and she'd crash.

It hadn't worn off for him. Desire still held him on a knife's edge of savage need. He wanted to strip her clothes off, throw her on the bed, and devour her.

Right, because *that* was how you handled a woman's first time.

But, unfortunately, he didn't have a whole lot of care left in him. His control was razor thin. He hated this town. Hated facing his past.

Hated what he feared lurked deep inside of himself.

What if I'm more like him than I want to be?

Alina had hit too close to an uncomfortable truth on the plane. She'd said that Midas's father killed while Midas protected. Midas had gotten into the bodyguard business because he wanted to be the opposite of his father. But what she didn't get was that he needed an outlet for the violence that breathed in him.

When you were the biggest one in the room, other people were always looking to prove something. They wanted to go against you. To challenge you. To take you down. He'd been fighting since he was thirteen years old.

It was his life.

Alina turned toward him. She hadn't touched him, not yet. Not when they'd disembarked from the plane or when they'd walked through the quiet airport. The car ride over to the hotel had been completed in silence. Tension had churned in the air between them.

Perhaps she'd changed her mind about him. About them.

Alina's hands went to the hem of her shirt. She pulled the blouse over her head and dropped it to the floor.

So, ah, she hadn't changed her mind.

She kicked away her shoes. Did a little hop and ditched her socks. He watched her pull in a deep breath, then she stripped off her jeans. She was left in her underwear.

Take them off, sweetheart.

She didn't.

"It's awkward for me." She gestured between them. "When you have on all your clothes, and I'm naked."

Oh, he could fix that. He tore off his shirt. Discarded his shoes. Stripped completely in about three seconds flat.

"Oh." Soft. "That was fast." Her gaze slid over him. First his shoulders. Then his chest. Down his abs.

Then to the dick that bobbed eagerly toward her. "Less awkward?" he asked.

A quick nod. She stripped out of her underwear. Her tight nipples thrust toward him. She still hadn't touched him. Yet as he drank her in, Alina began walking toward him. Her steps were hesitant, but her chin was up. She didn't stop until she was right in front of him. Then her hands reached out. She touched his chest. Feather-light. Her fingers skimmed over his heart. She teased his nipples.

Oh, sweetheart, be careful. He was not in the mood to play.

Then her fingers moved down. He could feel the tremble in them, but Alina didn't stop even though she was clearly nervous. Her silken fingers curled around his cock.

His breath hissed out.

"Tell me what you like. What I do right. What I do wrong. I want this to feel good for you."

His eyes were about to roll back into his head because it already felt good. She stroked him and pumped him and when she began to ease down in front of him... "*Alina.*"

"I've never done this before. Hope I don't mess up."

Mess up? *Mess. Up?* It was pretty much impossible for her to mess this up. He wanted her like hell burning around him, and she was putting her mouth on his dick. Her beautiful, slick mouth. Sucking him in. Licking him. His hands clamped around her shoulders even as his hips pushed toward her mouth.

Her lips parted more.

Alina, bent before him. His dick in her mouth.

A growl tore from him. He hauled her into his arms. Held her easily. Four steps and they were at the bed. He dropped her. She bounced a little and before she could sit up, he was on her. He'd shoved her legs apart. Put his mouth on *her*. He needed her wet and ready. Right then.

Control is shredding. Her mouth on me. Alina taking me...

His tongue swirled over her clit. His fingers parted her. Stretched her. Thrust in and out even as he kept licking with a furious intensity because he wanted her on the brink of release. She tensed and shuddered and rocked against him, and he knew she was close.

Not close enough.

His mouth became even more demanding as he lapped her up. Her taste was insane, and it just drove his hunger on more. His fingers were in her, she rode them, called his name and—

Right there. I feel you, baby. Now feel me.

He put his dick at her core and pushed. The head slipped in, and she cried out his name.

She also started coming. Her body arched and her hips slammed greedily against him. There was a quick moment of resistance, her body pushed back against him and she let out a startled cry, then he was inside.

All the way inside. Her inner muscles clamped around him. So tight that he knew he'd lose his mind at any moment. Nothing had ever felt this good. This hot.

But she'd gone still beneath him. No more cries of pleasure. No more shudders of need.

His hands slammed into the mattress on either side of her. Midas levered himself up. All he wanted to do was withdraw and thrust deep. Withdraw. Thrust. Rock the bed. Drive it into the wall as he plowed into her.

But she'd frozen on him.

Not happening.

"Does it hurt?" Midas swept his gaze over her face.

The lights were on. He'd left them all on for her, deliberately. Alina wasn't going to be in the dark.

Her lashes fluttered as the eyes she'd squeezed closed opened. "You're really big."

"Aw, sweetheart, thanks for noticing."

A laugh sputtered from her, and the instinctive movement of her body had her hips squirming against him.

Fuck, baby, you have no idea how close to the edge I am. But he was holding on by the tips of his fingernails for her. She mattered.

"Give me...a second?"

He'd do better. He'd give her an orgasm. His hand worked between their bodies. Went back to her clit, and he began to stroke her. Slowly at first. Carefully. Then faster, harder.

Her breath quickened.

Her hips dipped.

He held his cock perfectly still even as sweat slickened his shoulders. Her hips arched and angled. She rode him as she dipped and twisted, and his hand kept working her over and over.

He didn't withdraw. Didn't thrust.

Not until he felt the telltale quiver of her inner muscles around him. When the orgasm hit her, Alina tipped back her head as a long moan broke from her.

He was done. The last of his control obliterated as she came around him. The contractions of her hot core were too much for him. He withdrew and thrust. Withdrew. Thrust.

Wanted more. Deeper.

He rolled with her. Stopped when she straddled him and her hands splayed over his chest. His hands clamped around her waist as he lifted her up and down. Her breasts bobbed. So freaking sexy. Up and down. Faster and harder and she quivered around him. Her hips ground against his because there was no hesitation any longer. Only eagerness from her. Driving fury from him. His hips pistoned against her faster and faster.

Deeper.

"*Midas!*"

He emptied inside of her on the strongest climax of his life.

***

The warm water from the shower poured down on Alina. She couldn't seem to stop quivering. Every part of her body felt far too sensitive and aware.

And she swore that she could still feel Midas inside of her.

"There room for me?" Midas's deep, gravelly voice came from behind her.

She whipped around and saw him through the glass door of the shower. Technically, given his dimensions, no, there probably wasn't enough room for them both because the shower was so small, but her head dipped in a nod. She inched back more beneath the spray of the shower.

Naked, muscles flexing, he climbed in with her.

"Did I hurt you?" The water poured over him. Made those muscles gleam and tempt. He reached for the soap. Washed fast and thoroughly. Even cleaned his dick.

"Alina?"

She'd been watching the show. She'd had his cock in her mouth. And that cock had driven deep into her sex. *Still feel him.*

"Did I hurt you?" he repeated gruffly.

"Only briefly. Not like it could have been avoided."

He grunted. And then his soapy fingers were sliding between her thighs. She jerked back, but there was nowhere to go.

"Easy. Just want to make sure you're okay."

She was okay. No, okay wasn't the word. Alina didn't know what she was. She'd had three orgasms. At least, she thought she'd had three. They'd all sort of blurred together. And she should not want him again already.

But she did.

Or maybe she'd never stopped wanting him.

Her legs parted. His soapy fingers slid along her folds. Stroking carefully while his sharp gaze never left her face. She bit her lip to hold back a moan. Alina rose onto her tiptoes, and her hands flew out. One braced on the tiled wall beside her. The other hit the shower door. Steam drifted around her.

"I could eat you up," he told her. His voice was rough and possessive and sent need churning through her.

Was it normal to need him again so soon? Her sex pushed down against his fingers because she wanted so much more. He teased her clit. She jolted. Her hand slid down the shower door. Her head tipped back, and he just leaned forward and put his mouth on her neck. She loved it when he kissed her in just that spot. Right over her racing pulse.

"You feel so good, sweetheart. You gonna come for me again?"

Her eyes opened. His head had lifted, and he looked down at her with stark lines of need carved into his expression. She barely recognized her own voice when she dared, "Make me."

His pupils flared. In a flash, he'd spun her around so that she faced the glass shower door. It was a tight fit, but he'd maneuvered behind her. His hands cupped her breasts. Teased her nipples. Pinched lightly.

Her mouth opened wide in a moan.

His right hand dropped down her body. Went between her legs. No soft stroking this time. His fingers thrust into her. His thumb raked over her clit. Once. Twice. She squirmed because she wanted more, *more,* and that was when his hands both jerked away—only to immediately lock around her hips.

He lifted her up against him.

Her fingers slid over the glass door. Steam had covered it, and her hands left streaks on the glass.

His cock shoved against her ass, then he lifted her higher, and the broad head probed at her sex. He pushed into her. *Slammed deep.*

And his right hand moved again. Went to the front of her body. His left hand held her pinned against him as he caged her so easily between his body and the hard shower door. She should have been afraid of his easy strength. She wasn't. He was pinching and stroking and rubbing her clit. Pounding into her from behind. His mouth was on her neck. Licking. Lightly biting.

He had complete and total control over her and when the orgasm hit her, when he made her come, she could do nothing but cry out for him.

The pleasure was so intense that the whole world seemed to spin around her.

He came inside of her. She felt the powerful, hot jets, and it just made her pleasure hotter. Stronger. His hand flexed along her hip as he kept her imprisoned against him. He jerked behind her. And she thought his heavy cock would go down. That he'd slide out of her.

But he didn't.

Or, if his cock did soften, it thickened again almost immediately. Because when she shifted just a little, Alina realized she felt stretched. Filled.

Owned.

"What are you doing to me?" she whispered. The steam-covered glass was in front of her. She couldn't see beyond the foggy surface any longer.

"Destroying you for anyone else."

She felt pretty destroyed. Every muscle had gone limp.

He wasn't limp.

He kissed her neck. "That's sure as hell what you're doing to me."

He started thrusting again.

CHAPTER SEVENTEEN

He would not fuck her again.

Midas had, unfortunately, been telling himself that same thing for the last ten minutes while he watched Alina sleep peacefully beside him. She looked like some fairytale princess.

He felt like a freaking stalker.

A freaking horny stalker.

He'd made love to her over and over during the night. Something he should not have done. She had to be sore. He should have stopped.

But he'd never wanted anyone so badly. And as the dawn grew closer, his need for her had seemed to intensify.

Then she'd drifted to sleep. In his arms. Like she trusted him completely. The damn thing was, he'd slept, too. He'd pulled her onto his chest, locked one arm around her back, and held on.

When he'd woken, she'd been at his side. The sheet had been around her waist. One perfect nipple peeked at him, and his hungry dick stood at full attention.

He would not fuck her again.

She'd be too tender. She deserved more care.

The fury and the fear he'd felt after the scene at Kiera's had banked, for the time being. He could still hear the blast of the gunshots in his mind. When Bowie had first started swinging that gun around, Midas hadn't been sure that he'd be able to get to Alina in time. He couldn't remember ever being that afraid.

Not even when he'd been set up for murder.

Her lashes fluttered open. There was no dazed confusion in her eyes. Most people were confused or uncertain when they woke. But Alina just stared straight at him and smiled. "Good morning."

Oh, sweetheart, do not smile at me that way. Her high-voltage smile. The one that always seemed to pierce right through him.

"What are you doing?" Her hand slid over his chest.

"Trying not to fuck you."

Her hand froze.

Maybe he shouldn't have been so honest.

"Why?"

Not the response he'd expected from her. The sheet covered her thighs. Her sex. His hand moved down and caressed her lightly through the sheet. "Because I don't want to hurt you more."

"You didn't hurt me."

"Liar," he called. His fingers stretched a little. He liked touching her. Loved making her come. Could do it endlessly.

You have to get to the penitentiary.

His touch became a little rougher.

He caught himself. Stopped. His hand yanked back. Midas rolled toward the edge of the bed. He sat up and his long legs eased down as his feet touched the floor.

"Fine. You hurt me a little bit. I'm pretty sure that's to be expected." The bedsprings squeaked. Her hands curled around his shoulders before he could rise from the bed. "But the pleasure was more than worth any pain." She pressed a kiss to the curve of his shoulder.

Lust surged through him. White-hot. Electrifying.

"I love it when you kiss my neck," she added. Her breath feathered over him as she kissed him softly. "Do you enjoy it when I do the same to you?"

Enjoy wasn't the right word.

Her tongue slid over him. Her teeth scored him in a careful bite. His eyes closed.

The darkness pulled at him. Tempted him to slide down into the shadows that waited. But Alina kissed his neck once more. Her mouth was so soft and careful.

I should not be with her.

But he couldn't let go.

He turned and caught her around the waist. In a flash, he pulled her around him. His legs still hung over the side of the bed. His feet pressed to the floor. When he pulled her around, he positioned her so that she straddled his hips. Her legs were splayed wide over his thighs. He could see her. Every perfect inch.

His dick stretched toward her.

He didn't go in.

Her hand curled around his cock. Stroked him slowly from base to tip, then she heaved up, and pushed the head of his dick toward her. When Alina sank down, she took him inside slowly. Inch by tantalizing, drive-him-out-of-his-ever-loving-mind inch. Then he was in her fully. His hands were tight around her waist. Probably too tight. He should ease up.

He felt her clamp her inner muscles around him and squeeze.

His teeth clenched and his breath released on a hiss.

"Trying to learn some new tricks," she murmured. "What do you think of that?" Her inner grip relaxed only for her to tighten around him again.

What did he think?

He surged up to his feet.

"Midas!" Her hands flew to curl around his shoulders.

He took three steps forward. Trapped her between the wall and his body. And he fucked her. Fast and hard. Long and driving. Over and over as she writhed against him. His cock worked her. His gaze locked on her face. He wanted to see the pleasure turn her eyes blind. He wanted to see the way she looked when he obliterated everything else in her world.

He wanted to see the way she looked when she had her orgasm. The pleasure on her face that was for him alone. He pounded into her. Waited, waited—

When she came, when the pleasure made her eyes go even darker and flushed her cheeks, when her sex squeezed and squeezed, he let go and spilled deep inside of her.

He held her tight. His mouth pressed to her shoulder. His body shuddered. Her scent was on him. Her touch burned into him.

Mine.

Alina had given herself fully to him. Alina who was good and bright. She'd given herself to *him*. She wouldn't have fucked a monster. She'd waited her whole life for the right partner.

She would not fuck a monster.

Not her.

He needed that knowledge. He had to hold it tight, just the way he held her. Because when he went into the cage with the devil, he needed some kind of talisman against the dark.

***

"Is this going to work?" Alina stared through the glass. A one-way mirror. She'd been taken through the corridors of the penitentiary, and she'd tried hard not to show her fear. As soon as she and Midas had pulled up outside, though, she'd been afraid.

The imposing walls. The barbed wire. The armed guards. It was all far beyond her normal life.

DA Terrance Peters had met them at the entrance. He'd supervised their search before entry. Alina's personal belongings had been secured, as had Midas's. They'd been led through what felt like a twisting maze. Guards had been in front and behind them. Henry Monroe's lawyer—a sharply dressed man named Xander Palmer with close-cropped hair, a serious expression, and slightly nervous hands—had met them once they finally reached this little room.

An observation room.

They could see through the glass. But the people just beyond the glass? Those people couldn't see in.

Midas was in the room beyond the glass. He'd gone in there with Xander. Two guards had left to collect Henry Monroe and bring him to the meeting.

"I'm surprised he wants you to see this," Terrance said.

She turned at his low voice.

"Midas, that is." His stare slid over her, and she knew that he was taking in every detail of her appearance.

Do I look like I spent the night wrecking a bed with Midas? She didn't think so. Alina had taken special care with her appearance. Her hair was pulled back into a twist. She'd applied light makeup. Some blush to make sure she didn't look too pale. A small swipe of lipstick. She wore black pants and a white top. A turtleneck. It hid the faint mark Midas had left on her neck.

She'd removed the bandages from her wrists and ankles. Red marks still covered her skin, but the bandages weren't necessary. *I'm healing.* She was. Getting stronger every moment. Putting the closet and the damn darkness behind her.

Seeing Kiera had been a brutal wake-up. Alina didn't want to let her fear trap her. She wanted to live.

And I felt so alive with Midas last night. She'd actually never felt more alive, never felt happier, at any point. Not even when she'd won her first national title.

"He's your bodyguard, isn't he? Saw the story on the news about how he saved you after the abduction."

Her head turned back toward the one-way mirror. A small table waited in that room. A table with three chairs. One for Midas—he sat in it with his back stiff and straight. One for Xander—he perched on the edge of his seat as his fingers tapped along the top of the table. The third seat was empty. For the moment.

"He's my bodyguard," she agreed. *But so much more.*

"That why he brought you to North Dakota? He wanted to keep you close?"

He'd wanted her to stay with Memphis and Lane. "Coming was my choice. Midas believes my abduction is linked to his father. Since it's my life, I wanted to hear what his father had to say."

A low whistle escaped Terrance. "You are not going to like what he has to say." He sawed a hand over his mouth. "No one ever does. The man is as close to true evil as I've ever encountered."

Goose bumps rose on her body.

"If it gets to be too much, I can have a guard escort you to the warden's office." He motioned toward the warden. Warden Walker had been in the little greeting party that met them at the gate. Tall, fit, tan, Walker had been quiet during most of the trek to the observation room.

"I don't like this," Walker said now. "Henry is working an angle. He's *always* working one."

"Midas can handle him," Alina said. Her voice sounded confident. She had faith in him.

"Nobody can handle Henry." Terrance tugged on the knot of his tie.

She didn't get to say anything else because the door had just opened in that little interrogation room. A guard came in first. Squeaking steps. Keys jangling at his side. Slight paunch and nervous eyes.

The prisoner arrived next. Tall, as tall as Midas. With powerful muscles that stretched his prison uniform. His wrists and legs were shackled, and he walked forward with mincing steps.

Her breath sucked in when he turned to glance toward the mirror.

"Looks one hell of a lot like his son, doesn't he?"

Yes, he did. They appeared more like brothers than father and son. Same jaw. Same nose. Same cheekbones. But Henry had a buzz cut so you could barely see his dark blond hair. His face appeared harder, colder, than Midas's.

Henry smiled.

Her goose bumps got worse. The curve of his lips was the same as Midas's, but the eyes were wrong. The amber color matched, but there was no emotion in Henry Monroe's eyes. It was like staring into a void.

Then he blinked, and emotion flew into his stare. A deliberate trick? Because suddenly, he looked happy. So pleased.

Her stomach twisted. "Midas shouldn't be in there." She wanted to run in and pull him out. "He shouldn't be around that man." Alina was very, very afraid for Midas.

But Henry stopped focusing on the mirror. *I think he was smiling at me.* And he turned toward Midas. "Son," he announced in a deep, rumbling voice. *Midas's voice.* "I have missed you."

Another guard shuffled in behind the prisoner.

***

Midas unclenched his back teeth. Tension had his body so stiff that he practically ached, and it took all of his self-control not to leap across the table and wipe that smug smile off his father's face.

I have missed you. Such utter bullshit. "I think you missed freedom," Midas returned flatly. "Missed being outside. Missed good food. Missed...hunting."

The guards secured Henry at the table. Then they backed up.

"But I don't think you missed me," Midas finished. He didn't glance toward the mirror. Alina was beyond that glass, watching every moment. He hated for her to see his father, and he was adamant that his father would *not* see her.

Henry Monroe would never get close to Alina. Midas would make sure of that.

"You wound me." A dramatic sigh. "You are my only son. My flesh and blood. How could I not miss you? It's been *years*."

"You set me up for murder."

"Did I?" His brow furrowed. "I don't remember that. I just think the incredibly inept DA screwed the case. Terrance wanted to be famous, and he jumped the gun so he could be on TV. Why would I want my own family in a cell? It's not a fate I would wish on my worst enemy."

Midas had often felt that he was his father's worst enemy. "Bowie Dodge is dead."

"Am I supposed to know that name?" A shrug of shoulders that were as wide as Midas's. "Was he some friend of yours?"

"No." His father was such a good actor. Always had been. "He was a friend of *yours*."

A shake of Henry's head. "No, can't say that he was. Don't know the name."

"Five-foot-ten, about one hundred and eighty pounds. Twenty-seven years old. Dark hair. Hired himself out as a bodyguard."

His father's eyes narrowed. "Aren't you a bodyguard? I believe I heard a news story or two about you protecting a big actor and maybe a pop singer." His chest puffed up. "My son, running around with the rich and famous. You must know how proud I am."

Midas leaned forward. "The last thing I want is for you to be *proud* of me." That would be his nightmare.

Henry appeared pained.

"And we both know," Midas continued because he was not buying this BS act of Henry's, "that you would only be *proud* of me if I suddenly started following in your footsteps. You want me to be as much of a predator as you are, but that isn't going to happen."

Henry glanced down at his restraints. While tension held Midas in its feverish grip, Henry appeared completely relaxed. "I go to see a shrink twice a week." His stare rose to pin Midas. "Court ordered. But, you know what? As much as I originally hated the sessions, I've learned a few things from her."

Her? They had Henry going to see a female shrink? Surely, he wasn't left *alone* with her.

No, if he'd been left alone with the shrink, she'd be dead by now.

"Denial," Henry stated with a nod. "So many of us live our lives in denial. Denying who we are. What we want. What we need. You just can't move forward until you stop denying your true self."

"You've never denied your true self." Midas wasn't buying his crap. It might fool the shrink, but it wasn't fooling him. "You're a killer. A sadistic prick who gets off on torture and pain."

"And what are you?" Henry asked.

Screw this. "Bored." Midas rose to his feet. "If you aren't going to cooperate, I'm done."

Henry peered up at him. "All because I don't know your Bowie friend?"

"Not my friend. The bastard tried to kill me yesterday."

Henry's eyes widened. "Yet here you stand. Does that mean the bastard in question was the one to die? Hopefully by your hand?"

Midas slapped his hands on the table.

His father's lawyer flinched.

Henry's head turned toward him. "Xander." Said with a hint of disgust. "Why are you here? I asked to meet with my son, not with you."

Sweat dotted Xander's brow. He pulled a monogrammed handkerchief from his pocket and patted at the moisture. "I'm—I'm here because you need representation. I have to protect your interests." The handkerchief fluttered toward the one-way mirror. "The DA is in there, listening to every word that you say."

"I am well aware of who is in the observation room." A pause. His features tightened. "Why don't you go get your ass in there, too? Because I do not need you."

"But—but I'm trying to look after your—"

"Get the fuck out." Henry peered at the one-way mirror. "I waive my rights for an attorney right now. I just want to chat with my son and not have some pencil-pusher breathing on me and flicking his smelly sweat everywhere."

Xander whipped back in his seat. The chair legs screeched over the floor. "I—" He stood and clutched a briefcase to his chest. "I can go?"

"That's what 'get the fuck out' usually means," Henry said with a roll of his eyes.

Xander fled.

Midas continued towering over the table with his hands flat on the surface.

As soon as the door shut behind Xander, Henry sent Midas a small smile. "Lawyers, am I right? You can't trust them." He quirked a brow. "Gonna stand there all day? Or are you going to sit down so we can talk like two civilized men?"

"There is nothing civilized about you."

"I could say the same for you." Henry pursed his lips. "You look a little tired, son. You still not sleeping well?"

Midas remained standing.

"Still have those nightmares? You always had such nightmares as a kid. Used to wake up screaming. You would always yell and say that a woman was being attacked."

Midas's hands fisted. "You told me it was nothing. Over and over. *Nothing*. But I must have heard a scream at least once, didn't I? Something that made me start having those nightmares in the first place."

"Oh, hell, son, you didn't just *hear* a scream. When you were seven, you walked in on me killing a woman." His smile bloomed. "But I convinced you it was all just a dream." He whistled. "You sure had a lot of bad dreams over the years."

***

"My God." Alina's hand came up to her mouth. She feared that she might be sick right then and there.

"You do *not* have to be here," Terrance said. He remained on her right side.

The warden had come to her left. "I can take you out," he offered.

No, she could not leave Midas. She could see his fury, but beneath the rage on his face, she knew he had to feel so much pain. Midas had grown up with the monster across from him. No wonder he hadn't wanted to come back for this faceoff.

But he came back for me. She knew that truth. Because of Bowie's final words, Midas thought his father was involved in Alina's abduction. He'd come back to face the pain of his past, for her.

She would not leave him.

The door creaked open behind them. "What did I miss?" Xander asked.

CHAPTER EIGHTEEN

He would not let his father get to him. Henry's words could have been a sick truth or a dirty lie. Either way, Midas had to stay focused. "Bowie Dodge mentioned you before he died."

"You still haven't said, did *you* kill him?"

"Why does it matter?"

His father sighed. "You didn't. Still haven't killed anyone, have you? If you had, I'd see it in your eyes. Such a disappointment." He leaned forward. His shackles clinked. "One day, you will. After the first, there is no going back."

***

"He's supposed to tell Midas the location of the first victim." Terrance shifted from his left foot to his right. "Ask him, Midas. Dammit, do it now. Stop playing his game."

But Alina knew Midas wasn't going to ask, not yet. *He's doing this for me.*

He was trying to learn about Bowie. But Alina did not think that Henry was going to tell them anything useful. The man was just playing with them. Like a snake, toying with his prey.

She didn't like Midas being that close to Henry.

Let's leave. Midas. Let's just go. Please.

***

"Bowie told me, and I quote, 'Your father says hi.'" Midas slowly lowered back into his chair.

"Oh, I can assure you, I didn't say 'hi.'" A rolling laugh. "I would say something like... 'Get your ass to the penitentiary. We need to talk.' Or, 'You twisted sonofabitch, you left me to rot.'" Another laugh. "Not a 'hi.' I mean, what am I? Some flirtatious teenage girl with a crush?"

Was that supposed to be funny? "Three women have been abducted in Colorado recently." At least three. But until they had concrete evidence of the others, Midas was going to focus on the three victims that had been confirmed.

"Ooh." Henry's eyes widened with interest. "Do tell me more. Were they taken and murdered? Their poor, poor families."

"One died. One was returned. One was rescued."

Henry's head tilted. "Who did the rescuing? Was it any bodyguard that I might know?"

"Cut the shit or I walk out of the door right now."

But Henry merely shrugged. "I never agreed to talk to you about this Bowie person. I don't know him. Perhaps he *thought* he knew me. Maybe he even thought he was following my orders. He wasn't. Because, despite what you may believe about me, I wouldn't want you hurt."

"I've got six scars on my throat and jaw that say otherwise."

***

"What scars?" Alina asked. Her head whipped toward Terrance. "I haven't seen scars."

"They're covered by the beard. Midas started growing the beard shortly after he got out of the hospital." Terrance kept his stare on the scene beyond the glass. "Henry didn't exactly surrender with open arms when it was time for his arrest. Midas and FBI Agent Oliver Foxx tried to take him down, but Henry was ready. He tried to slit Midas's throat. Viewed what Midas was doing as a betrayal, even though Henry had set up his son. Midas fought back. Those two big bastards battled like it was a war. Midas didn't even realize how many times he'd been sliced until it was all over."

Her horrified gaze went back to the interrogation room.

"Henry is not exactly big on fatherly emotion. Or emotion of any sort," Terrance added.

Xander cleared his throat. "I believe my client has expressed his remorse for those actions. He was under a great deal of stress at the time and didn't even realize what he was doing to his son."

She was sure that Henry always realized what he was doing.

Henry's gaze flickered to the glass. To her. He sent her that faint smile again.

He doesn't see me. He doesn't.

Maybe if she told herself that enough, she'd believe it.

***

"I am sorry." Henry released a long sigh. "My shrink has told me that I need to take responsibility for my actions. Let people know I have caused them harm and that I regret their pain. It's the only way for me to grow as a person."

"You don't regret anyone's pain." He glanced at his watch. "Can we cut through the bullshit? Either tell me something useful or I'm walking."

"I don't know your Bowie Dodge. He thinks he knows me, obviously. He's wrong. Perhaps someone was playing a game with *him*."

Midas pulled the sleeve of his coat to cover the watch. He turned his attention back to his father. The man didn't exactly look as if he'd been wasting away in a prison cell. Quite the opposite. It appeared as if he'd been spending twenty-four, seven shifts in a gym. "You said you'd reveal the location of the first vic." Deliberately, he shifted the topic off Bowie. Midas had learned—long ago—that the best way to get Herny to slip up was to catch him off guard. He'd come back to Bowie in a few minutes. Try to catch his father in a weak moment. "I'm here. I did my part."

"Yes, you did. I have missed you." Henry's sharp stare swept over Midas's face. "Have you missed me?"

"No."

"Do you remember when you were little…how we'd have such great adventures? Surfing in California. Hiking the Grand Canyon. Skiing in Colorado."

"Do I remember that we barely stayed in any town longer than a few weeks? That we were always on the move? Living out of tents or cheap motel rooms?" He nodded. "Yes, I remember that. Didn't realize until much later that we stayed on the move so much because you were hunting. Killing women."

"I had fun surfing with you. My life wasn't just about murder."

"No kidding?"

"You've turned hard, Midas. Bitter."

"Yeah, well what did you expect—"

"I like it."

Fuck. He didn't want his father to like anything about him.

"I used to worry when you were a kid. You were so freaking soft. Big like me, sure. But you'd do the stupidest things. Remember that scrawny dog you found behind that motel in Phoenix City? You were feeding him scraps every morning and night. You even asked me if we could take him with us when we left town."

Midas did not move.

The shackles clinked as Henry lifted his hands and rubbed his chest. "Whatever happened to that mutt?"

"You killed him," Midas retorted. "Ran over him when we were going out one night, and you tried to say it had been an accident."

"Oh, yeah." A nod. He winced. "That wasn't an accident."

"I know."

***

"Would you like a tissue?"

Alina blinked. Her stare swerved toward Terrance.

"You have..." He motioned toward her. "Tears, on your cheeks."

She swiped them away.

***

"The first victim," Midas prompted. He wasn't going to let his father distract him. *Lucky. I named the dog Lucky. Thought it was so lucky that we'd found each other. He was a good dog. Sweet. His tail would wag whenever he'd see me coming.* Midas could feel his teeth grinding together.

"Right. The first. You never forget a first, do you?" Henry's gaze slid to the mirror.

"*Look at me.*"

Henry's attention jumped back to Midas.

"Don't look at the mirror. Don't play your games. Either keep up your part of the deal or I walk." *Do not look at Alina.*

"Is someone...special behind the mirror? I figured it would be our usual suspects. The DA. The warden—the man always likes to know everything that happens in his pen—and Xander, since I sent him running in there. Maybe a Fed or two in order to round things out. Perhaps your friend, Oliver Foxx? Oh, wait." His brows climbed. "Oliver is on his honeymoon, isn't he? I feel like I remember hearing something about that..."

"Who the hell would have told you about Oliver?"

His father strove to look hurt. "You might choose to ignore me, but I have friends. Actually, I have a large number of admirers. People send me letters all the time. They talk about the news. They talk about pop stars. The *bodyguards* of pop stars." A smile came and went on his face. "They ask me to marry them. To give them children. There is a very, very large subset of women who are fascinated with killers. Did you know that?"

Midas didn't respond.

"I think they like the thrill of fucking a monster. You ever met a woman like that? A woman who wanted to fuck a monster?"

Midas rose. "This is a waste of my time. You aren't going to tell me jackshit. You were jerking around the DA and now you're jerking me around." It was his turn to smile at his father. "Enjoy those life sentences. Since you don't have the possibility of parole, I hope you cherish every single second of your imprisonment." He marched away from the table.

"They tell me about current events." His father kept right on going with his list. "Chat with me about rock stars. Olympic contenders."

Midas stopped. His gaze jerked to the guard who stood near the door. The man stared back with a tense expression. Midas spun on his heel. *Olympic contenders.* "You told her father to hire me."

Henry glanced over his shoulder. Confusion clouded his gaze. "What do you mean? Whose father?"

"You knew Oliver was out of the country. You reached out to her father, and you told him to hire me. Why." Not a question. A demand.

Henry's brows lowered. "I'm just not following along. Perhaps if you explained who this woman is, then I might understand."

"You understand perfectly. You told her father—"

"I'm in a maximum-security penitentiary. I don't get to just pick up the phone anytime I want. If that were the case, I'd be ordering pizza deliveries every week. Remember how you used to enjoy extra cheese on your pizzas when you were a kid?"

What kid didn't enjoy extra freaking cheese? "You just told me that you get contacted by people all the time. Your fan club is quite extensive, I'm sure."

"It's good to be appreciated."

"You have people working for you, don't you? You give orders, and they jump."

Henry faced the front again. "My mail is checked by the warden." He sent a little wave toward the mirror. "Hello, Warden Walker. How is that lovely wife of yours doing?"

Midas stalked back toward his father. He reached out—

One of the guards grabbed Midas's hand. "You can't touch him."

He didn't want to touch him. Midas wanted to rip his father apart. Okay, fine, some touching would be involved in the ripping violence. But Midas pulled his hand back. Sucked in a breath. "Codes. You slipped codes in your correspondence. Or maybe—maybe you were giving orders to some cellblock mates. Telling them what to do. When to do it. And they passed along your messages for you."

Henry hunched his shoulders. "You're always accusing me of crimes."

"Because you always commit crimes!" Even though he wanted to storm out of that room, Midas returned to his spot on the opposite side of the table. He didn't sit, though. Just stood, glaring.

"Establishing dominance?" Henry nodded in approval. "I like it. Obviously, you are the dominant one. Because you're not the one in chains."

"No, I'm fucking not in chains. Despite your efforts."

"Hmmm."

"First. Victim." His voice vibrated with fury. Midas couldn't help it. The rage he felt as he stared at his father was too strong.

"There isn't anything of your mother in you. Not in your physical appearance, anyway." His father's head cocked as he studied Midas. "That's practically my face you're wearing."

"That's why it was so easy for you to set me up all those years ago."

"We were kids when I met your mother. She had a thing for bad boys. So, of course, she fell for me."

Like it got any badder than you.

"She wanted to fix me. Change me. Help me." Henry winked. "The shrink wants to do that, too."

"You can't fix something as broken as you are."

The shackles clinked once more. Henry touched his heart. "That hurts. Right here."

"No, it doesn't. You have to feel in order to hurt."

Henry's lashes flickered. "And that's what your FBI buddy told you, isn't it? That I don't feel. That I'm some kind of psychopathic monster. I mimic emotions. I don't actually love."

"You didn't love my mother, or you wouldn't have killed her."

A muscle flexed along Henry's jaw. "Your mother left us."

"No." Midas wasn't buying that lie any longer. "You always said that. But I don't believe you."

"Ah. Why not? Because you think she wouldn't have left *you?* You think she would have stayed with you, through thick and thin? *She left you.* She learned what I was. Your mother thought you'd be the exact same thing."

The exact same thing.

"So she ran. Took off when you were just a baby. Disappeared into the night, and I never saw her again."

Thud. Thud. Thud. Midas's heartbeat filled his ears like a blasting drum. "She would have taken me with her."

"That's what you've been telling yourself, huh?"

"She found out what you were. You fought. You killed her."

Henry raised his hands. "I'm a big guy. She was small. Always liked them small, you know. But you have to be careful. Small things break."

You are a twisted bastard. "Did you just want me in this room so I'd have to listen to your bullshit? Because I have better things to do. If you aren't telling me where my mother is, then—"

"What in the world made you think she was my first victim? Told you, she found out what I liked to do. She left us after that."

Thud. Thud. Thud. "You will never tell me where she is." Because his father liked pain and torture too much. He liked hurting Midas by keeping that information from him. Midas glanced at the one-way mirror. His reflection stared back at him.

But I just see my father. Every single time I look into any mirror, I just see him. He looked into a mirror and saw a monster staring back. Midas exhaled and stepped away from the table.

"Gonna pretend to walk away again?" Henry asked. "It's getting tedious. Back and forth. Back and forth."

Midas didn't answer.

"Gonna try and pressure me? Think if you don't respond, I'll spill a secret?"

The deal had been that Henry talked in exchange for Midas's presence. Midas had tried to tell Terrance that his father never kept his promises.

Midas didn't look at his father again.

"Why aren't you talking to me?" Henry blasted. "Midas, Midas, look at me!"

No, he wasn't going to look. Midas knew the one thing his father hated. *Being ignored.* So Midas used that last ace that he held, and he ignored his father. Midas's hand extended as he reached for the door.

"*Ice Springs Road.*"

Midas opened the door.

"*Aspen, Colorado.*"

He didn't look back.

"*She's right there, beneath the most beautiful aspen tree you'll ever see.*"

Finally, Midas turned to stare back at his father. Henry had swiveled in his chair and was glaring at him. But Henry didn't catch Midas's attention. What actually caught his attention—

The one-way mirror appeared to be vibrating.

What in the hell?

As he watched, it trembled again.

***

Her fist drove into the one-way glass again. Again.

"Alina!" Terrance caught her hand. "What is wrong with you? What's happening?"

Ice Springs Road. Aspen, Colorado. Her chest squeezed. No, it didn't squeeze. It was like a giant weight had just crushed onto her heart. "I have to get in that room." She yanked her hand from Terrance and ran for the door.

The warden blocked her path. "I think you need to relax. Something has upset you—"

"*Get me in the room. Now.*"

The warden looked over her shoulder. She knew he was eyeing Terrance and waiting for approval. He must have gotten it, because the warden turned around and opened the door. "Follow me."

***

"Ice Springs Road." Midas thrust back his shoulders. The door to the interrogation room remained open as he did a half-turn toward his father. "Am I going to find my mother there?"

"No. Told you. She wasn't my first victim." A slow smile curved his lips and lit Henry's eyes. "Of course, the woman under that aspen tree wasn't the first, either. In fact, no one knew she was mine. This is my first time to claim her."

Was he truly revealing another victim?

"She looked so beautiful when I left her. A broken snow angel."

Footsteps rushed toward the interrogation room.

Midas peered back at the open doorway just as he heard the warden bark, "You need to calm down, you need to—"

Alina shoved the warden out of her way. Tears streaked down her cheeks. Her breath heaved in and out. In and out.

"Alina," Midas whispered. "You...you shouldn't be here." *He can't see you. I don't ever want him looking at you. I don't ever want any of my father's evil touching you.*

"You bastard," she snarled.

Midas blinked.

Her hands slammed into him. Surprise more than anything else had Midas stepping to the side.

Alina turned her fury on his father. "Ice Springs Road." Her breath heaved again. "That's where my mother is buried. She's in the cemetery on *Ice Springs Road.*"

A dull roar filled Midas's ears.

No, no, this can't be happening.

"She's buried under an aspen tree," Alina said. "She had—she had a broken neck. We thought she died in a skiing accident. *We found her in the snow.*"

"No accident," Henry murmured. "Your mother was such a beautiful woman. You remind me of her."

A primitive scream of pain and fury erupted from Alina. She leapt for Henry, but one of the guards caught her around the waist and hauled her back.

"You bastard! You *bastard!*" Alina cried.

Midas stared in growing horror at the scene. Alina, with tears streaming down her cheeks. And his father—his smug sonofabitch of a father.

Henry winked at him. "Fiery, huh? Like mother, like daughter."

This time, Midas was the one to leap forward. His fist plowed into his father's jaw.

His father started laughing, and Midas punched him again. His fists slammed into his father over and over.

Until the guards hauled him off Henry.

And his father was still laughing.

CHAPTER NINETEEN

Two weeks later...

He watched as the limo left the Bellamy estate. Alina would be in the back, as she'd been each day since she'd returned to Colorado Springs. He waited a moment for the limo to go ahead, and then he pulled his motorcycle onto the road. He didn't get too close. Not like he wanted to be spotted. A careful distance was all he needed. The driver hadn't noticed him before, so it was doubtful the man would spot him this morning.

Not even four a.m. But that was Alina's schedule. She liked to be at the rink long before anyone else arrived.

There was hardly any other traffic on the road. A light rain had fallen during the night, and the pavement was slick. His hands gripped the handlebars easily as he navigated through the darkness.

The driver turned at the rink. Went straight to the entrance. He braked there, and the man exited the vehicle. Milo Shaw, Ryker's personal driver. Driver and bodyguard. The man had been special forces, once upon a time. Retired now, but still in fit condition. He would provide Alina with some protection.

Milo swept the scene. Never even saw the motorcycle or its driver.

Maybe retirement is hitting you too hard, Milo.

Milo opened the side door for Alina. She climbed slowly from the vehicle. Her hair had already been secured into a twist. She wore her training uniform. Her bag and her skates were slung over her shoulder. She didn't even glance around the area as she walked straight for the entrance.

Was she thinner? It looked as if she was. Alina couldn't afford to lose any weight.

He hid the motorcycle. Slipped into the rink. Watched her spin and soar. She didn't fall. She hadn't practiced her quadruple axel in days. Dmitri barked at her, but he seemed pleased. Half-hearted barks. Dmitri gestured wildly as he instructed her.

Five hours later, Alina finished with sweat soaking her body.

When she left, he followed.

She went to the gym. Worked out another hour.

He waited. Watched from across the street.

She left the gym. The limo driver took her to get lunch. She ate alone.

He waited. Watched.

She had a photo shoot. She was pampered and prepped, and she smiled, but her eyes seemed so sad.

He waited. Watched from the shadows. Stayed hidden.

Not too close. He couldn't afford to get too close. But he'd learned it was easy to watch from a distance. To watch. To yearn. To want what he could not have.

Dinner. She had dinner with her father. A swanky restaurant.

She prefers barbecue. A casual place where she could get sauce on her fingers then dance to soft guitar music.

The limo took her back home. She returned to the guesthouse. He waited and watched, and her lights eventually turned off.

All of the lights, except the one in the upstairs bedroom. Her room. Alina was still afraid to be alone in the dark.

He wished he could be in there with her.

Not a possibility, though. Since Alina hated his guts.

A long sigh escaped Midas. He lowered his binoculars.

He was such a fucking stalker.

***

Her skates cut across the ice. Music played, a classical masterpiece of emotion. Love found and lost. Her muscles bunched. She shot into the air. Spun. Over and over and over. Her skate touched down. One. The other. Her hands came out with a flourish as she skated backwards across the ice.

"Wow! That's fantastic!" Applause burst into the air.

Alina slowed to a stop near the side of the rink. Her right skate pointed downward as she balanced. The praise had not come from Dmitri. He'd been watching silently. The silent watching *was* praise from him. If he wasn't commanding her to do the routine again and again, if he wasn't pointing out mistakes, then he was giving her high praise. That was his way.

The thunderous applause slowly died, but Ophelia Raine kept grinning at her. "How do you get so high into the air?" Ophelia bounced in her sneakers as she stood just beyond the half-wall that circled the ice. "Are leg days like insane for you or what?" She grabbed a towel and tossed it to Alina.

Alina caught it and swiped away the sweat she could feel on her collar bone. "Or what," she said in response. She even forced a smile for Ophelia. She genuinely *liked* the other woman.

Ophelia had been Alina's shadow for the last two weeks. The last two wrenching, heartbreaking weeks.

When her father had learned about Henry Monroe's confession, he'd immediately fired Midas. Not that the firing had been necessary. Midas had already backed away from her. More like vanished on her. He'd called in his friends—Memphis, Lane, and Ophelia. They'd taken over her security detail in North Dakota. They'd even been with her on the flight home. Midas hadn't been there.

I don't know where he is.

"Hey." Softer. Ophelia inched closer to the half-wall. "Do not make me come out there and hug you. I'll bust my ass as soon as I step on the ice and we both know it."

Alina lifted her chin. "I'm okay."

"The hell you are." Low. Her gaze lasered over to Dmitri. He was busy reviewing his clipboard and making notes about the routine. Sighing, Ophelia's attention shifted back to Alina. "You're hurting."

Not physically, she wasn't. Or, maybe she was. It seemed like her heart might be breaking in a million pieces.

Memphis and Lane weren't in the bodyguard business. They were Ice Breakers. Cold case solvers. And who knew what the heck else? They seemed to have money to burn. But when Alina had gotten settled back in her father's guesthouse, Ophelia had come to her. She'd take over Midas's bodyguard position.

Funny, the first time she'd seen Ophelia Raine, it had been when the other woman came hurtling through the window at Kiera's home. Ophelia had proved to be an incredible distraction—and a lifesaver—that day.

Ophelia had a PI business. But in addition to her PI jobs, she'd revealed that she could provide protection services. She'd given her card to Alina and Ryker, and she'd offered to run point on Alina's protection detail. She'd also provided a list of high-profile references that stretched for days.

Ryker had vetted her, and then she'd become Alina's new best friend. Or at least, that was the story Ryker seemed intent on telling everyone. Another undercover ruse. But, at least this time, Alina knew the score.

Ophelia wasn't really her friend. Just as Midas hadn't been—hadn't been—

"There it is again," Ophelia murmured. "Gosh, you do this sad, doe-eyed thing that makes me want to burst into tears. Stop it."

She was trying to stop it. "His dad killed my mom."

"I know, sweetie. I'm so sorry."

"And he...Midas left me."

Ophelia winced. "I'm coming onto the ice, and I am going to hug you so hard. Give me just a second while I bust my ass, would you?" She sidestepped and started to reach for the door that would give her access to the ice.

"Alina!" A bark from Dmitri. "Skate, now!"

"God, that man is such a charmer. Don't know how he manages to fight off all the women who must be vying for his affection." Ophelia rolled her eyes.

"I-I need to get back to practice."

"You have been practicing for hours. Take a break." She opened the door. "We need to talk about Midas—"

Who are you? Dmitri's voice boomed. He wasn't talking to Ophelia. He'd grudgingly accepted her presence. Not like he wanted his star skater unprotected. When he'd learned about the abduction, the man had reportedly experienced a panic attack.

"Why are you in my rink?" Dmitri shouted. He rushed past Ophelia. "This is a closed practice! Security should have stopped you at the door!"

Yes, there was security stationed at the door. Two men at the entrance to the rink. Two at the rear. Her father hadn't just hired Ophelia. He'd gone all-in on protection.

But as her head turned toward the newcomers and fear had her heart rate accelerating, Alina realized why security hadn't intervened. She recognized the two people who walked toward Dmitri so determinedly. Detective Joyce Meriam and Detective Calvin Booker. They flashed their badges at Dmitri.

"Practice needs to pause," Calvin stated in what she thought had to be his official-business voice. "We have to speak with Alina."

Her breath shuddered out.

Dmitri did not move out of the detectives' path. Instead, he glanced over his shoulder at Alina. "Do you want to speak with them?"

"Uh, buddy, we're cops," Joyce informed him. "She has to speak with—"

"Alina does nothing she does not want to do!" Dmitri boomed. "Except skate. She skates when I tell her to skate." His eyes raked Alina. "Do you want to speak with them?" he asked again. His voice had softened. Marginally.

"Aw." Ophelia's voice carried only to Alina as she whispered, "Is he being protective of you right now? Like, nice in his angry Russian way? That is almost hot."

"He's not interested in women," Alina informed her, just as softly.

"Alina!" Dmitri thundered. "You want me to have them removed?"

"We are *police detectives,*" Joyce blasted—clearly raising her voice to match his volume—even as she tucked her badge back into the pocket of her coat. "You aren't removing us. You're going to remove yourself. We need to speak with Alina. It's about her case."

Dmitri held his position. One between Alina and the cops.

"I didn't think I was supposed to speak with you unless my lawyer was present," Alina temporized as she tried to figure out what was happening. *Why are they here?*

"We've already spoken with Bradford. Extensively." Joyce grimaced. "Him and your father. They are aware that we are here. I can assure you, there is no risk involved to you. We have an update on your case."

She nodded. "It's okay, Dmitri," Alina told her coach. "I'll talk with them." Especially if they had news about her kidnapping.

"Five minutes." A sniff from him. "Then you are back on the ice." He lingered. "I will be close, should you need me."

Then he marched toward the shadows on the left side of the rink.

Joyce watched him with a bemused expression. "Charming guy. Real people person." She closed in with her partner. "Working with him must be a nightmare."

"He's one of the top two figure skating coaches in the world."

"He's a dick." Joyce exhaled. She studied Alina, then winced. "You look tired."

Her spine straightened even more. "Practice can be intense. We're entering the final stretch."

"The Olympics." Calvin had been scanning the ice. Now his focus shifted to Alina. "Gonna bring home the gold?"

"I'm going to do my best." That was all she could hope for. Though she hardly felt at her best these days. She maintained her pose on the ice. Calvin, Joyce, and Ophelia were on the regular floor.

A chill skated over her because she'd known this visit would be coming. Her mother's body had been exhumed. A new autopsy ordered. A new investigation opened.

"You're still playing bodyguard?" Joyce asked Ophelia.

Ophelia laughed, as if the question had delighted her. "I'm not playing anything. I am her bodyguard. One of many. Her father has seen to it that Alina has an army at her beck and call. He wants to ensure her safety. After all, the mysterious leader of the kidnapping ring hasn't been apprehended." The words held definite censure. As in...*why haven't you caught him yet?*

"We think he has been." Calvin grimaced. "Not apprehended, but...taken down."

Alina jerked forward. "What?"

"Our investigation has concluded that Bowie Dodge was the man behind the abductions."

Her head shook. "But—"

"He was on the security staff for Kiera Thatch's father long before she was ever taken. He was already familiar with the family and their routine. He arranged her abduction, then stayed on as her bodyguard after she was released so he could make sure she never said anything that might incriminate him." Joyce hunched her shoulders. "It's cold in here. How can you stand being on that ice for so long?"

"I love being on the ice." When she skated, she didn't have to think about anything else. Not her past. Not pain. Not Midas...

I'm such a liar. I'm always thinking about him.

The ice had been her escape for years. After she'd lost her mother, she'd abandoned herself to the ice. She could soar and be free on the ice.

Except, she couldn't seem to free herself of Midas.

He left you. Stop this.

"We discovered Bowie was part of the security crew at one of the charity balls arranged by Maureen O'Sullivan." Calvin had picked up the story. His voice was emotionless as he continued, "He got close to her. Realized just how much money her family possessed and decided to try his abduction routine again. Only this time, it didn't work. She must have fought him and his men—Shayne and Fallon—and they killed her. They received a ransom for her, and her family received a dead body in return."

Ophelia stepped closer to the cops. "Why'd they pick Alina as their next victim?"

"Once upon a time, Bowie worked for Ryker Bellamy. A security job in one of your dad's real estate firms. But he was fired because he was accused of getting too rough with a coworker." Joyce shivered. "It's just cold near the ice, right? If I move back like, ten feet, I'll be warmer?"

Ophelia frowned at the blond detective. "You're saying Bowie was pissed at getting fired so he came after Alina?"

"Our theory is that he wanted her dad to pay." Calvin's hands dipped into the pockets of his dress pants. "The man seemed to hold one serious grudge. We linked him to Shayne and Fallon through their phone records. Looks like Shayne and Fallon were the ones to sabotage your car. Everything connects. We believe Bowie murdered his two associates to stop them from possibly ID'ing him, and then, when you showed up at Kiera's and started questioning her, Bowie realized he had to act."

She could still see all the blood. Smell it. Alina's nostrils flared. "Kiera is going to be all right." She'd called the hospital multiple times, but they'd refused to release any info on Kiera's condition to her. But then Ophelia chatted with a few of the nurses and somehow, she'd gotten the scoop.

Kiera had survived her surgery. She'd been in the ICU for days but had finally been transferred to a normal room.

"She's recovering," Calvin assured her. "A slow but steady process."

Alina exhaled.

"As for the man who shot Bowie Dodge..." Joyce rocked onto her heels. "We have learned that Ray Sader is the individual who actually contacted the Ice Breakers about Kiera's case."

"Huh. You don't say," Ophelia exclaimed. All wide-eyed innocence.

Alina slanted her a quick glance.

Ophelia shrugged. "What?"

"Memphis Camden confirmed to us that Ray was the concerned friend who wanted help with Kiera. Ray is not being charged in Bowie's death—"

"Uh, great to know," Ophelia cut in. "Considering the man stopped a murderer who was hell bent on shooting multiple people—"

"He is *not* being charged," Calvin repeated, voice stronger. "And we are currently viewing Alina's kidnapping case as closed."

Alina blinked.

"Uh, that's it?" Ophelia asked.

A wide smile curled Joyce's lips. "You're safe now, Alina. You don't need to look over your shoulder any longer. You can focus on the competition."

"But…" All the pieces weren't fitting for her. It seemed as if the detectives were trying to shove everything into a box and wrap it up with a neat, little bow. Only the box wasn't closing. "Bowie said that Henry Monroe was involved."

Calvin and Joyce shared a brief glance. "We believe," Calvin said slowly, "that was to throw everyone off the scent. A last dig, if you will. Bowie had replicated Henry's MO on Maureen O'Sullivan. The man seems to have been a—a fan of Henry's work. So at the end, we suspect he just tossed out Henry's name as a final way of hurting Henry's son."

Alina's brow furrowed. "But who told my father to hire Midas in the first place? It wasn't Oliver Foxx."

"Ah. Oliver." Joyce's mouth tightened. "He's been in the station quite a few times. He seems to forget that he's not technically a Fed any longer."

"I heard he did contract work for the FBI." Ophelia watched the detectives closely. "And the man is a profiling master. So if he wants to help you, shouldn't you be—oh, I don't know—*jumping* at the opportunity to work with him?"

"He is not, ahem, working with us any longer. Oliver Foxx has flown to North Dakota. He's working with the prosecutor up there to see if more of Henry Monroe's victims can be located." Sympathy softened Joyce's expression. "We're very sorry about your mother, Alina. Her autopsy results should be in soon."

"Her neck was broken." This was no surprise. "We've always known that. But...we...I was told she died in a skiing accident." Until Henry Monroe's confession had upended her world.

"It's possible he just said that to hurt you." Ophelia opened the door that led to the ice. She slipped. Cursed. Said something about her ass busting again. Then she grabbed for Alina. Grabbed her for support so she wouldn't fall but also...

Alina stared into Ophelia's eyes. There was no missing the concern in Ophelia's light blue gaze. "You don't know for sure what happened yet. You can't be certain he wasn't just trying to hurt you and Midas."

Calvin cleared his throat. "Henry has provided more details."

Ophelia spun to look at him. She almost fell, but Alina steadied her.

"He's spoken with Oliver. Described what your mother was wearing. How he first encountered her. How he—he set the scene after he killed her. All very specific statements." An exhale. "I'm sorry."

Sorry. She heard that from people a lot. Alina was sorry, too. Sorry that she'd lost her mother. Sorry that so many lies had been told. Sorry that Midas had such a monster for a father. "What will happen to him?"

"Well…" Calvin scratched his chin. "He is already serving multiple life sentences. Parole was never a possibility for him. In North Dakota, there is no death penalty. But we do know he and his son traveled all over the country. If Oliver Foxx can tie Henry to a crime in a different state—one with the death penalty, then you would—"

"Midas," she rasped. She hadn't been asking about Henry. "What will happen to Midas? He assaulted Henry." Punched him again and again. It had taken a small army of guards to pull Midas off his father. "Is he going to jail?" His father had been bound, unable to fight back.

He hadn't wanted to fight back. He'd just kept laughing and laughing.

She feared he'd wanted to push Midas into the attack. Goad him so that Midas would wind up a prisoner, too.

Once more, the detectives glanced at each other. And, yet again, Calvin cleared his throat. "No charges. Henry said he didn't want his son punished, and the DA was certainly sympathetic to Midas's, ah, situation…" His words trailed off.

"Henry wanted his son punished." Alina believed that with every bit of her being. "That's why he arranged for us to be together in the first place."

"Alina." Joyce winced. "I understand you've been through a stressful situation. I can empathize with you."

Ophelia snorted. "So glad you understand and empathize. It's great that you can relate to being kidnapped, stuffed in closet, terrorized, oh, and then you empathize with finding out that your boyfriend's dad killed your mom. Her situation is so super relatable."

Joyce's eyes narrowed.

Ophelia just tossed back her dark hair and met the detective's angry stare. "What?"

"I thought he was a bodyguard," Calvin noted quietly. "Not the boyfriend."

"Like you can't be both?" Ophelia huffed out a breath. "I'm her friend and her bodyguard, so there."

"Be that as it may…" Joyce's rose a bit as she tried to retake control of the situation. "We have found no evidence that Henry 'arranged' for you and Midas to interact. As I said before, we believe that Bowie Dodge was the mastermind of…"

She kept talking.

But Ophelia had turned her head toward Alina. "Bowie," Ophelia repeated. "You buying that?"

Alina didn't know what to buy. Her gut said no, though.

"The investigation has concluded." Joyce had wound up her summary. "We wanted to personally inform you and answer any additional questions that you may have."

Alina had plenty of questions. "Where is Midas?" Maybe that shouldn't have been the one that sprang straight to her lips. But it did. She'd feared he'd been behind bars. When she'd last seen him in North Dakota, five guards had been hauling him down a narrow hallway. They'd barely been able to restrain him.

Henry's blood-covered grin had been monstrous. *"See what he is? He can't keep his true self hidden, not any longer."*

And she'd realized that Henry had always intended to push Midas over the edge.

"We, um, are not quite aware of Midas's current whereabouts." A flat statement from Joyce. "We suspect he may still be in North Dakota, potentially assisting Oliver Foxx."

So...he wasn't close. He also wasn't locked up. He'd chosen to stay away from Alina. "Thank you for coming to speak with me."

Surprise flashed in Calvin's dark eyes. "No more questions?"

Too many to count.

"Time is up, Alina!" Dmitri thundered from across the rink.

"I have to skate." Quiet. "Thank you." She pulled from Ophelia. Her skates cut across the ice.

The investigation was over. The detectives believed the leader of the kidnapping ring was dead. That should mean that Alina was safe again. Her life could return to normal. She picked up speed as she raced around the ice. Faster and faster, she went. And she didn't feel the cold. Not at all.

In fact, she barely felt anything.

CHAPTER TWENTY

"Just how long do you intend to keep up your stalker routine?" Ophelia demanded. She yanked her coat closer and glowered at Midas. "Hiding across the street? Hunching in shadows? So creepy."

He glared at her. "You should not be here." And he wasn't hunching under a shadow. Not right then.

"Oh, what? Are you mad I spotted you?" Her eyes rolled heavenward. "Give me a break. I tagged you on day one. This isn't amateur hour. You're not dealing with Lane Lawson here. *Not my first case.* I'd be a real piss-poor bodyguard for Alina if I didn't notice the six-foot-six guy *stalking* her."

"I'm not stalking her. And you can't be guarding her if you're out here with me." *So go back inside. Now.*

"The case is over." She motioned toward the road. "I'm sure you saw the detectives arrive and then leave. They were sharing the fabulous news that Bowie Dodge was the kidnapping ring mastermind."

Midas narrowed his eyes.

"He's dead. Alina's kidnapping case is closed. All is right in her world again. Except for you. The stalker boyfriend who ghosted her." She shivered. "It's even colder out here than it is near the ice. How do you *stand* this temperature?" Her head tilted back. "And it's starting to snow. Wonderful." Small flakes landed in her dark hair. Growling, she looked at Midas. "She asked about you."

Do not show emotion. Do not. "Did she?"

"Wanted to make sure you weren't rotting in a jail cell somewhere. Wasn't that thoughtful of her?"

Midas didn't speak.

"She looked relieved to discover no charges were pending against you, but then...sad when she realized your fool-ass has been free for the last two weeks, but you haven't contacted her even once. Heartless jerk."

Anger beat inside of him. "What the hell am I supposed to say to her? *Sorry my dad murdered your mom? But, hey, let's move past it and fuck some more? I'm sure you'll love fucking the son of the man who broke your mother's neck.*"

She stepped back. "No." A definite shake of her head. "You do not say that. You do not ever say that. What is wrong with you?"

Like he would ever actually say those words to Alina. "Go back inside."

"You *should* try saying something like, oh, I don't know...just going out on a limb here... 'Alina, I love you. We're not responsible for the past. Let's try building a future together.'" She blinked. "That was good, right? I'm good."

Alina, I love you. "Alina does not need to be anywhere near me."

"But you need to be near her, don't you? Thus, the stalking."

"I'm not stalking! I'm keeping watch over her!"

"Because you love her. I just said that. Or something similar to it." She curled her shoulders and shivered. "So freaking cold. Let's go inside. You can grovel to Alina. Apologize for ghosting her. Tell her she's the best part of your life. Then you can take over primary bodyguard duty, and I can get back to the pile of other cases waiting at my PI office. Because bodyguard work is not usually my forte." Her lips twisted. "Though her dad pays me a ton of cash, so I'm not really complaining."

"Oliver Foxx actually *did* recommend you to Ryker."

"Well, sure. I'm awesome. Oliver knows it. So does Memphis. They're both references for little old me."

Midas had never learned the story of exactly how Ophelia and Oliver met. He'd been stunned when she came hurtling through the window at Kiera's place. Memphis had failed to mention that she was the pair of eyes he'd had on Kiera.

Midas's gaze slid beyond Ophelia and lingered on the entrance doors that led to the rink. "You should be in there with her."

"Why? According to the detectives, the danger has passed."

His jaw tightened.

"Unless you think they are pinning all of this on the wrong guy. If that is the case, I certainly expect you to tell me. As in, now."

He noted the two security guards who stood at attention near the entrance. Two at the front. Two at the back. And Dmitri was inside with Alina. "I don't have proof that anyone else organized her kidnapping."

"But...?"

"But Bowie struck me as a flunky, not a leader. And I don't buy that he was some fan of my dad's, who just tossed out that final line about my old man saying 'hi' right before Bowie took his last breath." His hands fisted. The snow fell harder. "My gut says there is more happening."

"Well, then go find some proof for your gut."

If he left to find proof...

"Or you could try talking to her. You know, before you cut out on your search for proof. Try telling Alina that you are still uber obsessed instead of leaving her in the dark about how you feel."

"She's better without me." Every time she looked at him, she'd just see his father. Twisted sonofabitch.

"I think that's her decision." Her teeth chattered.

Once more, he peered at the entrance. "Is she still falling?" *And getting up. Alina always gets up.*

"Falling?"

The surprise in her voice had his stare pinging right back to Ophelia.

She wrinkled her nose even as a snowflake landed on the tip. "Alina doesn't fall. She glides across that ice like a boss. She's perfection in motion. Even Dmitri has been grunting his approval."

His chest seemed to warm. "She's nailing the quadruple?"

"Who are you?" Ophelia gaped at him. "When did you turn into some ice-skating trivia master? The quadruple?" Another scrunch of her nose. "I'm assuming that means she spins four times, so, no, she's not nailing that. She's not even trying to nail that. She spins three times and lands flawlessly." A shrug. "Guess she's playing it safe now? No quadruples for her."

A blue Cadillac Escalade rolled into the lot. Midas tensed because instead of parking, the vehicle changed direction...and came toward him and Ophelia.

The Escalade stopped about five feet away.

"Way to attract attention," he snapped at her.

"You're going to blame this on my red coat, aren't you? Spoiler. You're the one who stood here talking to me for five minutes. And it's her *lawyer's* ride. Not like he's a threat to Alina. The man has known her and her family forever. Besides, the danger has passed. I repeat, it is over—according to the cops. You can stop lurking around. Just go in and talk to her. Man up."

Bradford exited the vehicle. He marched toward Midas. "You!"

Like he needed this shit. "Me."

Bradford pointed his index finger at Midas even as the lawyer's coat flapped in the breeze.

"You are to stay away from Alina Bellamy, do you hear me? Her father does not want you near his daughter."

"But what does Alina want?" Ophelia asked in her reasonable tone. "We should all go in and find out."

"*You* should be protecting your client, while you still have a job." Bradford glowered at her. "I need to speak privately with Midas, now."

Ophelia didn't rush away. She did send a sidelong glance at Midas. "Take the advice I gave you. Don't miss an opportunity. If you don't tell someone how you feel…well, let's just say that isn't the kind of regret I'd wish on my worst enemy." A long inhale. "You gonna be okay out here with him?" Her head bobbed toward Bradford.

"I think I can handle myself," Midas assured her.

She slowly backed away.

Midas knew it wasn't her fault that he'd been spotted by Bradford. When he'd seen the detectives arrive, he'd pulled out from his normal hiding position. And, yeah, he'd even been inching toward the rink. Thinking that, maybe, he should go see Alina.

So I wasn't staying properly hidden. It's my damn fault Bradford is currently glaring at me.

"The detectives have told Ryker and I that Alina is safe. They believe the danger to her is over." Bradford's lips thinned. "But I think I am staring at someone dangerous."

"I would *never* hurt Alina."

"You hurt her by breathing. You hurt her by existing. You hurt her by being the son of the man who took her mother from Alina when she was just a child." A puff of fog appeared in front of Bradford's mouth, testimony to the freezing temperature. "I have known Alina since she was a toddler trying on ice skates for the first time. I saw her go from a bubbling, always-smiling girl to a withdrawn woman who rarely makes new friends. Who prefers to spend hours on the ice because she's afraid to get close to anyone. Afraid of loving and losing someone." He pulled his scarf closer to his neck. "You are a threat to her."

"No."

"To her peace of mind. To her heart. You broke her heart, you understand that, don't you? When she learned the truth at that penitentiary? When she had to watch you attack your own father? You broke our Alina."

Midas didn't have a response. She had seen him at his worst. He'd been so angry. So enraged because...

He took Alina's mother. Alina. He hurt someone she loved.

And because...

My bastard of a father fixed it so I can never be with the woman I love. Ophelia hadn't been spouting BS. He did love Alina.

"Stay away from Alina," Bradford ordered yet again. "Don't talk to her. Don't try to explain. Don't try to make things better. There is no making this better."

Midas knew the last statement was true. There was nothing he could do to make this mess better.

"I will get a restraining order if I have to do so. You are clearly a violent individual. And, one who—I believe—has been stalking Alina. You are stalking her right now, aren't you? That's why you're outside her rink. Unhealthy. Dangerous. You cannot be near her. Her father and I will not let you near her."

Midas stared at the much smaller man. "You really think you could stop me from getting to Alina? You think a piece of paper would stop me?"

Bradford studied him. After a moment, some of the angry tension seemed to leave the lawyer's body. "No, I don't think I could physically stop you." Lower. Grim. "And you might not give a damn about what some judge says, either. But…" He licked his lips. "I think you care about Alina. She doesn't want to see you. She doesn't want you in her life. You are just a reminder of pain. So how about you try to do what's right for her? Stay. Away." He spun around and headed for the rink.

Every muscle in Midas's body had hardened. He wanted in that rink. He wanted Alina. He wanted—

For her not to hurt. For her not to hate me. For Alina to smile and be happy. I want…God, I want the past to have never happened.

His phone vibrated in his front pocket. Midas pulled it out. Not like he could ignore this caller. He put the phone to his ear. "Oliver." He knew Oliver had been in North Dakota. Working once again with the Feds and the DA up there, he was trying to get Henry to reveal more about his vics. "Has he told you anything?"

"Not a damn thing, and that's why I'm calling."

Midas grunted. "He's done sharing. It was all just a fuck-you to me."

"He hasn't *mentioned* you even once."

"Because he's done with his game." Obviously.

"No, I don't think so. Something else is happening. You're not going to like this but..." Oliver stopped.

"Spit it out." There was never anything involving his father that Midas did like.

"I want you here."

Fuck that. "I'm not leaving Alina." Hard no.

"You're not *with* Alina," Oliver threw back. "You think Ophelia hasn't been updating me? And by the way, she saw you the first day. You can't just hang outside of someone's bedroom window."

"I wasn't—" He stopped. He'd been about thirty feet away from the house. Hardly hanging by the window. "Her bedroom is on the second floor. I'm not freaking Dracula. I wasn't floating up there watching her."

"Uh, huh. Whatever. Look, Ophelia just texted me. The detectives have closed the kidnapping case. There is jack and shit for them to go on. We need to push Henry."

"Good luck with that."

"I don't need luck," Oliver responded instantly. "I've got you."

Oh, hell, no. "I'm not getting near him."

"It's like he's *waiting* for something. I can all but see the guy vibrating with anticipation. He's cocky and confident, and we have got to throw him off. That's where you will come in. He's not expecting you to come back. I want you with me when I—"

"First, the warden is not going to let me anywhere near Henry. Neither will the DA. And I don't know what kind of FBI magic you think you're working, but, dammit, you're not even *technically* with the Bureau any longer—"

"Working on a contractual basis," Oliver supplied, voice smooth. "The director and I understand each other."

"Wonderful for you. Truly. But I'm not coming. I have other priorities."

"Like keeping your eyes glued to Alina."

His eyes weren't glued to her. She was inside. And her lawyer had just threatened to slap him with a restraining order. "You ever want something so badly that you think about destroying the world to get it?"

A stark pause. Uncomfortable silence. Then, "Uh...Midas? That sounds like a statement your dad might make."

"I'm *not* coming to see him."

"What if he didn't kill Alina's mother? What if he's just jerking you around?"

Midas sucked in a deep breath. "I've heard he knew specific details—what she was wearing, how her body was found..."

"Sure, and he could have been *told* all of that. I can't say he's guilty yet. All I know is I need the man thrown off his game. I need you here to do that. I can get you on a private jet and have you here within hours. Come on, Midas, what if there is more happening?"

What if he didn't kill Alina's mother?

If his father hadn't killed her, if someone else was to blame... "I have to go."

"That's not a yes or a no. I really need one of those responses, my friend." Sympathy softened Oliver's voice. "I get this is your worst nightmare. I know what I'm asking, but there is a whole lot at stake here."

He knew what was at stake. "Get the private jet ready."

"Hell, yes."

***

Alina walked into the locker room with slow, tired steps. She'd put ear buds in after the training session, and the loud music blasted at her.

Classical music on the ice.

Driving beats after. She needed the furious rush of music to drown out everything else. Her skates were slung over her shoulder. Another bag weighing her down. The door shut behind her, and for a moment, she just stood there.

Finally, alone.

The showers waited to the right, yet she made no move to approach them.

The music kept blasting.

Her breath shuddered out. She could finally drop her mask, at least for a moment. She just *hurt* so much—

A shadow moved to the right. Coming out from the line of lockers with a rush of movement. Startled, terrified, Alina whirled and began to run back toward the door. But the shadow grabbed her. Caught her wrist in a tight grip even as she opened her mouth to scream her head off.

"Alina."

Soft.

Her head turned to look back at the man who'd caught her wrist.

"Alina, please," Midas said as his amber eyes burned with emotion, "give me five minutes."

CHAPTER TWENTY-ONE

"How did you get in here?" Alina asked. Her free hand snatched out her ear buds. Part of her wanted to wrench away from him. *Two weeks, Midas. Two weeks passed without a word.* And another part of her wanted to throw her body against him and hold on as tightly as she could.

"Security flaw at the rink." He grimaced. "Gonna text that asshole lawyer of yours to get it fixed. The guards in the back have a ten-minute window when they aren't doing their jobs properly. One guy goes to call his girl at this time—same time every single day—while the other is patrolling the left side of the parking lot. Really, he's just having a smoke break. If you know their routine, you can slip right in. As long as you have keys to the rooms and know the security codes, getting to this locker room is a snap."

Uh, not exactly sounding like a snap to her. "And you have keys because you were here before."

"Briefly in charge, yeah." A faint grin came and went on his lips. His thumb caressed over her racing pulse as he held her wrist. "You're not screaming for help."

"Because you wouldn't hurt me. At least, not physically."

He flinched and let her go.

"The detectives say that I'm safe. They believe Bowie Dodge was behind all the kidnappings." She dropped her bag and skates as she faced him.

"So I've heard."

"What do you believe?"

"I believe the guy struck me as more of a follower than a leader." His gaze swept over her. "God, I missed you."

Her breath caught.

"I'm so sorry, Alina."

Her chin lifted even as her lower lip trembled. "Sorry you ignored me for two weeks?"

"I didn't—" His hand yanked through his hair. "I've been protecting you."

That was the story he chose? "Your protection feels like you were ignoring me."

"I've watched you almost every damn moment. I had to be sure you were safe."

"Right. Because you take your bodyguard job so seriously. I hate to tell you this, but I'm pretty sure my father fired you. Watching me *isn't* your job any longer."

"Yeah, he did. Ryker fired me and told me to stay the hell away from you. And Bradford warned me that if I didn't stay out of your life, I'd get slapped with a restraining order."

Her eyes widened. "But—" She stopped, not sure what to say. Her father had told her nothing about ordering Midas away. Firing him, yes. But—*he told Midas to stay away?*

"They both want me far away from you, but here the fuck I am." His gaze seemed to drink her in. "I wanted to kill Henry."

Her heart slammed into her chest.

"When he confessed to hurting your mother, I could see your devastation. I could feel your pain. I attacked him, and I wanted to kill him." He sucked in a breath. "If the guards hadn't pulled me off him, I-I don't know what I would have—"

"Stop." She took a step toward him.

Midas backed up.

Alina blinked. "Midas, are you *afraid* of me?" Surely not.

"I'm afraid of hurting you more than I already have. God, baby, what is it even like for you to look at me? Do you see him?"

"No." She shook her head. "I see you. *You,* Midas." She took more steps toward him.

But Midas backed up again.

Oh, forget that. She rushed forward. She tossed the ear buds somewhere and grabbed his hands. "You are not your father."

"You saw me attack him. I am just as violent as—"

"How many women have you killed?"

"What?" Horror flashed on his face. "*None. I would never—*"

"What about torture? You do that a lot? Terrorize people? Torture them for fun?"

"*No.*"

"You hit your father. Yes. *But he'd just confessed to killing my mother.* I wanted to hit him, too. I was already running to attack him, but a guard pulled me back."

He'd turned to stone beneath her touch. "You hate me."

"No, Midas." Hate was the last thing she felt for him. "I'm mad because you left me without a word. I'm hurt. But I don't hate you." Alina didn't think she could ever hate him.

He looked down to where she touched him. "How can you put your hands on me?"

"Pretty easy to do." She didn't move her hands. "I missed you, Midas."

A low breath escaped him. Then he…

He bent down on his knees.

Stunned, confused, Alina started to retreat, but his hands reached out and curled around her waist. His head pressed against her as Midas held her and he said, "I'm so sorry."

Her hands fluttered in the air, then came down on his shoulders. "Midas?"

"I hate what he did. I want him to be lying. I'm going to find out—if…if he's lying, maybe we'll have a chance."

She didn't understand. Lying? "What are you talking about?"

"I'm sorry for what he did. I wish that I could have stopped him long ago. A nightmare that should have ended. I *never* want you to be in pain. And I know you can't be with me, knowing what my father did. That's why I backed away. I kept watching you. Kept protecting you. But I knew you didn't want to see me. I knew it would hurt you. Even though I missed being close to you. So damn much. Because..." She felt the shudder that shook him. "I love you."

Had he just said—wait... "Midas?" A whisper.

He rose in a rush. "If he didn't kill her, if it was just a lie, will you give me a chance? Give us a chance? I'm flying out ASAP. Oliver wants me in an interrogation with Henry. Thinks there is a chance Henry is playing one of his mind games. Maybe he didn't kill her. Maybe there's more here. *Maybe.* If Oliver is right, will you give me a chance?"

"You said you loved me." She went back to that because it was the certainty. There had been no *maybe* attached to those words. Midas hadn't said, "Maybe I love you." Everything else—lots of "if" parts and too many "maybe" choices.

But there had been no hesitation in his declaration of love. For me.

Midas swallowed. "I love you more than anything in this world. And all I want to do is protect you. But it seems like you need protecting from me."

No, she didn't. Not ever. "You are not your father."

Pain etched deep lines into his face. "That's the last person I ever want to be."

***

"How long have you been reporting to Midas Monroe?"

Aw, hell. Ophelia had known she'd have to face off with this guy sooner or later. Exhaling, she swung around to find Bradford Wells glaring at her. "Bradford!" she exclaimed brightly as if thrilled by the opportunity to chat with him. "Did you come by to watch Alina on the ice?" She shook her finger at him. "You know practice sessions are closed. Dmitri can get quite snippy about unauthorized personnel being here."

"You're fired."

Dammit. "Excuse me?"

"The detectives have closed the case. Alina is safe. Your services are no longer needed." So stiff. So annoying.

Her hands went to her hips. "This is because I was chatting with Midas, isn't it?"

"Want to tell me how long you've been reporting to him?"

"I wasn't technically reporting to him." She had been in contact with Memphis and with Oliver Foxx, but Ophelia didn't share those details with the attorney. They were need-to-know. She didn't see why he should have the info. "Firing me, huh? So what do I get? Two weeks to finish up?"

"You're done now. Collect your things." He motioned to one of the security guards who usually guarded the front entrance. "He will see you out."

Well, crap. "Here's your hat and don't let the door hit you in the ass," she muttered.

"Precisely." His stern features hardened. "Anyone with ties to Midas Monroe or his father is not welcome near Alina. Those individuals have caused enough heartache for the Bellamy family."

"Fine." Like she could win this fight. Ophelia knew a losing situation when she saw one. "But

I'm telling Alina goodbye first." She marched past him and headed for the locker room. Bradford was such a pompous prick. And, okay, *fine,* maybe she could see where he'd been worried about Midas. But only because the guy didn't *know* Midas.

Midas wasn't some out-of-control killer. She fully believed the man would take a bullet before letting anyone hurt Alina.

She pushed open the locker room door. "Alina!" Ophelia called. She didn't hear the spray of the showers. "Alina, I have to tell you—" Ophelia broke off. Alina's back was to her. Her friend—and, yeah, she thought of Alina as a friend and not just some client—had her arms curled around her stomach. "Alina, is everything okay?"

Alina slowly turned to face her. There were tear tracks on her face.

"Is there a threat?" Ophelia rushed to her. She locked her hands around Alina's shoulders and hauled her close. "What's happening?"

"Midas said he loved me."

Ophelia's eyes widened. He'd taken her advice?

"But he left before I could tell him that I love him, too."

***

"You are not to touch the prisoner."

Midas grunted.

"You are to remain two feet from him at all times."

Another grunt.

"You are to let Oliver Foxx lead the questioning. You are *not*," a vein bulged along Terrance's temple, "to let Henry goad you into another attack. Not under any circumstances, do you understand me?" The DA was sweating.

"We have this," Oliver assured him. "Midas is in full control." He slapped a hand on Midas's shoulder. "Aren't you, buddy?"

No, he was not. He'd left Alina when all he wanted was to stay with her, forever. She hadn't seemed to blame him for what his father had done. How could she be that way? So good? So warm? So...

Alina.

"He's not responding." Terrance began to pace around the small interrogation room. "I knew this was a mistake. My career is going straight down the shitter."

Oliver's hand gripped Midas's shoulder as he applied some pressure. "You are in total control. Tell the man that his, uh, career isn't going down the—his career is fine."

"You're fine, Terrance. I'm absolutely in control. Control is my middle name," Midas returned. "And I can't wait to see my dear old dad."

"Jesus." Terrance blew out a breath. "Jesus."

The door opened. Terrance whipped around. A guard came in first. Then the prisoner.

"Why the hell did you drag me out of my cell this late at—" Henry stopped. Stopped speaking and walking as he gaped at Midas as he sat in the chair at the narrow table that had once again been placed in the middle of the room. Henry shook his head. "You aren't supposed to be here."

"We've contacted your lawyer," Terrance informed him. "Xander will be here shortly. You don't have to say anything until he arrives."

"Fuck Xander. He's useless. I'll say what I want to say whenever I want."

It was the response they'd all expected Henry to give.

Another guard crowded in behind Henry.

Yet Henry still did not move. His gaze remained locked on Midas.

Midas smiled at his father. "Those bruises have healed nicely, though I did learn that you lost a tooth."

"You shouldn't be here."

"No? Where should I be?"

Henry shuffled forward as he lifted his bound hands. "You're going to mess everything up." Henry's glinting glare swept to Oliver. "This your doing, FBI man? You screwing things because you think you know how to get under my skin?"

"Am I under your skin?" Midas asked. He kept his tone mild. Oliver had asked Midas to do the bulk of the talking.

"Leave."

"Why?" Midas's hands were under the table. His pose appeared relaxed, but tension poured through every cell of his body. "Are you worried that I'll realize you've been lying, yet again?"

Henry blinked. "What lie?"

"You tell so many. It's hard to keep them all straight."

Another mincing step forward.

"But let's start with the big one," Midas decided. *I need this to be a lie. Because then I have a chance with Alina.* "You didn't kill Alina's mother."

Henry glared at him so hard and hotly that Midas was surprised the skin didn't burn off his body. Elation began to fill him. Henry had been playing a game. Just throwing out that confession in an effort to break Midas. It wasn't true.

Henry burst into laughter. Loud, raucous laughter. The same kind of laughter he'd been emitting as Midas punched him in this very room.

Terrance swiped his hand over his forehead. Oliver leaned forward in his chair.

And Midas felt his hope die.

Henry took mincing steps as he advanced. The guards secured him at the table. The grin still curled his lips as Henry said, "Oh, you poor bastard. Is that what you thought? That I was lying? No, son, I told you the truth. Hell, there was even a witness to the crime. Watched the whole thing. Why do you think I didn't get to finish with her the way I like?"

No knife wound to her heart.

"Thought he was gonna run to the cops. But he didn't. Realized later it was because he liked what he saw. It's that way, sometimes. You don't realize the beast is inside until something happens, and he gets a taste for death."

"What witness?" Oliver asked.

Henry's head angled toward him. "Am I talking to you or am I in the middle of a conversation with my son?"

Again, that response had been predicted. Oliver had said that Henry would view everyone else in the room as somehow less deserving of his time and attention.

But he'll talk to me. Henry loved trying to destroy Midas. "What witness?"

Henry's head swung back so that he stared straight at Midas. "Oh, you've met him." He hummed. "So has that pretty, little Alina. Of course, you carried her away before they could *really* get to know each other better. I suspect that Bowie person was actually working for him. Not me. Never me."

Midas jerked in his chair. The wooden legs creaked. He'd started to rise but caught himself. "Are you saying the man who organized the kidnapping was the witness?" And, no, they hadn't fucking *met*. Midas had gotten Alina out of the cabin before—

"You should not be here," Henry told him once more in a chiding tone. "I didn't ask you to come. In fact, I *gave* you a chance. I want you to remember that when it's all over. I put you in place so you could be the big, brave hero you always wanted to be. Making amends, you see. In my own way. My shrink tells me I have to do that."

Midas tried to focus on the words that actually mattered. "You're saying the person behind the kidnapping is still out there?"

"I'm saying that he's an admirer of my work. Occasionally, he likes to tell me about the work he does, too. Though he can't really compare with me. No one can. It's like seeing a master's work next to a novice's piece."

"We've checked your mail," Terrance said as he edged toward the table.

"So nosey of you to read other people's mail. Rude." Henry didn't seem concerned. "Didn't your mother teach you better than that?"

Midas knew he had to get more. But...

I want to get back to Alina. "Why do you hate me?" Again, Oliver had coached him about this question. He was supposed to keep Henry off balance.

Henry pushed back in his chair. His shackles banged into the edge of the table. "What makes you think I do?"

"Because you set me up for multiple murders. Because you're trying to wreck my life right now."

"Nah, son. I am trying to *help* you. If you lose everything, that's your own damn fault."

"Why did you kill my mother? You had a kid with her." *You had me. Why couldn't we have a normal life? Why did you have to be a monster?* "Having a child with her had to make her different from the others. Why did you—"

"I didn't kill her. You always get stuck on that. I told you over and over, she left us."

He would never get the truth. This meeting had been a mistake. Just like the last one. *A horrible mistake.* "You don't even know the truth, do you?" And maybe that was what this was really about. "You spin so many lies that you can't remember what's real and what isn't." He had a plane to catch.

Alina. He had to get back to her.

"I know exactly what is real." Henry's amber eyes glinted. "I remember your mother perfectly.

I remember every single moment we had together." His features seemed to soften. "And you're right. She was different. That made me different. I knew the first moment I saw her that she would be special."

Hadn't Midas thought the same thing the first time he saw Alina? That she was special?

I don't want to be like him.

"I could laugh. We went on hikes. She cooked dinner with me. Had dreams. Made me dream. And she was pregnant with you. Life. She was about *life*. You were born and you were Midas. Our golden boy." Henry licked his lips. "But it had been so long, and...the urge came again. I didn't think she'd know. I slipped out. She had to take care of you, and I slipped out," he said again, "but...she followed. Saw the body."

Henry had never said this before. Is this real? More lies?

"Your mom screamed and ran. But she ran—she ran right into the road. *Even though I told her to stop.* A truck hit her. Slammed right into her. *Boom.*" His shackled hands hit the table and made it bounce. "There was so much blood everywhere. *She left us.* Right then. If she'd just done what I told her, if she'd stayed in that motel room with you...*she left you alone.* What kind of mother does that to a son? Left you alone to follow me that night? Left us both when she ran? *She deserved what she got.* The truck kept going. Driver probably thought he'd just hit a damn deer or something. Too scared to stop on a dark road."

Midas made himself breathe.

"I walked to her." Henry's eyes had turned glassy. "Already gone. I buried her. Went back to the motel. Thought you'd be screaming your head off. You were...maybe six months then? You'd been alone for hours. Her blood was on my hands when I came back and picked you up. We had this—this damn little mini-crib thing that she'd bought for you. It let us go from town to town and was so easy to set up. You always had a safe spot to sleep. She wanted you safe." He looked down at the table. At his bound hands. "You weren't crying. You were still sleeping. She left you. If she'd stayed in that room with you like she was supposed to do, nothing bad would have happened. Not to her. I *loved* her. People are supposed to do what I tell them. It's so easy. So *easy*." Rage blasted in his words. "I didn't tell you to come here!" His eyes flew to Midas. Not glassy any longer. Shining with emotion. "Why the fuck aren't you doing what I tell you to do? I've given you everything. Nothing bad would happen. *Not if you just paid attention and listened to what I told you!*"

His father had broken. Midas could see it. In the pain that flashed in Henry's eyes. In the words that rolled out one after the other. This was the most vulnerable his monster of a father had ever been.

Because he loved my mother. Or, loved her as much as he could. The chink in his father's armor wouldn't last long. "I'm paying attention now."

And just like that, it ended. All emotion vanished from Henry's eyes. His mask returned. "No," Henry said. "But you will be when you bury her." He stood. "Terrance, I want to go back to my room."

Midas needed *more*. "Why didn't you leave me in that motel room? A kid could only slow you down. Why didn't you just abandon me long ago?" *It would have been so much better if you had.*

Terrance had motioned for the guards to escort Henry out. They'd unhooked his shackles from the table and were edging near the door, but Henry looked back. "Abandon my own son? What kind of father do you think I am?" An angry huff. "Now, these fool guards need to get me the hell out of here. I'm not saying another word without my lawyer."

One of the guards opened the door. But Henry didn't cross the threshold. He did throw an amused smile toward Terrance. "You really shouldn't lie. Aren't you supposed to be one of those upstanding individuals that fights for truth? For justice?"

"Don't know what you mean." Terrance pointed to the door. "Guards, I believe the prisoner said he wasn't cooperating any longer. Not without his attorney."

"That's the lie," Henry murmured. "You began by saying Xander would be here soon. Knew right then that you were trying to play with me. Nice attempt, by the way." Now he turned. The shackles strained as he maneuvered back to face Midas. "But how on earth could my lawyer be here when he's not even in the state?"

Midas felt his heart drop.

"I sent him on a very important errand." Henry nodded. "Very important. He's off to convey my sincerest apologies to Alina Bellamy. I do hope he gets my message across to her." A broad smile spread over his face and never reached his eyes. "Think he'll do the job just right for me?"

Midas leapt to his feet. "You—"

"*Out!*" Terrance bellowed. "Now! Get him out!"

The guards took him out. The shackles clanked and groaned, and the door closed a moment later.

"Midas?" Oliver's worried voice. "You okay, man?"

No. "Where. Is. Xander?"

"We'll find out." Oliver was on his feet, too. "And we'll call Memphis and Ophelia. We'll make sure they stay close to Alina."

He had to get to her. Tension pounded in Midas's temples. Boiled in his blood. "I need to get on a plane." He rushed for the door.

But Terrance stepped into his path. "Do we believe Henry about the witness to the Bellamy murder? Or is that some BS?"

Henry had been playing with them the moment he walked into the room. He'd known they were lying to him. Had he lied back?

And all that information he'd revealed about Midas's mother. Truth or lies?

Midas did not know. He was sick of the games. "Find Xander Palmer," he demanded as he spun back to glare at a frowning Oliver. "Use every federal contact you have. If he boarded a plane, if he rented a car—tell me. Let me know where that bastard is." And, the most important thing... *"Don't let him near Alina."*

Because his father never, ever apologized to anyone.

If he'd sent Xander to Alina, it wasn't because he wanted the lawyer to tell Alina how very sorry Henry was for his crimes.

But he might have sent Xander to kill her. Xander, the one person who would've had close contact with Henry. The person who could have carried out any orders that Henry wanted. Orders like...

Kidnapping. Hiring thugs to do the dirty work.

Hurting Alina.

"We find him," Midas said as he swallowed the fear and focused on the fury that churned ever hotter within him. "And we stop him."

CHAPTER TWENTY-TWO

Four a.m. Another day of practice. Another day on the ice.

Alina didn't wait for the driver to come around and open the limo door for her. As soon as the vehicle braked in front of the rink's entrance, she pushed on the door and stepped outside. Snow was falling, as it had been all night. Not as heavy now. At first, she'd feared the roads would be impassable.

But Milo had managed to get them through.

There wasn't a guard at the door. That gave her pause and she turned toward Milo.

"Everything's okay," he assured her as he came to her side. "After your father found out about the security issue yesterday, he hired all new guards. They'll be here soon. Dmitri is already in the rink, and I'll remain stationed out here in front."

The security issue, yes. The two guards who'd let Midas slip inside. As he'd indicated, Midas had texted Bradford, and Bradford had, of course, immediately informed her father of the situation.

"We didn't need to fire Ophelia." Alina hunched into her jacket. "I liked her."

Milo approached the front of the building. "I know, but she was reporting to Midas." He typed in the security code. Swiped his key card. "Your father doesn't want Midas near you."

Even though she shivered, Alina made no move to enter the rink. "It's my life." She hadn't told anyone about Midas flying to see Henry.

"He just..." Milo took her hands. Dependable Milo. He'd been driving her father's car for years. He'd started with them right after an injury had taken him from the military. "He wants you safe." His eyes swept over her. "You look so much like your mother."

That was what Henry had told her, too. And the words made her shiver even harder as she tugged her hands free of Milo's grip. "I'm not her." Milo had known her mother. He'd been their driver for several years before her mother's death. "Just like Midas isn't Henry." They were different people. And she was *not* going to just follow her father's orders.

She would have her own chance for happiness.

Milo held the rink's door open for her. Alina started to enter.

"Alina!" A man's voice. One that she didn't recognize.

She turned around and saw a man barreling toward them from the darkness. He wore a ski cap and scarf, and a long, dark coat billowed around him.

"Alina!" he shouted. "I must talk to you!"

"Get inside, Alina," Milo ordered as he drew his weapon. *Driver and guard.* He always had been. "*Now.*"

She stumbled over the threshold but looked back just in time to see—

Two other shadows erupted from the darkness. She sucked in a sharp breath as those two shadows hit the running man. They slammed into him and drove him to the ground even as the snow swirled in the air around them all. Alina backed up.

"It's okay!" A voice she *did* recognize. "We've got him, Alina!" Ophelia cried out.

Alina pushed against Milo. "Lower your weapon."

He did. But he brought out a flashlight. Milo shone it toward the group on the ground.

Ophelia and Lane Lawson had a man pinned in the snow. The man raised his head.

Xander Palmer. Her mouth dropped when she saw the lawyer's face.

"Midas had us looking for him! No way was he getting inside." Lane heaved Xander to his feet. "I think there are some detectives who will want a word or two with you, buddy."

"I just need to talk with Alina! Henry sent me with a message!" He fought Lane's hold.

"Do you want me to tase you?" Ophelia asked. "Because I can. I will."

"I'm an attorney! I've done nothing wrong. *This is a public place.* Let me go or I'll have you both brought up on charges and you—"

They let him go. But they didn't back up.

Milo still had his flashlight aimed at them.

"He wanted to apologize, Alina!" Xander stared at her. "Henry asked me to come here, to be face-to-face with you, and tell you how much he regrets his actions."

A sound of disgust escaped Lane. "So you're an errand boy for a serial killer? What a dream job. Lucky you."

"*If* you will come talk to him, he'll name more victims. That's his offer. His way of atoning. He wanted me to come to you and tell you—"

"Do not come any closer." Alina's voice rang out, strong and clear. "I am not interested in any offer from Henry Monroe. And, this isn't public property. It's private. My father owns this facility. As a lawyer, you really should know better." Her spine was ramrod straight. "Ophelia and Lane? I believe you mentioned something about detectives...?"

Xander backed away. "This is a mistake. I'm just relaying a message!"

"Message relayed. Stay away from me. Far away."

He looked at Ophelia and Lane.

"I will tase you," Ophelia said. "Give me a reason."

"I'll just knock your ass flat out," Lane stated. "I don't need a reason."

Footsteps rushed behind Alina. "Is everything all right?" Dmitri demanded. "Alina?"

"Unwanted company is being sent away." Her heart drummed. "And everything is fine. It's time for me to skate."

Accept an offer from Henry? Go see him in person?

Never.

***

Her skates cut across the ice. Faster and faster. The scene this morning had been chaos. The cops had arrived. The detectives had questioned Xander. They'd vanished with him.

Ophelia and Lane had vanished, too. Had they gone along for the questioning?

Her new guards had arrived. Two outside the front of the rink. Two stationed at the rear of the facility.

And she'd skated.

Dmitri had supervised. Been *almost* kind, in his way.

The lights around the rink were turned off. The only illumination fell on the ice itself. She skated faster and faster. They'd agreed not to attempt the quadruple. She hadn't been able to land it no matter how hard she'd tried, and Dmitri feared she'd injure herself if they trained too long with it.

But she skated faster and faster.

My mother...murdered.

Midas...saying he loves me.

Her muscles bunched.

The ice is so cold all the time...and I want to be warm.

She leapt into the air. Spun once. Twice. Three times. A fourth—

She slammed into the ice.

Her hands pushed against the cold surface. But she didn't get up. For a moment, Alina just stayed down on that ice. *What would happen if I just stayed down?*

"Alina?" Dmitri's voice. Worried. So unlike him.

Her lips pressed together. She rose on knees that wobbled. "I'm not hurt." A lie. *I hurt all the time. But it's on the inside. Midas said he loves me, and I think I love him, and I don't care what his father did.*

No, she did care. Of course, she cared. She just wasn't letting it stop her from loving Midas.

"Enough for today." Dmitri clapped briskly. "Go shower. Rest."

She should skate longer, but she didn't argue. Alina glided to him. He opened the small half-door for her.

"Why did you try the jump?" His eyes swept over her.

"Because I fall all the time. And I wanted to see what it would be like to fly." That probably made no sense to him. It didn't even fully make sense to her.

But Dmitri nodded.

She unlaced her skates. Swung them over her shoulder and headed for the locker room. She pushed open the door.

Then just sat down on a bench. Alina put the skates beside her. She brought her trembling hands up and stared at her palms. Still icy.

But she wasn't cold whenever Midas touched her. Not him.

Midas, when are you coming back?

A shadow moved. She saw it from the corner of her eye, and Alina leapt to her feet. Not in fear, but in joy. "Midas?" He'd gotten into the building again—

"No." Low. "Not Midas."

Terror spiked in her veins. Her heart thundered. She spun away. Her hand hit the skates. She leapt over the small bench.

But he caught her. One hand flew out and wrapped around her neck. He heaved her back against him. The bench fell in their struggle. She opened her mouth to scream.

A gloved hand slapped over her lips.

***

"You're not allowed entry." The two guards blocked the main entrance at the rink.

Midas narrowed his eyes. "I am not in a good mood." Far from it. "A snowstorm canceled my original flight. I had to drive my ass for hours until I could get to another airport where I could take a freaking nightmare plane ride here. The snow blasted us every moment."

"You're not allowed entry." A patiently repeated response.

Did he look like he was in the mood for patience? "I'm here to see Alina."

But they didn't move. "Mr. Wells specifically told us that you weren't to be allowed inside. You're on the list, Mr. Midas."

So they recognized him?

"Saw you on the news recently," the smaller of the two guards said. "You, ah, did a great job saving Alina." He had short, spiky, brown hair. "But we can't let you in. Orders are orders."

New guards. He'd already been briefed by Ophelia on the scuffle that had gone down this morning. *Xander was here.* And he was currently answering questions at the PD. Midas knew he should go there, but he had a desperate need to put his eyes on Alina. To make sure for himself that she was all right. He'd tried texting her several times, but she hadn't responded.

Probably because she is practicing. Alina doesn't have her phone on when she's practicing.

Memphis was currently at the police station with Ophelia and Lane. Midas would join up with them soon, but first...*I need to see Alina.*

"We don't want to have to get physical," the taller guard warned. Bright green eyes. A too-tough swagger. And he'd really sounded like he *did* want to get physical.

Midas smiled. "I would love to see you try."

"Don't, Drew," the smaller guy urged. "You do *not* want to tackle him."

"I'm going to see, Alina," Midas said. "You guys can either open the door for me, or I'll be opening it myself in about twenty seconds while you are groaning on the ground." After the talk with his father...

I need to see her.

"You're the one who will be on the ground," the one who'd been tagged as Drew retorted.

"He will wreck you, man," the smarter bodyguard warned his partner. "Let's just let him see her. Ten minutes. What will it hurt?"

"Are you *trying* to get us fired, Chip? You heard Mr. Wells! He went in like five minutes ago, and he specifically said that *no one* was to get inside. He warned us. I am not losing my job over this shit!" Drew puffed out his chest. "No one is getting inside."

So...Bradford was in there.

Midas turned and surveyed the lot. He didn't see the lawyer's normal ride. "Why is he here?" And something nagged at him.

His damn freak of a father and all the BS he'd said during both of their meetings...

Truth or lies? With Henry, it was always so hard to be sure what was real. But Midas did remember Henry saying...

"Lawyers, am I right? You can't trust them."

And...there had a been a witness to the attack on Alina's mother. At least, according to Henry, there had been. But again, truth or lies? If Henry had been telling the truth...If...

Someone had seen the attack but not reported it.

And *someone* had been in contact with Henry for a long time.

And...*Henry said we'd met the witness. Me and Alina...*

Henry had been specific about that. Certain.

"It's none of your damn business what Mr. Wells is doing! Now I told you to get out of here!" Drew shoved Midas in the back.

Midas didn't so much as stumble. *Bad mistake, new guard. Bad.* He turned. Smiled. "Do it again." A dare.

The fool did.

***

"It's all right, Alina." A whisper in her ear. "It's only going to hurt you for a moment. Just a brief moment." He spun her to face him.

Alina found herself staring up at Bradford Wells.

He smiled down at her.

One of his hands covered her mouth. The other now rested at her waist. A grip that bruised.

"I was going to just take his money. Just like I took the money from the others. And if you'd followed along, been good, I would have let you go." A pause. "Probably."

Her left hand gripped the laces of one skate. Her fingers had gotten tangled in the lace when she'd jumped over the bench. Her hand had flown out and knocked into her skates.

Slowly, she began to pull up that lace. Bringing the skate up higher and higher.

"They deserved it. Your father. Hayden Thatch. Leopold O'Sullivan. More bastards just like them. They acted so clean and upstanding. But I knew their secrets. Their crimes. I've seen all their dirty deeds. Corporate espionage. Shady deals. Like they are any better than the common criminals that you find on the street." His hand released her waist and rose to curl around her throat. "I've seen so much. I got tired of the secrets."

She kept pulling up that lace. Bringing the skate higher.

"People are always pretending to be different from what they really are. You know who doesn't pretend?"

Why was he asking her questions when she couldn't speak? That stupid glove pushed against her lips with bruising intensity.

"Henry Monroe."

She blanched.

"He tells the world he's a monster. He revels in it." A smile. "I watched him with your mother. I could have stopped him. I didn't. I watched, and it was the most beautiful thing I'd ever seen." His fingers tightened on Alina's neck. "He snapped your mother's neck. Brutal. Fast. She was like a bird in his hands. He dropped her onto the ground. The snow was all around her. I-I must have made a sound then. He turned and saw me. And you know what he did?"

Tears slid down her cheeks. The pressure on her throat had cut off her air flow. He wasn't snapping her neck. He was choking her.

"Henry smiled at me."

She pulled the laces...Alina felt the top of the skate touch her fingers.

"And he left her there. He walked away. I ran to her. She was still alive, can you imagine? So, I put my hand over her mouth...just like I'm doing to you right now. And I watched the life fade from her eyes as—"

She yanked up the skate, and she sliced the blade over the side of his arm.

Bradford screamed and let her go.

She drove that blade at him again. This time, she pounded it into his chest. The blade sank past skin and muscle and blood spurted onto her.

He heaved back, howling in pain, and the blood seemed to be everywhere. Alina whirled from him. She kept the skate in her hand and ran for the door. "Help!" she yelled. "Someone, *help me!*"

"*You bitch!*" Bradford roared.

She yanked open the door. Raced forward even as she heard the pounding of his steps behind her. "Help!" Where was Dmitri? Would the guards outside hear her?

The rink waited in front of her. She could cut across it. Get to the other side and get to the front doors faster. She jumped over the half-wall. Slipped a little but shot upright.

Bradford's hand flew out and grabbed her as he leaned over the wall. "You aren't getting away!"

She brought the skate down on him. She cut right across the top of his forearm.

More blood. He cried out, but his other hand yanked the skate from her.

And then he was coming completely over the wall.

Blood covered the ice. His blood. It soaked the ice and her. Alina spun and rushed over the ice. Her breath sawed in and out. She had to get away.

"Alina!"

Her head whipped up. *Midas.* He was on the ice and hurrying toward her from the opposite side of the rink. His eyes were wide with horror and that horrified gaze made her look back. Alina tossed a terrified glance over her shoulder.

Bradford was there. Swinging her own skate's blade at her. Alina ducked. She lost her balance, and she went crashing into the ice. Her body rolled and when she came up, she was staring at Bradford as he loomed over her.

Alina scuttled back, but he was bringing the skate's blade down and aiming for her neck. Her hands flew up. "No!"

Midas rushed by her. He slammed into Bradford. They both hit the ice with a shattering impact. They fought. Twisted. Bodies heaved.

There were more shouts in the air.

Dmitri. The guards? She looked over at them for just an instant. "Get help! Call the police!" Her wild stare returned to the battle.

Only it was...over?

Midas rose slowly and stared down at the lawyer. Blood spread from beneath Bradford, trickling out as it hit the ice. Kind of like a big spider web made of blood.

Bradford made no move to get up. She inched closer, but Midas caught her around the waist. "Baby, no..."

But she'd already seen. The unnatural angle of his neck...

Her gaze darted back to Midas.

His jaw hardened. "No one hurts you."

Once more, she peered down at the man who'd just tried to kill her.

Bradford struggled to breathe. Weak gasps. When he'd gone down, the blade had cut him again. Even deeper in the chest. Had it sliced his heart? Gone that deep? Past bone? It would take so much strength to deliver that kind of blow. And to break his neck...

Broken neck. And a blade to the heart.

"Like father, like son," Midas whispered.

"No." She shook her head. Alina held him tighter even as the others swarmed. "*No.*" Then she grabbed Midas's shoulders and hauled him down to her. Her mouth pressed to his. "You are the man I love."

"Alina..."

"I. Love. You." She ignored the tears and the blood and... "And I always will." Then she crumpled. Heaving sobs shook her body as the terror broke her right there on the ice.

But Alina didn't fall.

Midas scooped her into his arms and carried her off the blood-covered ice.

CHAPTER TWENTY-THREE

Another day, another interrogation.

Midas drummed his fingers on the scarred tabletop as his gaze darted between Detective Joyce Meriam and Detective Calvin Booker. The cops sat on one side of the table while Midas, Oliver Foxx, and a lawyer Oliver had hired, Toula Stratus, sat on the other.

Midas was pretty damn grateful for Toula's presence. Finding a good lawyer could be so hard these days, but Oliver had vouched for her. *Legitimately* vouched. Not just someone pretending to be Oliver…

As had apparently happened when Xander Palmer sent emails to Ryker Bellamy pretending to be Oliver. Or when Xander had even faked the phone call verifying Oliver's rec.

Yep, it sure was hard to find a good lawyer.

"How many more questions must my client answer?" Toula demanded. Her salt-and-pepper hair teased her temples. "You should be hailing the man as a hero. Yet, here we are." Toula glanced at her diamond-covered watch. "On hour four, and my patience is at an end."

So was Midas's. He wanted out of that room. He needed Alina.

She loves me.

She'd seen him at his absolute worst. And...

She still said she loved me. She kissed me...and she loves me.

That had been three days ago. The cops had questioned him over and over since that date. When Toula referenced hour four, she was talking about the four hours they'd wasted *that day* with the cops.

Oliver had advised Midas to stay away from Alina until the detectives were done with him.

His patience with *that* bullshit was at an end, too.

"Did you intend to break Bradford's neck?" Calvin asked.

Midas opened his mouth.

Toula put a hand on his arm. "Asked and answered already. Numerous times. My client tackled Bradford Wells because the man was intent on killing Alina Bellamy. During the course of the tackle—and ensuing fight—Bradford's neck was broken. The ice is slippery. Treacherous. There was very little control out there."

Calvin leaned forward. "What about the skate blade that got buried in Bradford's chest? Sure took a lot of force to do that, didn't it? To go so deeply?"

"As I said before," Midas growled, "he had the skate when I hit him. He was swinging it at Alina's neck. He wanted to slice her fucking throat open with that thing." *Not happening.* "When we collided, I think he landed on top of it."

Toula cleared her throat. Her hold tightened on him. A subtle...*I've-got-this.* "Obviously, the slice of the blade did not kill Bradford instantly. He kept fighting my client on the very, very treacherous ice. That's when the broken neck occurred. When my client was trying to fend off his attacker. A brutal end for a brutal man."

Now it was Oliver's turn to wade in. "Bradford confessed to witnessing Henry Monroe's attack on Alina's mother and to the fact that *he* was the one to suffocate her. He also confessed to being behind the kidnappings. He bragged to Alina about his crimes."

Because he intended to kill Alina. Midas locked his jaw.

"I know your department is working with the Feds on the investigation," Oliver continued smoothly. "Bradford's home has already been searched. Evidence was acquired that indicates there were potentially *more* victims. Not only that, but the Feds have been able to link Bradford *to* Henry Monroe. Bradford arranged for several different lawyers to work with Henry over the years. Those lawyers would send messages back and forth between Henry and Bradford."

"Is Xander Palmer cooperating with you?" Midas wanted to know.

Funny thing about Xander. Turned out, he was one of the few lawyers *not* linked to Bradford's crimes. Xander had been working his own agenda. One Midas damn well wanted to know more about.

Joyce nodded. "Xander swears he had no involvement with Bradford. He was only in town because Henry was so insistent. Xander thought if he followed Henry's order, he could get his client to reveal the locations of more victims." Her lips pulled down. "Xander seems to believe that Henry might have been involved in his aunt's disappearance. I believe he has a very personal stake in finding the locations of more victims."

And that explained why Xander was in Henry's web.

Someone needed to burn the web to the ground.

"Xander was following Henry's orders when he pretended to be Oliver and got Ryker to hire me." Midas shook his head. "Fool should have known he couldn't make deals with the devil." *My dad used him. Played with me. Wrought his usual hell.*

Silence.

"Ahem." Joyce cleared her throat. "For the record," she tucked a lock of hair behind her ear, "you did not deliberately break Bradford's neck and drive a skating blade deep into his chest?"

Midas stared back at her. *He was trying to kill Alina.*

"I don't think Bradford knew you were out of town," Calvin murmured. "If he'd killed Alina in that locker room, you believe Bradford would have tried blaming her murder on you?"

One hundred percent, I do. That's why my old man was so angry that I wasn't in town. I was the fall guy. "Alina isn't dead. Bradford is." His fingers drummed on the table again. "Isn't it strange, the way monsters can hide right in front of us, and we don't see them?" He raised his brows. "Chills you right to the bone, doesn't it?"

***

"You're not a monster, Midas," Oliver said as he braked the car in front of Midas's temporary home. The place that had—all too briefly—been Alina's safe house.

"Thanks for the ride, my friend." Midas unhooked his seatbelt. "And for the lawyer. And for all the Feds you pulled in to help so my ass didn't get tossed into a cage." He opened the door and climbed out.

"You killed to protect the woman you love. That doesn't make you a monster."

Midas leaned back into the vehicle so he could peer at Oliver. "No? Then what does it make me?"

Oliver's gaze darted to the right. "Why don't you ask her?"

Midas jerked back. He whipped around.

Alina stood on the porch. Her hands were behind her back. Her long hair blew lightly in the evening breeze. She watched him with her incredible, dark eyes.

"Don't fuck it up, my friend," Oliver cautioned. "And shut the door, would you? I've got places to be. Sadistic murderers to catch."

Midas slammed the door. He didn't look back when Oliver drove away. He was too busy staring at what waited in front of him.

"I hope you don't mind," Alina said as Midas closed in on her with lurching steps, "but this is where I want to be. Lane and Memphis let me in."

He would send them both an awesome thank you basket. He climbed one step. Stopped. Just drank her in. She stared back at him, and, no, Alina didn't look at him like he was some kind of monster.

But like I told the detectives, some monsters hide—

"If someone tried to hurt you, Midas, if someone tried to kill you, I'd do whatever it took to keep you safe." Her words were clear. Strong. "If that meant ending someone else's life in order to protect you, I'd do it."

He climbed another step. His hands reached out. Curled around her. He tugged her closer. Held her.

"I told the cops you saved me. That's exactly what you did. You're my hero. Like I've been telling you all along—you're my personal guardian angel."

His eyes squeezed closed. "I do not deserve you."

"I think you do. I think you've had enough pain and horror, and I think we both deserve to let all of that go." Her fingers brushed over his jaw. Seemed to linger over one of the scars he tried so hard to hide with his beard. "I think it's time we start dreaming, Midas."

His eyes opened. "You're in every dream I have." She *was* his dream. The only thing that mattered.

Her smile bloomed. The high-voltage smile that stole his breath and made him want to slay dragons.

Only, they *had* slayed the dragons. The bad guys were dead or in jail. She was safe.

"I love you, Midas," Alina told him. Beautiful, perfect words.

"I'd rip the world apart for you," he told her. Grim, growling words.

But she knew what he meant. Knew he loved her. He could see it.

And she sees me when Alina looks into my eyes. Oliver had been right. She didn't see a monster. Even if he was one.

She saw her protector. He *would* protect her. This day. Always. He'd fight. Kill. Destroy. As long as Alina was safe.

He swept her into his arms. The warm sound of her laughter eased the ache in his heart. They'd both lost too much. It was time to build a new life. Good memories. They'd make those. Over and over again. They'd get started right now. He carried her back into the house. Paused long enough to lock the door because...

You can't be too careful. Not when you have something so valuable to protect.

He took her to the bedroom. Lowered her onto the bed. Stripped her slowly. Kissed her neck. Her precious, beautiful neck. His lips skimmed over her collarbone. Then down, down he went.

His fingers teased her nipples. Then his mouth took them. First one. Then the other. Control wasn't an issue. He wasn't rushed or frenzied. This time was different for him.

Midas wanted to worship every single inch of her.

I almost lost her.
Never again.
Never.

He licked her nipples until she moaned and writhed beneath him. His fingers darted between her legs to seek out the sweetness that he craved so desperately. He kissed a path over her stomach. Then he spread her legs wide.

He feasted.

Light licks at first. Kisses. He played with her clit as she strained against him. His fingers dipped in and out, and he lapped her up. Every drop he could take. Over and over.

"Midas!" A quick shriek as she rocked against his mouth and came.

He didn't let up. He went deeper. His tongue swiped into her so he could savor every bit of her pleasure. Inside of her. Out. He teased her clit with his tongue. Went back in her. Repeated. Wanted more. Needed everything.

Her nails scraped over his shoulders and bit into him even through the shirt he wore. "What are you doing to me?" Alina cried out. "Stop torturing me!"

His head lifted. "Never." Never would he *ever* hurt her.

Her breath caught. Her gaze softened as her hand rose to cup his cheek. "Lose your clothes," she ordered, voice husky. "And make love to me."

He lost his clothes. Put his cock at the entrance to her body. His hands curled over hers, and he drove inside of her. All the way home.

He didn't rush. Not even when she arched frantically against him. This moment was special. To be savored. Next time, he'd go wild.

This time...*this time*...he needed to give her so much pleasure that she lost herself...

In me.

A second orgasm hit her. He felt the clench of her inner muscles around his dick. He hissed out a breath because she felt so fucking incredible. And he kept thrusting.

One of his hands moved down to wedge between their bodies. His thumb raked over her clit. Back and forth. Faster. Faster.

A third orgasm. Her whole body quaked.

"Come in me!" Alina demanded. Tempted. "Now, Midas, now!"

As if he could deny her anything.

He poured into her. Got lost.

In her.

His mouth pressed to her neck. Right over her racing pulse. "I love you."

EPILOGUE
PART ONE – MIDAS & ALINA

He could not breathe. Midas needed a damn paper bag or some shit like that. Sweat covered his body. Fear ate at his insides. And he watched as Alina leapt into the air.

One spin.

He was not made for this kind of pressure.

Two spins.

He was going to vomit. Jesus, one of the news cameras would probably record him.

Three spins.

Why wasn't she coming down into her normal position? Oh, shit. Oh, no. Oh, shit.

Four spins.

And she landed. Absolutely fucking perfect. The crowd erupted as everyone shot to their feet. He was jumping up and down, and her father was over in the corner wiping tears from his eyes.

Alina kept skating. She stopped when the music ended, poised perfectly in the middle of the ice. People were throwing flowers and stuffed animals at her, and she was *smiling*. A wide smile of such joy.

I would wreck the world for her any day of the week.

But he couldn't breathe yet. The judges had to show their scores. But they would be absolute idiots if they didn't give her—

His eyes widened as he saw the scores, and Midas let out a guttural roar of excitement. Alina was suddenly in front of him, and he hugged her as tightly as he could. She was laughing and crying, and Dmitri was crying, too, as he hugged Alina *and* Midas.

She'd done it. The gold.

His Alina had just won *fucking gold*.

And she stared at him as the cameras rolled. She didn't see a monster. She saw—

"I love you," Alina whispered.

The crowd cheered even harder when he kissed her.

EPILOGUE
PART TWO – HENRY

"I want a better view," Henry Monroe announced. "Bigger window. One that lets in the morning sunlight."

Oliver Foxx raised his brows. "Aren't you the demanding one?"

"I will tell you where to find the bodies of more victims. You just have to agree to my terms." Henry scanned the room with quizzical eyes. "Just you today? Where is the DA? And, of course, my son. Where is Midas?"

"Oh, I think your son is off celebrating. You know, what with Alina's big win and the wedding and everything." Oliver smiled. He planned to throw out some bait and see if he could hook Henry. "Gorgeous affair, by the way. Alina's father has even come around to Midas. But then again, how can you hate a man when it's clear he'd kill to protect your daughter?"

Henry stiffened. "Ryker Bellamy isn't some white-knight guy—"

"Because Bradford Wells told you he was evil? Nah. Bradford was wrong about Bellamy. Turns out, the shady deals were done by Bellamy's partner years ago. Not by the man himself."

"And you believe those lies?" A snort. "Typical."

"I believe Bellamy has cooperated fully with police. He confessed that he discovered what his partner was doing. And he proved that he already repaid the people injured long ago. He's not a perfect man, not by a long shot, but he's also not a homicidal maniac in prison for multiple murders." Oliver pointed at Henry. "That would be you."

Laughter. "We both know I'm not a maniac."

"Then what are you?" Oliver asked as if he was only vaguely curious.

"A concerned father. What I've always been. I wanted my son to live to his full potential." His smile grew. "And he has."

"Because he was forced to kill Bradford?"

"Broken neck. A blade to the heart." Henry sighed. "I am proud."

His words would horrify Midas. So Oliver would make certain that his friend never heard about them. "There aren't going to be any deals for you."

That news wiped the smile off Henry's face. "What?"

"You shared too much with Bradford over the years. He quite admired you, actually." *More like was obsessed with you.* "Bradford kept detailed notes of everything you ever told him. We located those in a safe-deposit box fairly recently. You told him exactly where you traveled over the years. A mistake. You see, Midas was able to confirm the locations on Bradford's list. The FBI is matching missing persons to those areas. Finding out who the victims were—"

"But you won't find them." Grim but pleased. "Not without my help."

Time to go in for the kill. "We found Midas's mother."

Pain flashed. A crack in Henry's mask.

"You revealed the keys we needed for that discovery. You said Midas was six months old. That he'd been left in a motel. We already knew that Midas spent the first six months of his life in Branson, Missouri." Oliver flipped through some files he'd brought along. "Want to know how we discovered the truth about Branson?"

Henry didn't speak.

"Midas's mom took him for doctor visits during those early months. There was a file on him in a local pediatrician's office…we found the file. The techs at the FBI can unearth just about anything. And, of course, since Midas teamed up with the Ice Breakers—have you heard of them? I'm part of their crew, too," he said, shrugging. "We work on cold cases. Finding victims who've been forgotten. Giving justice to families. Kick ass things like that." His jaw hardened. "We found his mother for Midas. She's being laid to rest, properly."

Henry looked away.

"We'll find the other ones, too. The victims that Bradford knew about. He made so many notes in his journal. All about you and your crimes. Like a twisted, fangirl diary. One that is going to bury you so deep in the ground."

Henry still wasn't meeting his gaze.

"Here's the thing," Oliver continued, and he didn't let any of his tension show. "I don't need to hear any of your lies. You're not going to jerk me around and you are certainly not going to play more mind games with your son." Oliver closed his file. He rose. "You're done." Then he walked for the door.

Now, if he'd played the scene properly there would be a response in *five, four, three*—

"Maybe I wanted him to save Alina."

"Guard, open the door," Oliver directed.

"Maybe I told Xander that Midas should be brought in as a bodyguard not because I wanted to pin things on him...but because I thought he could save her."

The guard opened the door.

"Maybe I knew he wasn't like me." Henry's voice rose a notch. Hard to do with such a deep voice. "Maybe I knew he could be...something else. If he just shook off the darkness I brought to him."

Oliver didn't turn around. "You expect me to believe that you care about Midas?"

"I told him everything he needed to know from the beginning. Told him not to trust the lawyer. When Midas came here the second time, I told him to go back. I knew Alina needed him."

"You were setting him up."

"I was trying to keep the woman alive."

Oliver's grip tightened on the file. "You wanted Midas to be a hero?"

"Better than being whatever the fuck I am."

Oliver finally looked back.

Henry had partially turned in his chair. His eyes met Oliver's. Henry raised his chin. "Jennifer Chestnut. Seattle. Buried off Juniper Avenue. Carly Shore. Wyoming. Left her on a little ranch outside of Gillette. Eza Jackson. Idaho. In Pocatello…"

The names kept coming.

Oliver went back to the table and began writing them down.

***

"You think he was bullshitting you?" Memphis Camden asked as he gazed at the list.

"I think I'm going to investigate and find out." Oliver paused. "But I need help." A lot of it.

"Right. Like the Feds aren't going to be all over this…"

"They will be," he allowed. "But I'd also like some people who specialize in cold cases."

Memphis's grin was tiger sharp. "I think I can help you out."

Oliver extended his hand to the man he considered a friend. "I knew you could."

THE END

A NOTE FROM THE AUTHOR

Thank you so much for reading ICE COLD KISS. I hope that you enjoyed stepping into the world of the Ice Breakers. It has been such a pleasure to write these stories. I love cold cases and mystery solving. And when you can add in some hot romance and happily ever after fun? Ultimate win for me!

If you'd like to stay updated on my releases and sales, please join my newsletter list.

https://cynthiaeden.com/newsletter/

Again, thank you for reading ICE COLD KISS.

Best,
Cynthia Eden
cynthiaeden.com

ABOUT THE AUTHOR

Cynthia Eden is a *New York Times, USA Today, Digital Book World,* and *IndieReader* bestselling author of romantic suspense and paranormal romance. She's a prolific author who lives along the Alabama Gulf Coast. In her free time, you'll find her reading romances, watching horror movies, or hunting for adventures. She's a chocolate addict and a major *Supernatural* fan.

For More Information
- *cynthiaeden.com*
- *facebook.com/cynthiaedenfanpage*

HER OTHER WORKS

Ice Breaker Cold Case Romance
- Frozen In Ice (Book 1)
- Falling For The Ice Queen (Book 2)
- Ice Cold Saint (Book 3)
- Touched By Ice (Book 4)
- Trapped In Ice (Book 5)
- Forged From Ice (Book 6)
- Buried Under Ice (Book 7)
- Ice Cold Kiss (Book 8)
- Locked In Ice (Book 9)

Wilde Ways
- Protecting Piper (Book 1)
- Guarding Gwen (Book 2)
- Before Ben (Book 3)
- The Heart You Break (Book 4)
- Fighting For Her (Book 5)
- Ghost Of A Chance (Book 6)
- Crossing The Line (Book 7)
- Counting On Cole (Book 8)
- Chase After Me (Book 9)
- Say I Do (Book 10)
- Roman Will Fall (Book 11)
- The One Who Got Away (Book 12)
- Pretend You Want Me (Book 13)

- Cross My Heart (Book 14)
- The Bodyguard Next Door (Book 15)
- Ex Marks The Perfect Spot (Book 16)
- The Thief Who Loved Me (Book 17)

Wilde Ways: Gone Rogue

- How To Protect A Princess (Book 1)
- How To Heal A Heartbreak (Book 2)
- How To Con A Crime Boss (Book 3)

Trouble For Hire

- No Escape From War (Book 1)
- Don't Play With Odin (Book 2)
- Jinx, You're It (Book 3)
- Remember Ramsey (Book 4)

Death and Moonlight Mystery

- Step Into My Web (Book 1)
- Save Me From The Dark (Book 2)

Phoenix Fury

- Hot Enough To Burn (Book 1)
- Slow Burn (Book 2)
- Burn It Down (Book 3)

Dark Sins

- Don't Trust A Killer (Book 1)
- Don't Love A Liar (Book 2)

Lazarus Rising

- Never Let Go (Book One)
- Keep Me Close (Book Two)
- Stay With Me (Book Three)
- Run To Me (Book Four)
- Lie Close To Me (Book Five)

- Hold On Tight (Book Six)

Bad Things

- The Devil In Disguise (Book 1)
- On The Prowl (Book 2)
- Undead Or Alive (Book 3)
- Broken Angel (Book 4)
- Heart Of Stone (Book 5)
- Tempted By Fate (Book 6)
- Wicked And Wild (Book 7)
- Saint Or Sinner (Book 8)

Bite Series

- Forbidden Bite (Bite Book 1)
- Mating Bite (Bite Book 2)

Blood and Moonlight Series

- Bite The Dust (Book 1)
- Better Off Undead (Book 2)
- Bitter Blood (Book 3)

Mine Series

- Mine To Take (Book 1)
- Mine To Keep (Book 2)
- Mine To Hold (Book 3)
- Mine To Crave (Book 4)
- Mine To Have (Book 5)
- Mine To Protect (Book 6)

Dark Obsession Series

- Watch Me (Book 1)
- Want Me (Book 2)
- Need Me (Book 3)
- Beware Of Me (Book 4)

- Only For Me (Books 1 to 4)

Purgatory Series
- The Wolf Within (Book 1)
- Marked By The Vampire (Book 2)
- Charming The Beast (Book 3)
- Deal with the Devil (Book 4)
- The Beasts Inside (Books 1 to 4)

Bound Series
- Bound By Blood (Book 1)
- Bound In Darkness (Book 2)
- Bound In Sin (Book 3)
- Bound By The Night (Book 4)
- Bound in Death (Book 5)
- Forever Bound (Books 1 to 4)

Stand-Alone Romantic Suspense
- Waiting For Christmas
- Monster Without Mercy
- Kiss Me This Christmas
- It's A Wonderful Werewolf
- Never Cry Werewolf
- Immortal Danger
- Deck The Halls
- Come Back To Me
- Put A Spell On Me
- Never Gonna Happen
- One Hot Holiday
- Slay All Day
- Midnight Bite
- Secret Admirer
- Christmas With A Spy
- Femme Fatale

- Until Death
- Sinful Secrets
- First Taste of Darkness
- A Vampire's Christmas Carol